# The Bear

# The Bear:
## California Dreamin'

*John Kerr*

# THE BEAR: CALIFORNIA DREAMIN'

iUniverse books may be ordered through booksellers or by contacting:

iUniverse
1663 Liberty Drive
Bloomington, IN 47403
www.iuniverse.com
844-349-9409

Because of the dynamic nature of the Internet, any web addresses or links contained in this book may have changed since publication and may no longer be valid. The views expressed in this work are solely those of the author and do not necessarily reflect the views of the publisher, and the publisher hereby disclaims any responsibility for them.

Any people depicted in stock imagery provided by Getty Images are models, and such images are being used for illustrative purposes only. Certain stock imagery © Getty Images.

ISBN: 978-1-6632-3900-6 (sc)
ISBN: 978-1-6632-3901-3 (hc)
ISBN: 978-1-6632-3899-3 (e)

Library of Congress Control Number: 2022907965

Print information available on the last page.

iUniverse rev. date: 05/03/2022

*This book would not have been possible without the constant love and support of my wife, Laurel. This one's for you, Babalu.*

# *Better Dead Than Red*

"Are you now or have you ever been a member of the Communist Party?" demanded Senator Nixon. The senator was one of four HUAC committee members questioning witnesses in an office in Los Angeles City Hall.

HUAC was back in town. The Hollywood Ten had gone to prison. Congress was controlled by the Democrats who, like their Republican counterparts, wanted to make headlines ridding Hollywood of the *Red Menace*. It was an election year and nothing got a candidate more ink than bringing down a silver screen icon.

Michael McGuire and his attorney, Leo Stone, sat at a table facing the panel of inquisitors. McGuire was the latest Hollywood producer called up to testify before the panel. Michael was middle-aged, and with his graying temples and thousand-dollar navy-blue Bond St. suit, he looked more like a successful businessman than a movie producer. Michael sat up in his chair and placed his hand over the microphone while conferring with his attorney.

"No," Michael replied.

Nixon appeared perplexed. "No what, Mr. McGuire?"

"No, I'm not a member of the Communist Party, nor have I have ever been a member."

"But you did hire writers who were communists?" Nixon replied.

"Are you asking or telling me, Senator?"

There was a chuckle from the gallery. Nixon frowned; his five o'clock shadow was already showing at 10 a.m. "Did you knowingly employ writers who were communists?"

"No."

The questioner cupped his mic and conferred with the other members on the committee, all of which were surprised when Michael McGuire had readily agreed to testify. Nixon thought it would be a slam dunk; ask a few questions and get the producer to give the committee some names. McGuire wouldn't be the first to rollover. Edward Dmytryk had, and so had Kazan. McGuire would make it three.

The senator didn't appreciate Michael's glib manner. He stared down from the long table he was seated at and frowned at McGuire.

"You employed Dorothy Parker, a known sympathizer and supporter of liberal causes. You also hired Waldo Salt to write the script for *Decision at Midnight*."

"Mr. Salt did indeed write the script for *Decision at Midnight*, a courtroom drama revolving around the guilt or innocence of a husband accused of murdering his wife's assailant."

"Then you admit that you knowingly hired a communist?"

"No, Senator. I did not know of Mr. Salt's political affiliations."

"What about Larry Parks?"

"What about him, Senator?"

"Larry Parks admitted before this committee that he was a member of the Communist Party."

Michael waited. There was no further statement coming from the senator. He leaned toward the mic and said, "Yes?"

Joe McCarthy had endured enough. He dabbed his brow with a handkerchief and grabbed his mic. "That's two known communists you hired, Mr. McGuire."

"I hired them for their particular skills, Senator, not their political affiliations."

McCarthy glared at Michael. "You mean to sit here and tell this committee that you had no idea either of these men were members of the Communist Party?"

Michael never flinched. He met Joe McCarthy's gaze and replied, "That is correct, Senator. As a proud Irish-American and veteran of a World War, I swear I had no knowledge of either man's membership to any political organization."

"Frankly, I find that hard to believe," remarked McCarthy.

Michael leaned toward the mic. "Believe what you like, Senator. I have testified under oath that I did not knowingly hire any communists on my films. I am not interested in a man's politics. I am only interested in their ability to perform their designated job. Did Walter O'Malley ask Carl Erskine what political party he voted for before he hired him? He's only interested in man's ability to strike out the other players. It's the same with me. I am only interested in a writer's ability to tell a story, hopefully a good one."

Michael McGuire was fifty-four. He had been a producer for nearly twenty-five years. That was a lifetime in Hollywood. Before making movies, Michael had been a bootlegger. Along with Jimmy Grazzi and Walter McGrath, the trio ran a successful operation that had included the swank *El Capitan* club on PCH. McGrath and Grazzi died in the Point Magu Massacre in '27. Jimmy Grazzi had actually escaped, got a face job in Tijuana, and reemerged as James Hagen, the owner of Allied Aircraft in San Diego the following year.

Michael turned and looked over his shoulder. His wife, Laurel, was seated in the first row of the gallery, along with their seven-year-old son, Nicholas. He smiled at them. Nicholas waved at his father. Laurel immediately grabbed the boy's hand and adjusted him in his seat. She knew the committee would frown upon any familiarity during the hearing, even from a child. Michael turned back and faced the panel.

John Rankin, an avowed segregationist and committee member, glared at Michael. He was a slender man with a shallow face and pale complexion.

"The committee isn't interested in Walter O'Malley or ballplayers. The committee is interested in writers and actors who are communists. You're telling this committee that you never knew those writers to be communists?"

"That is correct, Mr. Rankin."

"What about *Destiny on the Danube*?" Nixon interjected. He picked up his notes and read, "'The Legion of Decency found the film objectional for its gratuitous violence, vulgar language, and suggestive situations.' The Armed Forces refused to show the film to their servicemen. Patrick Callen wrote that script. Surely, you must have known if this writer had red leanings."

"Has Mr. Callen been named as a member of the Communist Party?"

"We will ask the questions, Mr. McGuire," Rankin barked. "The committee has not been able to locate Mr. Callen. When we do, he will be brought in for questioning. Now answer the good senator's question, did you know that Patrick Callen was a communist?"

Michael knew Callen didn't exist. "I did not," he replied.

A page leaned down and whispered something to Senator McCarthy. Joe frowned. He jotted something down on a piece of paper and handed it to the page. Rankin leaned close to Nixon and whispered something. The page handed Nixon the note. He then glanced at McCarthy's message— "McGuire wrote the script." Nixon gave a nod and then scowled at the producer.

"It has been brought to my attention that you are the author of that script."

"I am."

"Why did you use a false name?" snapped Rankin.

"Writers have a long history of employing pseudonyms. The name is not false. Patrick is the name of my great uncle, and Callen is my grandmother's maiden name. It was my way of honoring them."

The room hummed with reporters and spectators. McCarthy hammered his gavel for order. The committee conferred for a long moment. Rankin finally leaned toward his mic. There was a loud honk. Feedback blew the ears off of the audience in the gallery. Rankin backed off the microphone.

"It is apparent that you have no intention of cooperating with this committee at this time. It is our decision to recall you for further questioning at a later date."

"I beg to differ. I have answered every one of the committee's questions," Michael protested.

"The witness is dismissed," said Senator Nixon

Michael stood. Flash-blubs burst. Reporters hurled questions like the rat-a-tat of a machine gun.

"You dodged the bullet on that one," said attorney Stone, picking up his briefcase.

"They'll be back," Michael replied matter-of-factly.

Stone looked at Michael and gave him a pat on the shoulder, then walked out ahead of his client. The pack of reporters followed. Michael went over to Laurel and Nicholas.

"That was boring," said Nicholas.

Michael chuckled. "Out of the mouth of babes." He grabbed his son's hand. "Let's go face those bastards down, boy."

Leo Stone stood on the steps of City Hall and faced the phalanx of reporters who peppered him with questions. The attorney held up his arms. The din died down.

"You heard my client. Michael McGuire answered the committee's questions. He stated he was not a member of the Communist Party under oath. Mr. McGuire's films have been some of the most popular Hollywood has produced. This is nothing more than the committee fishing for headlines and bullying an innocent man whose only goal is to entertain Americans."

Michael, Laurel, and Nicholas came out of the lobby and stood by the attorney.

"Mister McGuire, Howard Silver, L.A. Tribune. How'd you feel about the hearing?"

"Optimistic," Michael replied, not missing a beat.

"Even though the committee has reserved the right to recall you for questioning?" asked a second reporter.

He shrugged. "Live to fight another day and make another movie."

"What will that be?" asked a third scribe.

"You'll have to wait and see."

Michael gave the reporters thumbs up and quickly maneuvered Laurel and Nicholas down the steps and into an awaiting car. As soon as they were in the car, the driver pulled away from the curb.

"Well, that went rather well," Michael replied glibly.

"The committee wants to recall you. That means they can still find you in contempt," said Laurel.

Michael put his hand on Laurel's arm, reassuring her. "Semantics are everything, and I am better than they are when it comes to semantics."

"They make up the rules as they go along, Michael. Are you too blind with pride to see that?" Laurel asked.

Nicholas looked at his parents. He had never seen them argue before. "Why are you mad at Daddy?"

Laurel caught herself. She wiped her eyes and forced a smile. "Mommy and Daddy are just having a disagreement."

Michael smiled at his son and tousled his hair. "We've got the press on our side, Nick. That's better than half the battle won. You always want the press on your side."

Laurel looked at her husband. "By the way, what is your next project?"

Michael gave his wife a million-dollar all-American grin and winked. "You'll just have to wait and find out."

The car slowed down.

"What is it, Raymond?" Michael asked the driver.

"There appears to be some type of demonstration going on."

Nicholas peered out the window. Dozens of people carried signs.

"What does 'caw' mean, Daddy?" asked the boy. Nicholas pointed to a man carrying a placard with C.A.W. in bold black letters at the top. Below it read, "Public Housing is Socialism. Stop Elysian Park Heights Project."

Michael looked at the masses of people crossing Fifth Street. Most were working class men in their twenties and thirties, some older. A few women were in the group as well. All were white. They chanted, "Better dead than Red. Commies go home."

Michael turned and looked at his son. "C.A.W. stands for Committee for the American Way, Nicholas. They would like to—"

"Daddy, look they're beating up that man."

Half dozen protestors had encircled a Hispanic teenager and were pushing him around on the sidewalk near where the car was stopped in traffic. Michael's first instinct was to get out of the car. He glanced at Laurel and rolled down the window instead.

"Hello, can you please tell us where the parking is for the rally?" Michael asked.

The group was caught off guard by the well-dressed man.

"Don't you fellas belong to the Committee for the American Way?" Michael addressed them.

The group of protestors stopped hitting the Mexican teenager and looked at the man in the Cadillac.

"Yeah," said a man wearing a checkered shirt and khakis.

The teenager used the moment to break free of his captors and race away.

Khaki slacks frowned. "Let the greaser go," he said to his companions before leaning on the Cadillac and looking at Michael. "There's a lot just down the block."

"Thank you," said Michael.

Traffic started moving again, and the Cadillac continued west on Sunset.

"I thought you were going to beat up those guys," said Nicholas.

Michael grinned. "Sometimes you get better results with honey."

Nicholas gave his father a perplexed look. "Were you afraid of them?"

"No. You see, son, the people who belong to C.A.W. are full of hate. Beating them would only make them hate more. They could've hurt you and your mother. It was better to let them think I was like them. That boy they were hurting was able to get away."

"Yeah, I guess so," Nicholas replied with a thoughtful expression.

"Only resort to violence when your options are limited." He held his son's chin and looked him straight in the eyes. "Nicholas, if you go down that road, make sure your opponent never gets up."

"Michael!" Laurel barked at her husband. She turned and adjusted Nicholas's jacket. "Disregard what your father just said. Violence only begets more violence."

"Yes, Mother," replied the young boy.

It took another light before the Cadillac got through the intersection. Michael looked out the window. The United States had won the war with Germany and Italy. The fascists were now here in the streets and in the government. A cold chill ran down Michael's back as traffic finally broke and the car picked up speed and made a right on Vermont.

*　*　*

Chester Dockery stood on the small stage at Elysian Park. He was middle-aged, had a thinning hairline, and wore a brown suit. Dozens of people had gathered to hear him speak. A large banner that was strung overhead between two posts read: *Californians for the American Way. Committed to Life, Liberty, and the Constitution.* Dockery looked out at the crowd gathered and smiled to himself.

Chester Dockery had once been just another Kluxer from El Cajon. He had purchased time on KDEK, a small radio station in Santee, to preach his gospel of hate, and he became a celebrity of sorts. Chester preached a Horatio Alger doctrine mixed with white supremacy. The show was a hit. In two years, Chester Dockery's program was syndicated on over a dozen stations in California and Arizona. Chester preached prosperity through hard work and an America free of foreigners and blacks.

Chester looked at the crowd gathered and said, "Communism is a threat to our American way of life." He paused for a moment to allow his words to sink in before he continued, "Communism is a threat to our neighborhoods, our children, and the very core of what it is to be an American. Now the commies will tell you that the Negro has the right to buy a home in your neighborhood and have his children go to school with your children. When coloreds move into a white neighborhood, property values go down and crime goes up. This is a fact. Are we going to allow coloreds to destroy our neighborhoods?

The crowd responded with a loud, "No!"

"Are we going to allow the commies to take over our government?"

"No!"

"Behind every commie cause is a dozen Jews. They own the banks and they run Hollywood. The Jews are responsible for the coloreds moving into your neighborhoods. Are we going to let them?

"No!"

"Are we better than the Jews?"

"Yes!"

"Are we better than the commies?"

"Yes!"

"We are Americans. We will not allow the Jews and communists to destroy our communities and this great country!"

A thunderous "Yes!" came from the crowd.

Chester Dockery looked out at the group of people chanting, "We're better than the Jews," and smiled. Chester knew in his heart that he and his followers would win the righteous war against the Negroes, communists, and Jews, the Axis of Evil.

# 2

## *The World is a Ghetto*

Every muscle in Angela Camacho's body ached as she climbed onto the bus. She was glad her shift was over at the cannery. It was Friday, and she would have the weekend to herself and Johnny. Johnny was eighteen months old and the only thing Angela had to remind her of happier times.

The bus was nearly full. Angela made her way down the aisle and found an empty seat by the window. A bum was asleep in the aisle seat. Angela stepped over him and settled into the seat. Normally her brother, Ezekiel, drove them home. He had left work early that day to go to the demonstration at Elysian Park. Angela needed the money and worked till the end of her shift. Now she had to take three busses and walk a mile to get home.

The bus pulled away from the curb. Angela sat back and listened to the hum of the motor while she watched the blocks pass by.

After graduating from high school, Angela had lived with her parents. She took night classes and cleaned the houses of wealthy residents in Los Feliz during the day. Three years after the war ended, Angela met Daniel Hudson at Los Angeles State in a business law class. Daniel was attending on the G.I. Bill and grew up in Glendale.

His father, Lloyd, was a contractor who was busy building homes in Lakewood. His mother, Betty, worked as a secretary for a downtown law firm. The Hudson family opened their home to Angela and treated her well. Angela didn't have many gringo friends and was surprised at the Hudson's liberal attitudes. Lloyd and Betty were unfazed that Angela's parents lived in Chaves Ravine. The city had passed a bill that year declaring Chavez Ravine as the site of Elysian Park Heights, a new housing development created for low-income families.

Angela was twenty-three and was due to attend Loyola Law School the following year. She had met a man who loved her and saw her life laid out before her: law school, marriage, career, and then possibly children. That summer, Angela discovered she was pregnant. Daniel suggested they go to Tijuana and have it taken care of. Angela refused. Daniel stopped taking her calls. The Hudson family closed ranks. Angela was now persona non grata.

Law school was out of the question. Angela told her parents of her pregnancy. Richard and Olivia Camacho took the news calmly. Johnny came into the world in the same house as his mother had. Daniel Hudson was not present at his son's birth. War had broken out in Korea. Daniel was drafted. Two months after arriving in country, he died at the battle of Unsan. Angela did not attend his funeral. She was a single mother and had to work her shift at the cannery. Her brother, Ezekiel, was a line supervisor at Pacific Cannery and had gotten her the job. Angela had to cut and gut the fish as they traveled down a conveyor belt. It was long, hard hours, but it paid better than cleaning houses. Olivia remained at home and took care of her grandson.

A man from the City Housing Authority came and talked to the residents of Chavez Ravine. He explained that the city needed their property for the Elysian Heights project and that they would be paid the going rate for their home. When the man offered Richard Camacho nine thousand dollars for his home, he took the money, packed up the family, and moved to a nice three-bedroom home in Lincoln Heights.

Richard believed he made a killing. Their old home was paid for. Richard had purchased the two-bedroom house in La Loma for seven hundred dollars nearly thirty years before. Angela pointed out to her father that he would now have a six-thousand-dollar mortgage. Richard waved his daughter off. He had made over ten times what the Chavez Ravine home cost him. Angela was sad to leave the neighborhood. She and her brother were born in the house. Moving would mean a new start.

Ezekiel came with his wife, Carmen, and their young daughters, Leticia and Lucy, to help with the move. They lived in La Loma just up the hill from Richard and Olivia. The furniture and belongings were packed into Ezekiel's truck and moved to the new house.

Angela was her father's favorite. The fact Johnny was the first grandson only set him on a pedestal in Richard's eyes. Johnny walked on water as far as Grandpa was concerned. Richard loved to sit on the porch of the new house with Johnny on his lap. He would sip a cold beer and share it with the young boy. Johnny would take a sip, make a face, and squeal. This always made Richard laugh.

After four months, the family had settled into their new home. Angela enjoyed having her own room. She could put Johnny down for a nap and close the door. Every Sunday the family got together and Richard would barbecue chicken or carne asada along with corn and frijoles. Angela had given up law school, but she had Johnny. She had her family. Then St. Patrick's Day happened.

Richard and Olivia went to mass that day to celebrate San Patricio. They were coming home when a driver ran a red light and hit their car. Richard and Olivia died at the scene. The driver of the other vehicle lived. He was a doctor who lived in Laughlin Park, an exclusive area of Los Felix where Cecil B. de Mille and Anthony Quinn had homes. The doctor claimed he was on his way to an emergency and had honked his horn as he raced through the intersection. The police never bothered to check the doctor's alcohol level. They never bothered to verify the emergency he claimed to be racing to. The DA didn't press charges. The doctor was an honored member of the community and on the board at Cedars of Lebanon Hospital. The deceased were two Mexicans. It was a tragic accident, but nothing to ruin a man's reputation and career over.

Angela was unable to make the mortgage payments, and the bank foreclosed. She and Johnny moved in with Ezekiel and his family, who had remained in Chavez Ravine. Many of the families in the neighborhood had moved out. The City Housing Authority was busy buying up properties. Ezekiel resented the fact that the city could take his house. He drank and vowed to remain until the bulldozers arrived.

Angela trudged up the hill, finding Carmen was sitting on the porch. Even with two young daughters, Carmen had kept her youthful figure. Her thick black hair was kept just above her shoulders. Ezekiel's truck was conspicuously absent from its spot next to the home. Carmen stood when she saw Angela walking up the path.

"Angie, EZ didn't bring you home?"

Angela sat down on the step with a tired huff. "No. He went to that demonstration at the park. I wanted to finish my shift. EZ isn't home?"

Carmen shook her head. "No."

"How was Johnny?"

Carmen smiled. "A perfect angel. Come on, let's get you some dinner."

Angela stood and followed her sister-in-law into the house. Carmen heated the frijoles while Angela went in to check on Johnny, who was asleep in his crib. Letty and Lucy were dead to the world on the bed next to the crib. Angela tip-toed out of the room and quietly closed the door behind her.

Carmen heated a flour tortilla on the grill.

"I can do that," Angela said, walking into the small kitchen.

"Sit. You've been working all day," Carmen retorted, waving her off.

Angela didn't argue, instead taking a seat at the dining table.

"A man for the Housing Authority came again today," said Carmen.

Angela looked at her sister-in-law. "He offered nine thousand dollars. He said we had until Monday to decide."

"What are you going to do?"

"I don't know. EZ refuses to leave. Me, I'd take the money." Carmen gestured to the window with her hand. "Look out there. Half our neighbors have already gone. It isn't the same place anymore."

Carmen placed a plate with a quesadilla and frijoles in front of Angela and took a seat across form her.

"This is so good," moaned Angela after taking a bite of the quesadilla. But then she saw the look of concern in Carmen's eyes. "What?"

"I think if we don't take this offer, there might not be any more."

"That would make EZ happy," Angela kidded. She realized Carmen didn't see the humor in her remark. "The Vargas aren't moving."

"That's fine for Aurora and her family. I've got to think about the girls," Carmen replied.

Angie saw that Carmen was upset. She reached across the table and took her sister-in-law's hands. "We will get through this, Carmen."

Carmen wiped her tears. Angela got up and hugged her. Headlights beamed through the front window. There was the rumble of Ezekiel's truck parking next to the house. The baby awoke. Angela went into the bedroom and picked up Johnny, cradling him against her shoulder. He quickly quieted down. Letty and Lucy were still asleep. Angela put Johnny back in his crib and went out to the living room.

Carmen stood in the kitchen staring into the sink. Ezekiel was now seated at the table drinking a beer, a cut over his left eye. He still had on his blue work shirt with his name and Pacific Cannery stitched in red on the front. Ezekiel's arms were thick and muscular from years of loading crates of fish.

"What happened?" Angela asked carefully, frowning at the cut.

Ezekiel looked at his sister and gave her a faint smile. "George, Louie, and a couple of the other fellas, we went down to protest Dockery's rally."

"And they kicked your culo," Angela shot back.

Ezekiel meekly nodded his head. "There were too many gringos."

Angela laughed at her older brother. "Ha! When will you realize there will always be *too many gringos*? Sleepy Lagoon and the riots weren't enough? I love you, EZ, you're my brother. You can't keep doing this sort of thing."

Ezekiel gave his sister a quizzical look. "What else were we supposed to do?"

Angela hugged him. "You're thirty years old and act like a kid. You have a wife who loves you and two daughters. You wear that shirt with your name and the place you work. You make it easy for the police."

Ezekiel grinned. "You were always the smart one, Angie."

Angela glanced over at Carmen and then looked at her brother. "A man from the Housing Authority came and offered you nine thousand dollars for your home."

Ezekiel looked at Carmen. She nodded her head but remained silent.

Angela fixed Ezekiel with a hard look. "Take the money, EZ. You and Carmen and the girls can move and start over."

"Like Papa and Mom?" Ezekiel asked, not bothering to hide the snide tone in his voice.

Angela nodded. "Yes, like Papa and Mom."

"What about you and Johnny?"

"We'll be all right, especially if my brother doesn't get thrown in jail for picking fights with *gueros*."

Ezekiel signed and nodded his head and put his arm out. Carmen came over, and Ezekiel hugged her close.

Angela patted her brother's arm. "Papa understood, EZ. It's just a place. Nobody really owns the land. We're all just passing through this life. Let the Vargas family stay if they want. Chavez Ravine died when the city decided to build Elysian Heights. It will never be the same. Better to go and make a new home for your family."

Ezekiel took a sip of his beer and looked at his sister. "Listen to her, miss smarty pants."

"Angie is right," retorted Carmen.

Ezekiel sighed. "I know." He flashed a big smile. "We just don't want Angie to get a fat head on us."

He laughed loudly, and Carmen and Angela smacked him on his shoulders.

"Quiet, you'll wake the children," the two women admonished in unison.

Ezekiel threw up his arms and then grabbed both Carmen and Angie and hugged them. He knew Angela spoke the truth. He knew that for the sake of Carmen and the girls they would have to move.

"Do you have the man's card?" Ezekiel asked

Carmen retrieved it from the drawer where she put it and handed the business card to her husband.

"I'll call him first thing Monday," Ezekiel promised.

Carmen kissed him on the cheek, then she and Angela went out and sat on the porch steps. The two women didn't say anything. They knew the survival of the family required them to leave Chavez Ravine. Carmen placed her arm around Angela, and they looked up at the evening sky, counting the stars.

Ezekiel sat and drank his beer in the darkness of the kitchen and wondered why it was so hard to maintain his machismo. His father had never lost his. After a while, Ezekiel finished his beer. He decided that he would worry about his machismo another day and went out to sit on the porch with his wife and sister. Familia trumped machismo.

# 3

# *A Gig*

The war had changed everything. Los Angeles had changed, and so had the music business. Many of the clubs had closed once the soldiers returned home. Those that continued to operate booked only small combos. The era of big bands was gone. That made it hard for working players.

Cosmo Turner was a player. He had a band before the war. He even had his own club for a brief while. Then he got drafted. Cosmo spent three years fighting Germans in Africa, Sicily, and France. When he came back, Cosmo moved into a studio apartment on 36ᵗʰ Street and quickly discovered landing steady work as a piano player was hard to come by. He spent his days at the union hall but was lucky if he picked up three gigs a week. Most of those were playing back-up in a burlesque joint, four sets for twenty-five dollars. Back in 1942, Cosmo had his own club and band, but now he was reduced to hustling pick-up gigs for peanuts. Cosmo was thirty, had fought in the *Good War*, and could hardly pay his rent.

Cosmo hated to seek a handout. He hated going hungry and being tossed out on the street worse. He considered hitting up James Hagen for a job, the wealthy owner of Allied Aircraft. Their paths had crossed when a Cosmo was hired to locate a grifter named Nicole Sullivan. She had taken Hagen for ten big ones, stolen Cosmo's heart, and then disappeared. Cosmo never forgot her.

While Cosmo was battling fascists in Sicily, Sullivan had slipped after pulling another con. She was grabbed by Mexican gangsters who had worked with Hagen when he was Jimmy Grazzi and partnered with Michael McGuire. Nicole Sullivan found out the hard way that crossing a man like Hagen had severe consequences. He had left her to the Mexicans, who put her to work. After the war, Cosmo spent three months scouring dives, bars, and brothels for Sullivan. He wasn't successful and returned to L.A.

By the time things got desperate enough for Cosmo to seek Hagen's help, the man wasn't able to do much. James Hagen was currently under investigation for misappropriation of funds during the war. His wife of ten years had divorced him. It was in the papers. Cosmo knew you didn't hit a man up when he was getting kicked. He got by hustling gigs and living low. There were only three things that interested Cosmo: the next gig, 100 proof bonded whiskey, and good-looking women. He might have been living in a single room apartment, but he was living the life.

Cosmo wasn't a churchgoing man, but he took to going when his neighbor, Mrs. Williams, a septuagenarian, asked Cosmo to fill in for her at the First Baptist Church. Mrs. Williams was the church's piano player and lately her arthritis prevented her from playing. Cosmo took the gig. He didn't much care for the fire and brimstone preaching of Reverend Elias Howard, however. The gig paid six bucks a Sunday. As a rule, a musician would generally do just about anything to avoid what was commonly referred to as *real work*. Cosmo was no exception to that rule. A gig was a gig as far as he was concerned.

It didn't take long for the church ladies to circle their wagons. Cosmo was single, and while not gainfully employed, was good looking and a sharp dresser. This frightened Cosmo more than running into a Klan meeting on a Saturday night. The ladies loved to cook. Cosmo was a musician and used to living on a steady diet of roadkill and booze. No woman would get to him through his stomach. What Cosmo was interested in the church ladies weren't offering.

When one of the ladies pressed him, Cosmo handled that issue with a smile and the diplomatic reply, "Now, how can I faithfully devote myself to you when you know there are a dozen of your lady friends and fellow worshippers who would like me to say, 'yes' to them as well? It would be unjust for me to take a side." He would give them a wink and tell them that he would silently dedicate his next performance to them. The women loved it. Cosmo was forbidden fruit. Propriety dictated behavior. After three months, a general détente emerged between Cosmo and the church ladies.

Reverend Howard knew Cosmo wasn't a believer. That didn't faze him, though. The Reverend believed that God would not give talent like Cosmo possessed if it wasn't for a purpose. The minister knew Cosmo played burlesque houses, as well, but Elias Howard was a patient man. He knew Cosmo had been sent to the church for a reason. That Sunday, he had asked Cosmo to remain after services.

Cosmo knocked on the office door, which was open. Reverend Howard was removing his robe.

"Come in, Cosmo."

The minister hung up the robe and turned to Cosmo. "I will make this brief. Wendall Shorter is a horn player and a member of this congregation. He informed me that a producer at Royal Studio is in need of a piano man for a recording session." Howard handed Cosmo a card.

"Wayne Jackson," said Cosmo, glancing at it.

"He's the man in charge of the session. I have no idea what they're paying, but I'm sure you can handle the job."

Cosmo slipped the card into his coat pocket. "Thank you, Reverend." He turned to go and then looked at the minister. Howard was pushing sixty and certainly didn't strike Cosmo as a club hopping gentleman. "Why are you telling me this?"

Reverend Howard gave Cosmo a questioning look. "What do you mean?"

"Well, don't get me wrong, Reverend, I truly appreciate the gig, but you know I don't fly with all that hosanna business."

Reverend Howard grinned. "You have a gift, Cosmo. Go see the man. What have you got to lose?"

Cosmo patted his pocket. "I will. Thank you." He tipped his hat and exited Reverend Howard's office, waving to the ladies as he left the church. There was a light step in Cosmo's walk as he made his way to his car, a blue pre-war Buick sitting on the street. He got in and started the engine and headed north up Western.

# 4

# *Courier from Hong Kong*

Lee May Sing glanced out the window of the limo. The sky was a slate gray. New York had changed since she was last there before the war. It was bigger and noisier, but much of its sophistication was worn and tarnished. 42$^{nd}$ Street was a seedy ghost of its former self. Lee May much preferred California to New York. She had grown up there, the daughter of a man whose family had been partners with Michael McGuire's grandfather, Sean. California was open and held vast vistas of coastline, desert, and mountains. New York was concrete and steel. The only vista was the building next door. But New York was where the work was. Hollywood wasn't calling the Chinese actress any longer, as Lee May was forty-four. Outside of Hepburn, Davis, and Crawford, it was hard for an actress over forty to get roles. It was especially impossible for an actress who was Chinese.

The Mutual Network had offered Lee May the lead in a television series with a guarantee of sixteen episodes. She was paid six thousand per episode. Lee May Sing was pragmatic, so she took the job and moved to the Big Apple.

The war had broadened Americans' interest in countries beyond their borders. The executives at Mutual Network hoped that by combining a former big screen star with exotic locals and action-packed scripts, they would have a winner.

Most Hollywood stars looked down on television. They considered it a distinct step down from making movies. Lee May had pitched the series herself to Lee Ketchum, a vice-president at the network. She suggested they do a TV series based on her character, Ann Kwan, in *Daughter of Canton*. This had been a film she made with Michael McGuire during the war and had been very successful at the box office. Her character of Kwan was now a courier for the Hong Kong Consulate. Each episode took her to a new locale, all of which were shot on a soundstage at Kaufman Astoria Studio.

The network also allowed Lee May to write her own scripts. She would no longer play the China doll that the Hollywood moguls had crafted for her. Miscegenation was still the law in many states when it came to Asians. Lee May overcame this issue by always having Ann Kwan depart one locale and leave any romantic interest with a broken heart as she sailed off to another adventure as the *Courier from Hong Kong*.

Lee May was surprised at how swiftly the episodes were shot. One day of rehearsal. Two days for principal photography, one day for pick-up shots, and one day for editing. Lee May didn't mind the pace and rather enjoyed it. In seven more weeks, she would be back home in California, which made her happy. Her friends lived there. Michael McGuire was there.

Lee May found New Yorkers cold and rude. She eschewed Chinatown. To some Chinese, she was a hero, the first Asian female to get star billing in a Hollywood film. To others, Lee May Sing was loathed for her portrayals of villains and maids. Lee May hadn't helped herself when she glibly quipped to a reporter, "It's better to play a maid than be a maid." Many Chinese took offense. To them, Lee May Sing was the Asian equivalent of an Uncle Tom. At the time, however, Lee May Sing didn't care. She was twenty-six and had much of her career ahead of her. Eighteen years later was a different matter.

It had been nearly a decade since Lee May was cast in a major role. She was no longer a Hollywood star. There were many Chinese who reminded her of that fact. Lee May spent her days at the studio or at her apartment on West 30th. She didn't entertain much and rarely went out, instead preferring the company of her cat and a good book to dinner at Sardis. This gave Lee May plenty of time to work on scripts and prepare for the next day's shooting. She would often make suggestions for lighting and for camera set-ups and blocking. Lee May Sing was a pro.

The car stopped, and the driver got out and opened the door for Lee May. She thanked him and entered the studio. Donald Beaumont, the director, was seated with the rest of the cast at a table. He was in his fifties, and his gray hair only made him look more sophisticated than he had in his younger days. He wore gray slacks, a navy-blue sports coat, dress shirt, and tie.

Beaumont had cut his teeth directing B pictures on Poverty Row. Television production demanded a director who could shoot fast and on a tight budget. Don Beaumont was now the go-to guy for an action-packed drama series.

The director rose when Lee May Sing approached the table.

"Lee May."

Beaumont and star shook hands. Lee May gave the director a chaste kiss on the cheek. She remarked, "It is so good to work with you again. It's been years, *Singapore Sally* at Republic."

Beaumont grinned. "My God, you do have a good memory. That must be…"

"Thirteen years ago," Lee May interjected.

The director chuckled and shook his head. "You really do know how to hurt a man. Let me introduce you to our guests this week, Clifton Webb, Ben Johnson, and Agnes Morehead."

"It is a pleasure to meet you," greeted Agnes.

"You really are more beautiful in person than on the screen," Webb quipped.

Ben Johnson tipped his head. "Miss Sing."

"It is so nice to meet you all," said Lee May. She noticed a young man in a t-shirt and dungarees sitting at a table alone studying his script.

Beaumont leaned close and said in a hushed tone, "That's James Dean. He is playing the role of the mechanic. Rather intense little fellow. Word is leave him alone and he'll give a us a hell of a performance."

Lee May sat down. Beaumont took his seat and picked up his script. "All right, folks, we have this morning to do a read through. We're shooting in three hours on the New York set."

Dean laughed.

"Might I inquire what is so funny, Mr. Dean?" asked the director.

Dean sat there for a moment and regarded the other actors in front of him and gestured to a window. "We've got all of New York right outside this studio. Seems sort of foolish to use a set."

Beaumont glanced at Lee May, who had a bemused look on her face. The director faced the young actor and gave him a stern look. "Be that as it may, we will be shooting Murray's garage and the exteriors for Attorney Dawson's office and the flower shop on Stage 6. Now, Mr. Dean, would you care to join the rest of the cast as we do a read through?" the director said more as a statement than a question.

Dean sighed. He got up like he carried the weight of the world on his shoulders and slowly ambled over to the table where the others were seated. He slouched in his chair and said, "I'm ready when you are, boss."

Beaumont took a deep breath. "Okay, let's start."

The read through went fine. Dean surprised Beaumont and did his part well. When it came to shoot, however, Dean was decidedly different.

The cast and crew were assembled on the set. The scene called for Lee May to enter the garage and inquire how long it would take the mechanic to repair her car.

"Why does it have to be Murphy's Garage?" asked Dean.

Beaumont gave the young actor a questioning look. "What do you mean?"

Dean grinned. "I don't feel like a Murphy. I think the place should be called Stoney Stonewall's Garage. I feel more like a Stoney than a Murphy."

The director had worked with difficult stars before, but they were stars. This twenty-year-old smartass hadn't made a single film. Beaumont smiled and said, "Thank you for that suggestion, James. Unfortunately, the sets have already been designed."

Dean nodded his head and continued chewing his gum.

"Please get rid of the gum," said Beaumont.

Dean chuckled. "This is my prop."

The director held back a roll of his eyes. "Fine, let's take our places and see if we can't get one in the can."

The actors took their places. Beaumont called for action.

"Rolling," called out the D.P.

"Speed," called out the sound man.

Lee May entered the garage. Dean had his head under the hood of a Chrysler.

"Hello," said Lee May.

Dean kept his head under the hood. This wasn't in the script.

"Hello," Lee May repeated.

Dean continued to keep his head under the car's hood.

Lee May took a step. She was still close to her mark and tapped Dean on the shoulder.

Dean feigned banging his head on the hood. He grinned at Lee Sing and said, "You spooked me there for a moment."

The line wasn't in the script. Lee May didn't miss a beat.

"I am sorry to disturb you, Murphy. When will my car be ready?"

Dean picked up a rag and wiped his hands slowly. "Well, that depends, ma'am. I gotta get a part from the warehouse in Jersey."

Dean had gone totally off script and was adlibbing lines.

"Cut!" shouted Beaumont.

The crew stood silent. Clifton Webb took out a silver case from his breast pocket and removed a cigarette. He offered a cigarette to Agnes, who took one, and one to Ben who declined. Beaumont stood up and looked at Dean.

"I must have a different script than yours, James."

Dean grinned. "Ah-h no. I just thought my character was more realistic adlibbing than just reciting these lines. They're pretty lame."

Lee May had written the script. She remained silent, leaving it to the director.

"Well just to humor me, let's try it as written, James."

"You can call me Jim."

"Fine, Jim, please just deliver your lines as written."

Dean saluted Beaumont. "Yes, boss."

The director turned to the crew. "All right, let's do it again."

Dean hadn't taken his position under the hood.

"Yes, James…Jim?" asked the director.

"What's my motivation?" asked Dean

"Your what?" asked Beaumont, briefly dumbfounded.

"My motivation, I'm Murphy the mechanic. What is my motivation for this scene?"

Beaumont took a deep breath. There was an entire episode to shoot. Thankfully Dean was only in one other scene. The director looked at the actor. "Your check."

"Excuse me?' asked Dean.

"You repair cars. Ann Kwan left her car for you to repair. You do the job, you get paid. You don't do the job; you don't get paid. That's your motivation."

Dean winked at Beaumont. "Got it. Thanks, boss."

The actor took his place. Beaumont took his seat. He leaned close to the Pauline Lippmann, the script girl, and whispered, "If that little shit needs any more motivation, he's going find a size eleven up his ass."

Pauline forced back a laugh.

"All right, let's do it again," said the director. "Action."

# 5

# *Needles*

Los Angeles Tribune Headline – May 9, 1951

## Investigation at standstill with Allied Aircraft CEO vanishing act

### Howard Silver

The Congressional investigation into James Hagen's misappropriation of funds has all but come to a standstill since Hagen vanished from his San Diego office three months ago. Police are at a loss to say exactly what happened to Hagen or where he might be. Claire Hagen, the former wife of the missing executive, said, "I haven't seen or spoken to Jimmy since our divorce." Senator Knowland was quoted, "Hagen can only run so long. We'll get him. This is a complete disrespect to Congress and the laws of our fine country." So far, the FBI has not been called upon to investigate Hagen's disappearance, which leaves this reporter wondering just what type of shenanigans Mr. Hagen thinks he can get away with.

"Fuck 'em." James Hagen tossed the paper on the floor in disgust. He was seated at a table in a private Pullman car. The Pullman was one of three attached to a locomotive. All three cars were fitted with cut glass and ivory door handles and contained more luxuries than a pasha's palace. The train was stopped on a sidetrack some twenty miles north of Needles between the California and Nevada border.

Hagen shot Tom Hollister, his fixer, a perturbed look. He was dressed in a dark suit and sat in a plush chair. After Hagen's run-in with Nicole Sullivan, he hired Hollister to tend to the type of business that needed a discreet but physical response. Tom had worked for the Gambino family and was a trusted soldier.

"Fuckin' reporter," snorted Hagen.

"Relax. The Heb is talking out his ass," said Hollister. "I spoke to Cheney this morning. He said that the committee is more than likely to move on if you can't be located in the next week or so."

Walter Cheney was Hagen's attorney and had no knowledge of his client's whereabouts.

"Fucking shyster said the same thing a month ago." Hagen took a sip of his coffee. "Fuckin' lawyers. I'm tired of sitting out in the middle of nowhere waiting for this shit storm to blow over."

Hollister gave Hagen a reassuring pat on the arm. "You needed to disappear so the Feds couldn't serve you."

"Yeah, Walter wanted me to take the *Oso Oro* and head out beyond the three-mile limit," chuckled Hagen, referring to his fifty-foot sloop. "Could you imagine being stuck out at sea for three months? Instead, I'm sitting in the middle of the fuckin' desert."

"It's the smart move, Jimmy. The authorities can't subpoena you, and you're not out at sea."

Hagen shrugged his shoulders. "Easy for you to say. Walter needs to get on the fuckin' stick and make those assholes in D.C. lay off. When the war was going on, nobody said a fuckin' thing about budgets as long as we got the planes made. Now Congress wants to go over billing that's ten years old with a fine-tooth comb. Fuck 'em."

"That's why Cheney decided to send a couple of reporters to interview you. You can give them your side of the story."

Hagen gave Hollister a look like the man had just lost his mind. "Reporters coming here?"

"Relax, it's been arranged.'

"The whole point of being on this fuckin' train is so nobody will know my whereabouts. You bring reporters out here; the FBI will show up the next day. What the fuck was Walter thinking?"

Tom Hollister offered a reassuring smile. "Don't worry. Bobby and Vincent are handling this. They picked them up in Dago, and they're bringing them out here blindfolded." He gestured to the windows. "Nothing out there will identify your whereabouts. It's desert."

"What do we do when they leave?" asked Hagen

"We go to Vegas for a couple of days and then head to Kansas City."

Hagen frowned. "No. Not Kansas. We're going to take this train to Arizona instead."

"Fine.

The two men sat down at the table. As if on cue, a waiter wheeled in a cart and served them steak, eggs, and hash browns with a large pot of black coffee.

An hour later, a yellow school bus pulled up on the frontage road next to the tracks. All the windows were blacked out except for the windshield.

"This is them," said Hollister.

James Hagen stood up. He walked over to a mirror and checked his appearance, smoothing back his hair and adjusting his tie. Satisfied Hagen followed Hollister into the next car. The second Pullman was just as fancy as the previous car, except this one had more of a feeling of a private club with its bar, card table, and ticker-tape machine. Hagen took a seat in a plush silk stuffed chair, and Hollister stood behind him.

Vincent Drysdale led the contingent of four reporters into the Pullman. Drysdale was forty-two and Allied Aircraft's vice-president of marketing. He had worked for Thompson—Mitchell, one of the biggest agencies on Madison Avenue for over a decade. He handled the Chevrolet and Chesterfield Cigarettes accounts. Hagen hired Drysdale away from the ad company. He knew the aircraft industry was dependent on D.C. and the Pentagon. He'd wanted the best New York huckster and got him. Drysdale was eloquent. Drysdale was smooth. Drysdale could sell oil to the Saudis.

Robert Sardi was at the tail end of the group. Sardi was twenty-six and was Drysdale's copywriter and right-hand man. Sardi was actually Robert Sarducci formerly of the Murray Hill area of Cleveland, Ohio. He came from a working-class family that placed a high value on education. After the war, Sarducci got a degree in English and sought out a job in the newly burgeoning advertising industry.

Bob was smart enough to know that Sardi sounded smart. It drew a connection to the famous Hollywood restaurant. Robert Salvatore Sarducci became Bob Sardi. Nobody was interested in hiring a kid out of college as a copywriter. Sardi labored in the mailroom of Walter & McKenzie and hated it. After six months, he asked his uncle, Tony, for a favor. Tony worked for Alfred Calabrese. The man made a call. Calabrese affirmed that a young Bob had a gift for words and knowledge of *the business*. He would be an asset to James Hagen. Bob Sardi was on a train to San Diego two days later.

Sardi and Drysdale quickly removed the reporters' blindfolds. These men worked for the *Examiner, Chronicle, Telegraph,* and *Daily News*. A representative for the *Tribune* was conspicuously absent. The reporters grumbled as they rubbed their eyes. All were astonished to see James Hagen seated before them.

"I assure you I am not a phantom, gentlemen," Hagen said. This got a chuckle out of the group. Hagen gestured to the bar. "There is a full bar at your disposal."

The men walked over and helped themselves to the scotch, whiskey, and gin at the bar. They then turned their attention to Hagen. Sardi picked up a humidor and offered cigars to the men.

"I'm sorry for all the secrecy, boys. The Feds want to serve me, and I'm not ready to dance with that bunch of hooligans."

"Why are they so interested in you?" asked a short man in a brown suit.

Hagen threw his arms open in mock surrender. "Why else? Politics. Nobody cared when Allied Aircraft was rolling out plenty of planes for the war. Now that the war is over, some folks on Capitol Hill believe they can make a name for themselves by dredging up accounts from a decade ago. We won the war. Time to move on."

Bob Sardi stepped up and gave the group and warm smile. "The reason we brought you gentlemen out here was to show you that Mr. Hagen is indeed among the living and that he is more than happy to talk to you fellas. You have to realize that due to National Security Mr. Hagen is limited in the scope of what he can answer. Mr. Drysdale will supply you with a complete dossier on Allied Aircraft's current projects and our policies."

The reporters were smart enough to know the score.

"Who do you think will win the series this year?" asked a reporter from the *Chronicle*.

"It's still pretty early in the season to call that one, Charlie," Hagen replied good naturedly.

The men talked sports. They talked liquor. The talked cars. They talked women. An hour later, Bob Sardi and Vincent Drysdale replaced the blindfolds on the reporters and loaded them up in the school bus.

James Hagen poured himself a scotch as the bus disappeared down the frontage road. "What'd you think?"

Hollister shrugged his shoulders. "I wouldn't worry. Bobby can handle that bunch."

"Kid's smart."

The engine started. The train slowly backed up and then pulled forward, coming off the sidetrack and onto the main track and heading east. Cactus, scrub, and rocks disappeared as the train rolled started a slow climb. Lizards, snakes, and rodents were left to rule the desert kingdom.

Hagen glanced out the window. "A change of scenery will be nice."

# 6

# *Hooray For Hollywood*

Royal Studios sat on Santa Monica Blvd just west of La Brea. The backlot once covered twenty-six acres. Now it was half that. Irving Schulman, the former studio head, was gone, heart attack, dead at the tender age of eighty-nine. Schulman died at his desk the week after the Chinese crossed the 38th Parallel. Sarah Royal remained as acting head for the time being. The New Yorker bankers wouldn't allow that for long. They were fine with Sarah as head of production, but they weren't about to allow a woman to run the studio her father had founded.

Julius Solomon, a graduate of Brandis University School of Business, was sent to oversee the studio until a new studio head could be appointed. Julius had convinced his uncle, who sat on the bank's board of directors, that he was just the man for the job. Abraham Weisman had no interest in movies. He preferred a good book or going to the symphony. He did know that the right movie produced a tremendous profit, however, and Weisman had a great interest in making money. He sent his twenty-six-year-old nephew to Los Angeles with the single order, "Come the end of the year, the balance sheet better show black."

Julius had a wild mop of red hair and the complexion of primer paint. He stepped off the train at Union Station wearing a pair of khaki jodhpurs and carrying a riding crop. Julius lost the crop two days later when he nearly put his eye out with it. Michael convinced him to lose the jodhpurs as well. Julius kept his boots. There were lifts in the boots which brought him an additional three inches. At five foot three, the young man needed all the help he could get. Julius encouraged people to refer to him as Julie S. He thought it had a modern feel to it. Michael called him Mr. Solomon without the slightest bit of sarcasm. The new studio head took to Michael.

Julius was smart enough to know that if he wanted the studio to show a profit, he had to garner the cooperation of Sarah Royal and Michael McGuire. He also had to clean house and wasn't sure how they would take to such an act. They were both much older than he was and had worked together for years. McGuire was a producer with a record number of films that had made money. They might not have been blockbusters, but not one his films had lost a dime.

As the first order of business, Julius sold off two thirds of the studio's backlot. Real estate was more valuable than having fifteen acres of open land. Sarah didn't object. She knew that if she fought Julius, the bankers would more than likely remove her as head of production, a position she had held since her father died.

Michael remained silent and kept his head down. He preferred to shoot on location. It kept the crew away from the prying eyes of studio management. The fact that Julius sold the backlot to developers didn't bother Michael. It now gave him the perfect excuse to do more location shooting.

The sale of the studio's land and Michael's film, *For the Love of Mike*, put the studio in the black that year. It was Michael's most profitable film yet. He was smart and knew many of the former GIs were tired of war pictures. They had been in the real deal and didn't need Hollywood handing them another reenactment with a star who had been four thousand miles close to the front. Instead, Michael gave them a fish out of water story about a New York reporter sent to do a story on a female zoologist studying mountain lions in the Rockies.

The film not only did very well at the box office, but it also captured the best screenplay Oscar in April.

The morning after the Oscars, the bankers in New York informed Julius he was now the head of Royal Studio. Julius was well aware that retaining his position was directly contingent upon Royal Studio remaining profitable. Julius loved Los Angeles and he loved his job. He knew that to succeed he needed to keep a talented producer like Michael McGuire close. He needed to keep Sarah Royal close as well. Julius Solomon, formerly of Brooklyn, allowed the pair the freedom to work. Then HUAC returned to Los Angeles.

The House on Un-American Activities had come to Hollywood in 1947. Ten of the most talented writers, producers, and directors ended up going to prison. The committee went back to Washington. Joe McCarthy, a freshman senator from Wisconsin, saw HUAC as his personal road to fame and glory. He also saw Hollywood as an easy target. McCarthy's anti-Hollywood rhetoric appealed to Midwesterners and many others. They viewed California as the land of fruits and nuts and Hollywood as a hedonistic haven for Jews, homos, and Reds. It was an election year, and nailing Hollywood commies meant headlines.

Michael loved making movies. He even loved them when he was a young bootlegger running a highly profitable nightclub. Michael was blessed with a foresight that most men lacked. It wasn't that he could tell the future; Michael had the ability to not only see the forest for the trees, but he could also see a path through the forest. Michael knew bootlegging was not a venue one grew old in. At the top of his game, he had sold his business interests and contacts to Joseph Ardizzone, the head of the Los Angeles rackets, and "retired" honorably from organized crime.

Royal Studios was in turmoil at the time with Joseph Royal's death. Michael used the opportunity to set up shop at the studio. He smoothly made the transition from bootlegger to producer, employing many of the same skills. It was the year of *The Jazz Singer*. Talkies had come to town and changed everything. Actors had to speak their dialogue. Michael knew that if you made a villain interesting enough, the audience would root for them. His pictures generally dealt with flawed characters who were regular folk. Michael didn't make epics; he made meat and potatoes movies. The films were made on small budgets and made money. Michael knew the road to survival in Hollywood was to remain profitable to the studio. You were only as good as your last film.

Michael knew he had detractors, of course. One couldn't remain a major entity in Hollywood for as many years as Michael had without raising a crop of them. Jealousy and fear were the two biggest motivators. Michael was also prone to progressive politics. His aunt had been a suffragette and died in the firebombing of the Los Angeles Women's Clinic where she had worked as the agency's attorney. Michael's wife, Laurel, worked for Planned Parenthood. Michael produced films starring Asians, Negroes, and Mexicans. Michael did not put his name to petitions or join political organizations. His grandfather, Sean McGuire, had taught him to be circumspect when it came to such things. It was precisely because of his flying below the political radar that HUAC initially missed him.

The committee was running on overdrive. Joe McCarthy planned to kick ass and take names. Joe was going for broke. He had a list, and he was going to squeeze the balls of every producer, director, writer, and actor he could. If they weren't commies, they were homos, dykes, and malcontents. All of it was juice for Joe's political machine. He and his right-hand man, Roy Cohen, perused lists, pressured stoolies, and pimped the press. The public ate it up. They were shocked to discover Ty Power was a gay blade and Marlene lunched at the *Ladies*

*Club.* The committee and its revelations tantalized, scandalized, and sensationalized the public's love for salacious innuendo.

Hollywood folk were rich. They had it coming to them. They were homos. They had it coming to them. They were Jews. They had it coming to them. Joe and the committee killed careers and marriages like swatting flies. McCarthy did the rumba at the Mocambo. He dished dirt and consumed pasta at Perino's. He smiled and sipped scotch at Cicero's. Wannabe starlets rubbed their tits in Joe's face. He loved it. Roy Cohen cruised for bum boys in Santa Monica. A promise of a screen test got Roy laid every time. Hollywood was a godsend of political mana and sexual shenanigans far beyond anything Wisconsin could ever offer. Joe and Roy were having the time of their lives. Then they set their sights on Michael McGuire.

The committee had called Larry Parks in and put him to the question, "Are you now or have you ever been a member of the Communist Party?"

Parks objected. The committee squeezed Larry's cajones. They threatened his wife, Betty. Parks squirmed. He squawked. He squealed. He was pilfered in the press. Park's career went from leading man to persona non grata in sixty seconds. Anyone who worked with Larry was now suspect. Guilt by association was the committee's mantra.

Michael McGuire had produced *Pacific Convoy* in '42 with Parks playing a supporting role of a ship's lieutenant. The film was a hit. Michael went on to produce other films. Parks went on to play Al Jolson, twice. Parks was pink. The committee decided that McGuire was probably a pinko too. They subpoenaed Michael. He appeared on the appointed date and answered their questions. The committee didn't care for Michael's answers. They classified Michael McGuire uncooperative and reserved the right to call him back and put him to the question again.

It was a beautiful day as Michael pulled up to the studio gate. He waved to Ernie Becker, the guard. Ernie had a solemn look on his face as the black Lincoln Cosmopolitan passed the gate. Michael drove across the lot, parked, and walked into his office. Joyce Wentz, his secretary, looked up.

"Sarah wants to see you."

Michael picked up the mail and leafed through the envelopes. "Did you get in touch with Bob Mitchum?"

"Yes. He said he'll do the film with one exception. He doesn't want to play against Cooper."

Michael looked at Joyce in surprise. "Gary Cooper is a real get for this picture."

Joyce nodded and forced a smile. "Mr. Mitchum said, 'Please tell your boss I won't play second fiddle to a stoolie.'"

Michael sighed. "Damn politics. Get Bob on the line, please."

"Sarah said she wants to talk to you."

"Yeah, fine. Get me Mitchum first."

Joyce gave Michael a look that said, "Now."

Michael set the mail down and rolled his eyes. "Fine."

Michael didn't wait for Sarah's secretary to announce him. He walked right into the executive's office and took a seat. Sarah was on the phone. As soon as she saw it was Michael, she excused herself to the person she was talking to and hung up. Sarah got up and closed the door to her office.

"Oh, it's going to be one of those meetings," said Michael with a glib tone.

Sarah resumed her seat behind the desk. "Unfortunately, yes."

"If this is about the budget for—"

"This is about your survival." Sarah looked at Michael and allowed her words to sink in.

"My survival, what are you talking about? *Vegas Shakedown* is on budget and due to wrap next week, four days ahead of schedule. *Badge in the Dust* is set to begin shooting in two weeks."

Sarah folded her hands. "Michael, the committee labeled you uncooperative."

"I answered their questions."

"Obviously not to their satisfaction."

Michael frowned. "Come on, Sarah, you know as well as I do all they wanted from me were names. The committee is interested in only one thing: getting people to name others. The more names they collect, the more it aids their fascist cause."

"Careful, Michael. It's a good thing you are saying these things to me and not someone else."

Michael chuckled, "Well there goes our First Amendment rights. Jaysus, Sarah, McCarthy and Nixon are a pair of political punks looking to make a name for themselves."

"You need to play ball with them."

Michael arched an eyebrow. "Are you suggesting I give them names?"

"I am suggesting that you cooperate with the committee. Being listed as uncooperative makes it very difficult."

"For whom?"

"For the studio, for me."

Michael sat silent for a long while. "I won't name anybody," he finally said.

She pursed her lips. "I can give you some names."

"Damn it, Sarah, I don't want them. You think I don't know who works on my pictures? The point is, I don't give a damn. If they can act, direct, write, or sew a costume, I don't give a tinker's fart what they do when they leave the set."

"The committee is going to want you to give them names. I can supply you names of people it won't hurt."

Michael looked at Sarah with disbelief. "Damn it, you don't understand. Informers have been the bane of the Irish for eight-hundred years. I will not join that club. You of all people should know that."

A silent tension filled the room you could cut with paper.

"I don't know if I can protect you," Sarah finally said, breaking the silence.

Michael gave the executive a warm smile. "Sarah, I value your friendship. I certainly don't need you to protect me."

"Don't expect Julius to protect you. He will abandon you faster than a rat on a sinking ship."

"So, I'm a sinking ship."

Sarah averted her eyes. "I hope not."

Michael realized then that the meeting was going nowhere. He stood up. "I can handle the committee, Sarah."

Sarah looked at Michael. "Not without giving them names, I'm afraid you won't."

He gave her a devilish wink. "A hundred dollars says the committee won't give you or the studio any trouble on my behalf."

Sarah sighed and retorted, "I hope you're right, Michael."

Michael smiled and exited the production executive's office. He had put up a good front. Michael knew that if the committee didn't reclassify his standing that Royal Studios would fire him. All of the studios had signed an agreement pledging that they wouldn't hire any know communists or their sympathizers. Michael had miscalculated the committee. It was time to checkmate them. He walked off the lot and went down to Lucy's Adobe, where he placed a called from the phone booth in the restaurant.

"What' da hear what' da ya say, ya fuckin' Mick?" said James Hagen. He had given Michael his number. McGuire was the only man besides Tom Hollister who knew how to get in touch with Hagen. The pair had served together in the Great War. Michael had saved Hagen's life and was the only man James trusted with knowledge of his whereabouts.

"I see you're in the news again," Michael shot back.

"Fuck 'em," said Hagen. "I heard HUAC decided to crawl up your ass."

"Yeah. That's why I'm calling. I could use some help from our friends." Michael replied with a sigh of resignation.

"I'll make some calls. Don't worry."

When Michael sold his interests to Joseph Ardizzone, Jimmy Grazzi, Michael's partner, decided to do the same. He decided to "retire" in a much flashier fashion and "died" in a blaze of glory at Point Magu. The bootleggers were landing a load of bonded scotch on the beach when the police showed up. Jimmy and William McGrath crashed their car into the lead police car, allowing the truck loaded with contraband hooch to escape.

McGrath had been the third partner in Michael's bootlegging enterprises. He was dying of cancer and came up with the plan. He drove his vehicle, which was rigged to explode on impact, straight into the police car. When the dust settled, he and two other policemen were dead. They had put a body obtained from USC's medical school in the front with McGrath. The authorities believed it was Jimmy Grazzi. He had escaped on the truck with the illegal Canadian scotch.

Six months in Tijuana with a new face and name change, James Hagen became the owner of a small aircraft company. Then the war came, and the rest was history. Hagen became a very wealthy man. He had never completely severed his ties with the underworld and was on good terms with the Italian and Mexican families operating on the west coast.

"I gotta tell you, Frankie Bomp loved that movie, *Gangster Alley*," said Hagen, referencing Frank Bompensiero, the head of the San Diego family.

"I made that back in '44," replied Michael with a tone of disbelief.

"What can I tell you? Frank doesn't go to the movies like most folks. Don't worry about those fucks. Cohen is a fag who takes it up the ass, and McCarthy is a lush."

"I also need the *Tribune* to lay off. The studio depends on the paper for positive coverage of their films."

"Done."

"Thanks."

There was a brief pause. Then Hagen said, "You will owe these people a favor."

"I expected as much. Tell them I won't kill anyone. Other than that, I'm sure I can accommodate them."

"Understood."

"Be well, Jimmy," Michael said, hanging up the telephone.

# 7

# *All the News That's Fit to Print*

The department editors were gathered around the long table in the office. Harry Chapman, owner of the *Los Angeles Tribune*, sat at the head. The *L.A. Tribune* was the paper of record for the city. Once, there had been over a dozen newspapers that competed for readers. Discounting the local rags, now there was but two, the *Tribune* and Hearst's, *Examiner*. Otis Grayson had once reigned as owner of the *Tribune*. Grayson was big on boosterism, big business, and inside deals. His son-in-law, Harry, cut one of the best inside deals of the century, picking up for pennies thousands of acres in the Valley thought to be worthless. William Mulholland built his aqueduct and stole the water from Owens Lake. Harry and Otis made millions. Otis died shortly after WWI. Harry was now the owner and managing editor of the largest paper west of Chicago.

"First order of business," said Harry. "I want us to downplay Senator McCarthy and his committee."

"The *Examiner* is going to scoop us, Harry," retorted Max Duncan, the Metro editor.

Harry gave a nod. "Let them. The committee will eventually return to Washington, just like they did before. They're attacking an industry that will remain here, an industry that would be injudicious to alienate. The *Tribune* depends on the studios' advertising and access to their stars. We shall leave the naming of names and innuendo to Mr. Hearst and the tabloids."

There was a chuckle from the group of men.

"What do you want me to do regarding Michael McGuire?" asked Duncan. "The committee declared him an unfriendly witness. Howard Silver is working on a background piece on McGuire for the Sunday edition."

Harry looked at the Metro editor. "Scratch it."

The editor looked perplexed. "Scratch the McGuire Story?"

"Leave sleeping dogs be, Max," Harry Chapman replied.

Duncan gave a nod. He knew Michael had once run a popular speakeasy, but that had been years ago. McGuire was a successful movie producer and had been one for over two decades.

What Max didn't know was that prior to the editors meeting, Ben Draper, the paper's Manager of Sales and Circulation, had received a phone call. The caller didn't elaborate. He merely explained that unfavorable coverage of Michael McGuire would result in the *Tribune* losing the business of a dozen companies that advertised in the paper. Allied Aircraft was mentioned as one. Draper informed Harry of the call. Harry thanked his manager and proceeded to the editors meeting. Business was business, and Harry saw no profit in going after Michael. He had much bigger fish to fry.

"What about the story on Elysian Park Heights?" Harry asked.

"We're working on it," Max replied.

"I want it in shape by Sunday. Put Silver on it. We've got an election coming up this year, and I want every reader to see that development for exactly what it is. This is Socialism at its worst. I want dirt on Neutra, the architect behind the project. This is nothing more than the taxpayers footing the bill to subsidize a bunch of Mexicans."

The editors nodded their heads.

Steve Garrison, the sports editor, raised his hand. Garrison was younger than the other editors and readily deferred to them in these meetings.

"Yes, Steve?" said Harry.

"Sir, my boys have been hearing a lot about the city approaching Paul Brown to move his team here."

Harry flashed a smile. "I'm glad you brought that up, Steve. As you all know, Los Angeles has no major league team. It has been the dream of many to see a ball club move here. I am going to have to ask your indulgence on this subject, though. Negotiations such as these are tricky and require a delicate handling."

Garrison gave a nod. "Understood, Mr. Chapman."

"Fine, then I'll leave you men to it." Harry stood and walked out of the conference room.

Harry had lunch with Dennis Ryan that afternoon. They dined at the Ambassador. Ryan was a major player in the city and was also quickly gaining entrance to the oligarchy. Ryan came from humble beginnings. His father had been a working man who died seven months after Dennis's birth. Ed Ryan left a wife with five sons. Dennis was the youngest.

All the men in the Ryan family pitched in to do their part. Dennis worked a paper route and did odd jobs. Helen Ryan always stressed education and made sure each of her boys went to college. After graduating, Dennis opened a gas station with his brother, Allen. When the war broke out, Dennis enlisted in the Navy. After the war, he entered politics. His first try at a city council city failed. In 1947, however, he was successful. Dennis Ryan got a new jail built, passed major smog legislation, and fought to keep war time rent control laws in place. He fought for city employees and pushed for them to get raises, calling their situation "indentured city servants." He also supported the Elysian Heights public housing project.

Ryan was a hero to the working people. Harry needed Ryan on his team, which was why he had invited the rising political star to lunch. Harry had learned to play the long game from his father-in-law. Cultivating Ryan was part of that game.

"I want to thank you for meeting me today," said Harry as they finished their lunch.

Dennis was thirty-one and had the rakish good looks of a man about town. He smiled and said, "I'm sure you want something, Harry. Why don't you just tell me what it is?"

Harry took a sip of his scotch and glanced at the man seated across from him. "I would like you to change your support for the Elysian project."

"Might I ask why?"

"I would prefer not to say. The city needs that land for other purposes."

"Those purposes wouldn't have anything to do with a major league team, would they?"

Harry scratched his jaw, hesitating. "Someone has been talking out of school."

Dennis sat back in his chair. "Give me your pitch, Harry. I'm listening."

Harry looked at the councilman and chuckled. "Fine, lad, it's very simple. If Los Angeles is going to take its rightful place among other major American cities, we need a major league ball club. All cities of prominence have a major league team. Ball clubs, especially winning teams, attract followers from out of the area who will come to the city to see their team play. They are good for business, and they certainly would say Los Angeles has arrived."

"I agree," said Dennis.

The councilman's response caught Harry off guard for a moment. He hadn't expected Ryan to agree that quickly. "Well, that is good news, Dennis," Harry stammered.

"I would like something in return," said Dennis.

"Of course."

"My brothers, John and Louis, have a construction company. Whatever you plan to build on that land, they get a contract. The housing project, wherever you plan to move that, they get the contract on that project too. They get your support in your paper as well. They're not as good looking as me, but they both have fine families that would look nice in the Sunday features."

Harry was silent for a moment. He picked up his scotch and held it in a toast. "To great beginnings, councilman. Very well played."

Dennis Ryan picked up his glass and joined Chapman in his toast. "To great beginnings."

"If you don't mind my asking, why are you willing to change your vote?"

Dennis set his glass down. "Family. You just agreed to give my brothers a heck of a lot of work. I will champion the people, but family always comes first. I would ask that you go easy on the Mexicans in your paper."

"Why? They don't live in your district."

Dennis met the publisher's eyes. "They will eventually. If you haven't noticed, Harry, they are having more children than we are."

"They overbreed like dogs."

Dennis shrugged his shoulders. "Be that as it may, one day they will outnumber us. It is best to pet a dog you wish to control than beat it with a stick."

Harry sat back in his seat and looked at the councilman. "They told me you were whip-smart."

"Then we have a deal?"

The newspaper publisher reached across the table and shook the councilman's hand. "We have a deal."

# 8

# *Par for the Course*

The ball sailed high into the clear blue sky, then curved and began its decent before finally landing in the rough.

"Son of a bitch," cursed Dick Nixon, looking where his ball had landed.

Ben Patchard, a wealthy farmer from the Central Valley, grinned. He set his ball down and teed off. The ball fell short of the green, but was in a better position than Nixon's.

Harry Chapman was next. His ball sailed straight and fell on the green. The final player, Ross Goodwin, a developer, nailed it. His ball landed on the green and rolled to a foot from the cup. Goodwin specialized in family home developments in the southland. Nixon had beaten Helen Douglas to win the Senate race. Chapman, Patchard, and Goodwin were three of the biggest Republican donors in the state. The four men headed down the green. They had no caddies, however, as they did not want prying ears.

Harry and Ross allowed Nixon and Patchard to take the lead. This was more than a game of golf. This was where business was conducted.

Patchard was older than the senator, but he had retained his athletic good looks. "You know you guys were pretty hard on, McGuire."

Nixon gave Patchard a pained look. "You're saying that because he's related to your wife. If I didn't know you better, Ben, I'd say you wanted me to give McGuire a break."

"That's exactly what I'd like you to do," laughed Patchard. "Sure, Emily is his cousin, but that's not the reason. Michael McGuire is no communist. You won't be able to prove otherwise."

"The man is tricky, I'll give you that," sighed Nixon.

Patchard shrugged. "Think about it."

Nixon smiled and went over to play his ball. He was two over par by the time the group moved on to the next hole.

None of the men mentioned politics for the rest of the game. They talked baseball. They talked the market. They talked cars. After the game, they adjourned to the club house. A round of Bloody Marys was ordered. The group tallied up their scores. To his surprise, Dick Nixon won the pot. This had not occurred because Nixon was in Ben Hogan's league. It was in the other men's best interests to put the senator in a festive mood.

Ben Patchard had received a call informing him that he would have trucking issues getting his produce to market. Russ Goodwin had received a similar call, regarding the strong possibility of an electricians' strike. Both were told they could avoid these problems if the senator and his colleagues changed their designation of Michael McGuire from uncooperative witness to cooperative.

The drinks came. The trio paid the senator his winnings and toasted him. The men joked. They jollied. They joshed. Goodwin looked at Nixon and said, "What do you think about what Ben spoke to you about?"

Nixon gave the developer a bemused look. "I am but one man on the committee."

"Your word carries weight, Dick."

Nixon peered around at the three men. "Why McGuire? I know Ben here has an interest because of his wife, but what makes you, Harry, want to give this pinko a break?"

Chapman met Nixon's gaze. "The man is well liked in the film industry. My paper depends on their advertising. It depends on the studios' goodwill to have access to their stars."

Goodwin wasn't a man to make longwinded speeches. He pulled out his check book and wrote a check for five thousand dollars to the senator's re-election committee. The developer tore the check from the book and handed it to Nixon. "This isn't a bribe. It's an advance on your next term. There are people who believe in you, Dick. They expect great things of you."

Dick Nixon's eyes widened when he saw the amount. He folded the check and slipped it in his pocket. "Like I said, gentlemen, I'm just one man."

Goodwin gave Nixon a reassuring look. "We have no doubts in your capabilities."

Two days later, Robert Hillsbury, the arts editor at the *Tribune*, received a call from a clerk working for the committee. The man would not give his name; he merely informed Hillsbury that Michael McGuire had been reclassified as a cooperative witness and that HUAC was closing their investigation on the producer. Hillsbury hung up and called his boss, Harry, to inform him of the news he had just received.

"Was that it?" asked Harry.

"Yeah, the guy just said the committee was closing their case on McGuire."

"Fine."

"Do you want use to run a story on this?"

"No. I'm sure Mr. McGuire is well aware of his good fortune. We'll leave it up to him to spread the good news among his colleagues."

Hillsbury chopped on his cigar. "Kind of strange the committee doing an about face like that."

"I suppose they saw Michael McGuire was just a dead end." With that, Harry Chapman hung up the phone. He was pleased the matter was settled. He didn't need a movie producer getting in the way of the city acquiring a ball club.

# 9

# *Chavez Ravine*

Ezekiel watched the line. The women gutting the fish worked fast and with mechanical proficiency, sending the fish down a conveyor belt. The women had to cut the head and tail, gut the fish, and replace it on the conveyor belt every six seconds as another fish would come down the trough. That meant ten fish per worker every minute cleaned and prepared. That meant six hundred fish per hour, forty-eight hundred per shift per worker.

Ezekiel knew the new quota was pushing the line. The fish were packed in ice when they arrived at the cannery, and the water in the trough was cold. The workers' fingers frequently turned blue before the noon break. Ezekiel also knew that to protest would be futile. He would be fired and management would simply replace him with someone who would supervise without complaint.

Angela worked her five-inch knife fast as she first chopped the head and then the tail. It had been Ezekiel's blade when he was a gutter. Many of the other women had smaller ones with dulled points. This made it less likely to get injured but harder to gut the fish. Angela's knife was made of fine stainless steel and had a sharp point. She worked fast and hard, as the conveyor of fish never ceased. It was just after ten, and her hands were already numb. The tips were completely white, all the blood having vanished. Many of the women wore gloves, but Angela didn't. She claimed they slowed her speed.

Angela reached down in the trough and grabbed another fish before chopping the head and tail. She stabbed the knife into the fish and it slipped in her hand. The blade pierced her palm, going all the way through with the point protruding out the top of her hand, making her cry out in pain. She pulled the blade out, and blood sprayed into the trough. The woman working next to her pulled a rag from her smock and handed it to Angela. Two fish went by untouched. A third worker grabbed the fish and swiftly gutted them, but three more were already at that workers station.

Angela stepped back from her station. Blood continued to seep through the rag wrapped around her hand. Ezekiel looked at his sister, noticing she was injured. He ran over to her.

"Angie."

She waved him off with her good hand. "I'm all right, EZ."

The rag was now soaked with blood. Ezekiel unwrapped the rag and inspected Angela's hand. There was a jagged cut over an inch long. Blood continued to seep from the ugly wound. He quickly rewrapped the injured hand.

"You can't work."

She fervently shook her head. "I can."

"You need stiches. You can't work," the supervisor replied with a tone of finality.

Angela hesitated, then nodded her head.

"Clock out. I'll take you to the clinic."

Angela gave her older brother a pointed look. "Don't. You can't afford to lose the wages. I'll take the bus."

Angela was right. Ezekiel had signed the papers with the Housing Authority agent two days ago. He had to hand over the deed, and they would have thirty days to vacate their home. Every penny was needed.

"Are you sure?" Ezekiel asked.

Angela nodded her head.

"What the hell is going on here?" bellowed a voice.

Ezekiel turned. It was Ralph Kragen, the department supervisor. He was tall, chunky, and had white skin with freckles covering his arms and face.

"Angie cut herself," explained Ezekiel.

Kragen's gaze cut to Angela, and she unwrapped the rag. The large man's face went pale.

"Go get it taken care of." Kragen looked at Ezekiel. "You'll have to make due until I can get you a replacement at noon."

"I understand."

Kragen glared at Angela. 'Get moving. We're not paying you to stand around and bleed."

Angela looked at her brother, and a silent moment passed between them. Then she turned and left the floor.

Two buses later, Angela was at the Downtown Clinic. The room was packed, and Angela had to stand. The fact that she was dripping blood on the reception room floor got her in to see the doctor ahead of many other patients. The physician was an elderly man with gray hair and a well-trimmed moustache. He cleaned the wound and stitched Angela's hand.

"You won't be able to use that hand for two weeks. We don't want you to break those stitches."

"I must work," protested Angela.

"What do you do?"

"I work at Pacific Cannery."

"Not for two weeks. Come back next Wednesday and we'll take a look at those stitches."

Angela looked at the doctor in earnest. "I have to work."

He frowned. "You nearly severed a tendon. If the stitches open, you'll bleed again. I can write a note to your employer."

"That's okay," Angela said with a heavy tone of resignation. She picked up her purse and left the doctor's office.

Angela and Carmen were seated on the steps when Ezekiel pulled up and parked his truck. He jumped out and hurried over to the two women. He kissed Carmen and then looked at Angela's bandaged hand.

"The doctor said I can't work for two weeks," Angela muttered sadly.

Ezekiel eyes flashed from Carmen to his sister. "You know they'll fire you, right?"

Angela nodded her head. "I'm sorry.'

Ezekiel wrapped his arm around her. "Will you be able to use it?"

"Yes."

He kissed the top of his sister's head. "Good."

"We need the money."

"Your hand is more important, mija."

A helicopter flew overhead, kicking up dust. Ezekiel stood up on the porch and watched as it passed. Besides the pilot, he could see two men in business suits. One on the men wore glasses. Both seemed to be surveying the area from their perch in the helicopter. Ezekiel waved to the men. The chopper banked slightly, rose, and flew off in the direction of Palo Verde.

"What was that?" asked Carmen.

"Probably gringos from the Housing Authority," said Ezekiel.

Tom Mendoza, a stout man about Ezekiel's age, walked up the path. He had a quart size bottle of beer in his hand. "You see that?"

"Yeah," Ezekiel replied.

Mendoza belonged to a car club. The members would cruise Sixth Street and Whitter Blvd. with their vehicles on the weekends. As far as Carmen was concerned, the *Lobos Solitarios* was a gang. She wanted no part of them and preferred that Ezekiel didn't hang around Tom Mendoza and his friends.

Carmen and Angela walked up the steps and into the house before Carmen stuck her head back outside. "Dinner will be ready in ten minutes."

Ezekiel gave a wave of acknowledgement.

"Pendjos from the city," said Mendoza. He took a long swig from the bottle and then handed it to Ezekiel.

"No, I'm good, thanks."

Mendoza shrugged his shoulders. Like a magician, he produced a pack of Lucky's from his rolled-up shirt sleeve, shook one out, and flipped it up to his lips. He pulled a Zippo from his pants pocket, threw the lid back, and struck it in a single stroke. He lit the cigarette and returned the Zippo to his pocket, all in what appeared to be a single fluid move.

"You sell your place to the city?" Mendoza asked, exhaling a cloud of smoke.

"Yeah," Ezekiel replied with resignation.

"Damn, ese, I thought you were staying."

Ezekiel gave Mendoza a pained look. "You can't fight city hall."

"EZ," Carmen called out.

"You can't fight the chicas, EZ." Mendoza chuckled and gave his friend a pat on the back. "Adios." The hefty man made his way back down the dirt trail, and Ezekiel walked into the house.

The table was set. Leticia and Lucy sat in their chairs as Carmen set the pot of beans on the table and Angela placed a basket of warm tortillas next to the pot. Then the women took a seat. Johnny was in an old wooden highchair next to his mother. The family ate with little conversation. After they were done, Leticia and Lucy went outside to play. Ezekiel looked at his wife.

"Maybe we can tell the agent we can't sell the house right now," he suggested.

"I'm sorry, it's my fault," sighed Angela, her expression turning sad.

"It is not your fault," Carmen replied sharply. "It is the people who make you work faster that are responsible." Her dark brown eyes burned at Ezekiel.

"If I say anything, they will fire me. Then we won't have any money."

"EZ is right, Carmen. Don't worry. Take the money from the agent." Angela forced a smile. "Johnny and I will be okay. We can get a place of our own."

Ezekiel stared at his sister in surprise. "How will you get a place if you don't have a job?"

"I have some money saved. It is my left hand that is injured. I'm right-handed. I can look for work."

Ezekiel frowned. "I don't want to hear that. We are *familial.*"

Angela placed her good hand on her brother's. "Johnny and I are a family too. It is time that we got our own place."

Ezekiel and Carmen both began to protest. Angela held up her hand and cut them off.

"I love you both. EZ, you are my brother. Carmen, you are my sister. It is time you had your own house. Johnny and I will be forever grateful for your kindness. It is time for me and my son to find our own place."

Ezekiel was going to say something, but Carmen gave her husband a look. He nodded and remained silent.

Johnny giggled, kicked his legs, and messed his pants.

Angela picked up her son and carried him into the bedroom to change his diaper.

Carmen cleared the table and washed the dishes.

Ezekiel took a beer from the icebox and went out and sat on the porch. The moon was coming up; it was a full moon. Ezekiel sat and sipped his beer and listened to the crickets chirping.

* * *

The helicopter landed on the top of the Los Angeles Tribune building. Harry Chapman and Roy Haines got out. Roy was younger than Harry and had the build of a retired athlete. Haines was Paul Brown's point-man. The two men kept their heads down as they hurried across the pad and into the newspaper building.

Eli Bronstein was waiting in the executive conference room along with Kenneth Colby and Warren Edding. These three men represented the downtown oligarchy. All were multi-millionaires who had made their fortunes through nepotism, insider knowledge, and the exploitation of the impoverished. They stood by a portable bar telling stories of glory days in the market. The group turned when Harry entered with Haines.

"Well, I can see you men had already helped yourself to my liquor," Harry quipped.

The men chuckled.

Eli Bronstein wasn't a man for small talk. He looked at Haines and asked, "So, what do you think of our fair city?"

Roy took the drink Harry handed him and smiled. "Quite different from Cleveland."

Harry forced a smile. He hadn't wanted to pressure Haines. "I showed Roy the area we have planned for a stadium."

"And?" retorted Bronstein.

"That's quite a bit of real estate," replied Haines.

There was a moment of silence.

"I thought that area was earmarked for low-cost housing," said Haines.

Bronstein gave Harry a look that said, "Did you spill the beans?"

"I did my own research," said Haines.

"I wouldn't be too concerned about the housing project," offered Kenneth Colby.

Haines gave the group a questioning look.

Warren Edding was the oldest of the group and a banker, though his gray hair and demeanor gave him the air of an elder statesman. He looked at Haines, then smiled and said, "What was given in one election can be taken back with another."

Haines chuckled. "I see."

"I hope you do," said Bronstein. "We are prepared to offer Mr. Brown a very handsome deal to relocate his team here."

Roy Haines wasn't the team owner's point man for nothing. He finished his drink. "I will take your offer to Mr. Brown. I would like to thank you gentlemen for your time." He tipped his hat and left the conference room.

Bronstein glanced over at Harry. "What the fuck just happened?"

Harry bounced on the balls of his feet. "I believe that was a polite 'no', Eli."

Bronstein frowned and growled, "I told you that we should only talk to the owner."

"Brown wasn't coming to Los Angeles, Eli," Harry replied calmly.

"Well, he should've, and it was your mistake to talk to that putz," Bronstein groused.

Edding refilled his glass. "Laying blame is not going to help us. What's our next move?"

Harry looked at the three men. "I understand Walter O'Malley is unhappy with his stadium in Brooklyn."

* * *

The Housing Authority office was on the third floor of the City Hall building. Ezekiel was surprised how small the office was for something that held so much power over the lives of his family. He had arrived early and was the first in line. Ezekiel had told his supervisor he would be in late and didn't want to get docked more than an hour from his pay. Even still, he nervously watched the clock on the wall.

A clerk finally called his name ten minutes after eight. Ezekiel followed the short man in the rumpled gray suit back to a desk. He had a pale complexion and looked as if a good wind could blow him right over. The clerk gestured to a metal chair next to the desk.

"I am Mr. Dershowitz. I will be handling the transfer of your property," the clerk explained as he took a seat behind the desk. "I hope you have brought the deed of ownership."

"Yes." Ezekiel handed the clerk a folder of papers.

Dershowitz took the file and quickly scanned the contents. "H-m-m." He looked at Ezekiel. "It appears your paperwork is in order." The clerk placed a document in front of Ezekiel. "Just sign here and you should receive a check in seven to twelve business days for eighty-two hundred dollars."

Ezekiel frowned. "Mr. Draper told us we would get nine thousand dollars."

Dershowitz looked at Ezekiel with a blank expression. "The field agents have been told not to discuss sales amounts with clients." He indicated to a map hanging on the wall. "Payment for property is based upon the plot map and the assessed value of the neighborhood. Eight thousand two hundred is what the city will pay for your house."

"That's less than what my father got a year ago."

Dershowitz frowned. "That was because the city was paying a bonus to those who filed first. Just sign the paper, Mr. Camacho," the clerk replied dismissively, pronouncing the name *Koo-ma-choo.*

"This is my home," snapped Ezekiel.

The clerk folded his arms, rocked back in the chair, and glanced at his watch.

Ezekiel stared at the contract.

"There are other people waiting," said Dershowitz.

Ezekiel took the pen and signed where the clerk indicated.

Dershowitz tore a carbon copy and handed it to Ezekiel. "You have thirty days to vacate the property."

Ezekiel looked surprised. "You, said it would take twelve days to get the check. We need that money in order to be able to move."

Dershowitz waved him off. "That would be the longest. Most likely you should receive it in seven days. That gives you nearly three weeks to vacate the property. Surely, you don't need more than a few days to move your belongings."

Ezekiel glared at the officious clerk. He grabbed the copy of the contract, turned, and stomped out the office.

Traffic was light, but Ezekiel was still two hours late for work. Ralph Kragen was not happy when Ezekiel told him that Angela was sick and wouldn't be in that day.

"Get down on the floor and get to work," barked the supervisor.

Ezekiel gave a nod and headed down to his station.

The day dragged on. Ezekiel wasn't sure why he had told Kragen that Angela was sick. Kragen had seen her hand. He knew that if Angela didn't come in tomorrow, they would fire her. Ezekiel was too occupied with the fact that they were getting less money than he and Carmen had expected for their home. They certainly didn't have enough for the house in Glassell Park that Carmen liked.

"Be sure that sister of yours shows up tomorrow," Kragen admonished when Ezekiel clocked out for the day.

He gave a nod and walked to his truck. The drive home seemed to take forever. When he arrived, Carmen was waiting for him. His look told her everything.

Carmen didn't say a word. She hugged Ezekiel and gave him a kiss. "There is a cold beer in the ice-box, and I fixed menudo for dinner."

Ezekiel smiled. He was grateful Carmen had not pestered him with questions. "Where is Angela?"

Carmen spread a big smile. "She got a job with Planned Parenthood."

"What?"

"Your little sister is going to be a secretary for the agency director."

"How?"

Carmen laughed and shrugged her shoulders. "Pure luck. Angie went to the post office and ran into one of her old classmates. She told Angie about the job. Angie went down and the director hired your sister on the spot."

"Planned Parenthood, that's a women's clinic?"

Carmen nodded her head. "Yes. Angie will be doing a good thing."

"Well, why isn't she here to celebrate?"

Carmen tenderly ran her hand down the side of Ezekiel's cheek. "She thought maybe we might enjoy the evening. Angie took Johnny and the girls to see *Song of the South*. You want that beer?"

Ezekiel looked at his wife and held out his hand. "I think I'll pass."

Carmen smiled and took her husband's hand and led him into the bedroom.

# 10

# *The Session*

Cosmo gave his name to the guard at the studio gate, who handed him a pass and told him where to park. Cosmo followed the guard's directions, parked his car, and walked across the lot to Studio B. He was surprised at how large Royal Studio was. His mother had been in films shot at the old studio on Hyperion back in the thirties, but this was much grander.

"You must be Cosmo Turner. I'm Wayne Jackson," the producer said when he saw the piano player enter the studio. Jackson was a short man who wore black framed glasses with thick lens. He was dressed in brown slacks, a yellow shirt, and a lime tie.

Cosmo extended his hand, and the two men shook.

"Wendell said you could play anything," Jackson said.

Cosmo grinned sheepishly. "I try."

Jackson handed Cosmo his charts. "Here. Today is an easy session. We're going to lay down eight incidental music tracks. Each runs approximately sixty seconds." He pointed to the screen on the wall. "They'll run the clips and we lay down the track. It's really very simple." He clapped Cosmo on the shoulder. "You'll do fine. If you need anything, just ask Eddie Moore; he's the first trumpet and band director."

With that, Jackson walked off. The studio was quickly filling up. There was a full rhythm section along with strings and horns.

Cosmo walked over to the piano and sat down. He set the charts on piano and stared at them. No one had said anything about playing with charts. Cosmo had always played head arrangements with the other players. Art Tatum was about the only piano man who could out play him, but Cosmo couldn't read a line of notes to save his life. He picked up the charts and walked over to the horn section.

"Which one of you is Eddie Moore?"

A lean man with a friendly face gave a nod.

"I'm Cosmo Turner."

The two men shook hands.

"The thing is, no one said anything about charts," said Cosmo.

The two other horn players rolled their eyes but remained silent.

Eddie smiled. "You a head man?"

Cosmo grinned and looked down at the floor. "Yeah." He looked up at Moore. "I need this job. I can do it. I just need you to play me the melody."

Eddie studied Cosmo then gave a nod. "Come on."

Eddie took Cosmo outside the studio. He played each of the charts for Cosmo in quick succession on his trumpet. "Got it?"

"Yeah."

The two men went back inside the studio.

Michael McGuire stepped inside the control booth and stood behind Jackson. "We need to nail this today, Wayne."

"No problem, Mr. McGuire."

Wayne leaned forward toward his microphone. "Okay, let's do one, folks. And...the film is rolling."

There was a five count on the screen before the movie played. It was a scene on the beach. The musicians played their parts. Cosmo tread lightly on the keys. The film stopped after about sixty seconds.

"Let's try that again with a bit more piano this time," said Wayne Jackson.

Cosmo glanced over at Eddie. The trumpet player gave him a slight gesture with his hand that let the piano man know all was cool.

"All right, we are rolling film and in five, four," said the producer.

Cosmo nailed it on the second take.

Eddie Moore gave him a nod of approval. He turned to his mic and said, "Maybe we should do a quick run through before a take so that everybody is on point," he suggested to the producer.

Jackson gave a thumbs up to Moore. "You're the director, baby."

Eddie Moore grinned. "Don't you forget that."

Cosmo nailed each take on the rest of the session. In one case, he added a small flourish that was barely noticeable at the end.

Michael looked at the man sitting behind the piano. "Who's the piano player?"

"Cosmo Turner. I don't think he reads," said Jackson.

Michael recognized the name. This was the man who had been involved with Nicole Sullivan. James Hagen had told him about Turner. Michael looked at the producer. "Keep him. I knew plenty of head players back when I was running a nightclub. They usually can play rings around those that can read."

Wayne Jackson gave Michael a look. "We're lucky we've got Eddie handling the band. If the guy was playing for Bernstein or Steiner—"

"He isn't," Michael said, cutting off the producer. "Get his number and address."

Jackson threw up his hands. "Whatever you say, boss."

Cosmo was surprised and relieved that the session went as quickly and smoothly as it did. Eddie Moore was satisfied. He had signed Cosmo's chit. He was two hundred dollars richer and it was only noon. Cosmo felt like he had gotten away with murder. He chuckled to himself as he drove off the lot.

# 11

# *Home*

Lee May Sing was glad to be back in California. The last few weeks of shooting in New York had seemed to go on forever. Los Angeles was far better than anything the Big Apple had to offer. Now she could get some much-needed rest from the hectic pace of being on the set at 6 a.m. for a makeup call.

Lee May sat on a chaise lounge. The warm morning California sun felt good. The patio overlooked a beautiful garden complete with a koi pond and meditation circle. The maid showed Michael out to the patio, where Lee Sing was reading *Catcher in the Rye*. She looked up as Michael walked over and greeted her.

"Glad you're home." Michel took Lee May's hand and kissed it.

"Michael!" The actress jumped up and gave him a hug. "It's good to see you."

Michael glanced at the book sitting on the table. "Any good?"

Lee May Sing made a face and held her nose. "An affluent male adolescent fantasy masquerading as literature."

"Then it must be good."

"H-m-m. If they gave awards for triteness, this would be the winner."

Michael took a seat on the lounge chair next to Lee May. "Never underestimate the masses when it comes to art, my dear. I read it. You're right; it's a lousy story."

The maid returned with a food cart containing chinaware, silverware, and a large Kowa wood bowl containing a salad. Next to this were a crystal pitcher of water and another of orange juice. The maid bowed and returned inside the house.

Lee May began serving the salad. "I do hope you will join me for breakfast."

Michael cocked an eye.

Lee May grinned back. "A late breakfast." She handed Michael a plate of salad.

"Thank you."

"I know this isn't one of your cowboy meals."

Michael speared a cucumber. "I already had my cowboy breakfast."

"The food back east is heavy. I've been feeling slow lately. I thought eating light and getting some sun would help."

Michael noticed for the first time that Lee May was thinner than he had remembered.

"You look great."

Lee May crinkled her nose and held up a small carrot before thrusting it in Michael's direction. "You used to be a better liar, Michael McGuire. I'm forty-four, soon to be forty-five. I haven't made a film in years, and unless the network can find a new sponsor, *Courier from Hong Kong* just wrapped for good. I look and feel like hell warmed over."

Michael somberly filled his glass with water from the pitcher. "I'm sorry."

Lee May waved him off. "I should be the one to apologize. The committee…how thoughtless of me to forget. How did that go for you?"

Michael poked at his salad and sighed. "It went. I'm cleared, but it cost. The studio is probably not going to renew my contract. Sarah said they will have to go one picture at a time." He looked up from his food. "Funny, but outside of running a saloon, this is the only job I've ever had."

"Does Laurel know?"

"Yeah. This isn't good for her, me drawing attention."

"You said it cost you."

"I owe some people."

Lee May Sing's grandfather had been a Tong leader. Her father, Walter, had been one as well. They had both been partners with Michael and Sean McGuire long ago. The actress knew what it meant to owe someone.

Michael chuckled and shook his head. "I'm sorry, but I can't offer you a role in my next picture. I have no idea if there will be a next picture."

"What will you do?"

Michael tugged his ear lobe and grinned. "What will you do?"

Lee May set her fork down and gazed out at the garden below. "Live."

* * *

There was a loud knock at the door. Nine-year-old Nicholas McGuire rushed over and opened it. He was brushed aside by two men in gray suits who were followed by a cadre of officers. Laurel rushed into the living room at the sound of the invasion.

"Who are you and what is going on?" she demanded.

One of the men in a gray suit flashed his buzzer like a Deadwood sheriff and returned it to his breast pocket just as quickly. "Special Agent Randall, FBI. That's my partner, Special Agent Warren."

Randell was short and chunky with a fat face highlighted by very pink cheeks. He had a toothpick that he rolled around in his mouth like a professional juggler. By contrast, Agent Warren was medium built and looked like he had once been a BMOC a decade or so ago. Warren gave a nod to the officers, who fanned out through the house.

Nicholas starred at the men as they went through drawers and dumped books and papers on the floor.

"I want to see a warrant," Laurel growled.

Agent Warren shoved Laurel down in a chair.

She jumped right back up. "The committee cleared my husband! You have no right—"

Laurel was cut short when Warren shoved her back in the chair, harder this time.

Agent Randall glared at the woman. "Sit the fuck down and shut the fuck up. I don't care if Truman himself gave your commie husband a pass. If you give us any trouble, one call and we'll shut down those clinics of yours faster than a cat's ass on fire. Do you understand me?"

Laurel nodded her head, her eyes swelling with tears. She looked at Nicholas, finding the young boy had a blank expression. She motioned for him to come to her. Nicholas remained and stood silent, watching the men tear apart the house. He took in every detail of the two men who stood over his mother. Nothing missed the young boy's eyes, their worn brown shoes, their faded Fedoras and coffee-stained ties. Nicholas wanted to remember every detail of the men who had aggrieved his mother in such a fashion in his father's home. He would not forget.

* * *

The maid hurried out onto the patio where Lee May and Michael were seated. "Mr. McGuire, the studio called. They said you need to call your wife."

Thirty minutes later, Michael walked into his house. The agents and police were gone. Nicholas was playing with his set of toy soldiers in the living room. The place was still in a state of disarray, but Laurel had done much to straighten things up from the raid.

"Where's Mom?"

Nicholas pointed upstairs.

"Are you all right, son?"

Nicholas nodded his head.

Michael raced up the stairs. He found Laurel putting things back in the dresser. She dropped the stack of dress shirts on the floor and stared at Michael.

"They came into our house. Those men went through our things," Laurel cried.

Michael walked over and held his wife tight. "It's all right. You and Nicholas weren't hurt."

Laurel pushed away from Michael and gaped at him in disbelief. "The FBI came into our house and went where they pleased. They threatened to send officers and close the clinics. Nicholas saw it all. Don't tell me we weren't hurt."

Michael sighed and held his arms down at his side.

"What is going on here, Michael?"

"This isn't about the committee or my films. This is about getting even for something that happened a long time ago."

Laurel stared at her husband. "Maybe you should tell me."

"You know I had a nightclub before I became a producer, but you don't know the rest of the story." Michael sat down on the bed and for the next thirty minutes explained to his wife exactly how he and Jimmy Grazzi had left their bootlegging enterprises behind and reinvented themselves. He told her how it was only William McGrath who had died when he drove the truck into the police squad car at Point Magu that night.

When Michael finished, Laurel stood with a blank expression. Her arm suddenly flashed out, and she slapped him hard across the face.

"Do you realize the danger you've put Nicholas in?"

Michael remained silent.

Laurel got up and walked out of the room. Michael sat down on the bed. The stack of dress shirts was scattered on the floor. He heard Laurel's footsteps descend the stairs. A few moments later, the front door opened and then closed. The sound of a car engine started, and the vehicle drove away.

The house was silent. Michael was alone in the large bedroom. He sat silently staring at the colorful shirts that lay strewn across the floor. The telephone rang. Michael let it ring until it finally stopped. A minute later, the phone rang again. Michael reached over to the nightstand and answered the call.

"Yes?"

"This is Anthony Bono calling for Mr. Gambino. He would appreciate it if you would put Frank Sinatra in the war movie."

"I'm not doing a war movie. Buddy Alder is."

There was a moment of silence on the line, and then Bono came back on. "Mr. Gambino would like you to speak to Buddy Adler about casting Frank in his film."

"Buddy is a good producer—"

"Mr. Gambino will take it as a personal insult if Frank doesn't get the part."

The line went dead.

# 12

# *A Revelation*

Harry Chapman and Chief Parker had lunch at the Ambassador. William Parker had been elected on an anti-corruption platform. The downtown oligarchy liked "Wild" Bill Parker, who had grown up in Deadwood. Los Angeles needed a square jawed police chief. The last three had resigned the position during corruption investigations.

Parker knew his place in the city food-chain and acted accordingly. He had vowed to rid the city of criminal gangs and make the streets of Los Angeles safe for its hard-working residents, which meant white folks. Wild Bill hated Mexicans, Chinese, and Blacks.

More importantly, Bill Parker hated Sheriff Biscailuz. The sheriff had jurisdiction of the west-side of the city, Mickey Cohen's territory. The sheriff and Cohen were as tight as Siamese twins and turned a blind eye to his and Jack Dragna's dealings. Chief Parker wouldn't get in bed with criminals. He formed an elite squad of detectives whose purpose was to dissuade certain Italian, Irish and Jewish visitors to the fair City of the Angels. The oligarchy loved it.

Harry Chapman cut into his steak. It bled on the plate. "I want to thank you for coming to lunch, Bill."

Parker took a drink of water and dabbed his lips with a napkin. "The pleasure is all mine. Now, what did you have on your mind?"

Chapman grinned and speared a piece of bloody meat. "Right to the point. I like that." He popped the steak in his mouth and downed it with a sip of scotch. Harry smiled and looked across the table at the police chief. "I know your boys are handling Cohen and the rest of his bunch admirably. There is a growing need to deal with similar factions that are disrupting our city."

"What might those be?"

"We need to do something about the Elysian Heights Committee."

"I wasn't aware that this group—"

Harry held up his hand, effectively cutting the chief off. "It's a bunch of socialists. They formed a committee to support Richard Neutra and the Elysian Heights Project." The reference was to the renowned architectural designer tasked with building the low-income housing development. Neutra had been called before the Committee and cleared, but it had put a dark shadow on the project.

Chief Parker poked at his mashed potatoes. "I'll look into it."

Harry cut another piece of steak. "We would appreciate it if you gave it your personal attention."

Wild Bill understood. "Certainly."

"Fine. We don't need a bunch of rabblerousing reds creating problems if that project fails to come to fruition."

The chief arched an eyebrow. "I was under the impression the deal was done."

A bemused look spread over Harry's face. "What can be given can be taken away." He took a sip of scotch. "It really is rather simple. The federal government purchased the land from the city. We got it for peanuts when the city council used eminent domain to obtain it from the Mexicans living there. If the project is defeated in another vote, the Feds will be stuck with the land. The city plans to offer to purchase back Chavez Ravine at a reduced price of course. We come out winners at both ends."

The chief took a drink of water, set the glass down, and looked at Harry. "The department will do whatever is required."

Harry smiled. "Good."

* * *

Michael McGuire watched the crew set up in front of the Vista Theater. Fred Zinnemann was the director. He was impressed with the director's speed and ability to get the right shot. It wasn't quite noon and they had already nailed a dozen pages of the script. Michael hadn't missed a step, either. When Royal Studio failed to renew his contract, he brought a project to Warner Bros. They went for *Federal Squad* in a heartbeat. It was a tough compact story about the FBI fighting a group of spies in the Long Beach shipyards. Jack Warner hated Reds, and he knew McGuire's pictures made money. He gave Michael three weeks to shoot the picture and a solid director.

Zinnemann talked to the camera operator and then walked over to where Michael was seated. "What do you think?"

"Looks fine."

"We can get this scene in the can before we break for lunch."

"Good." Michael stood up. The producer and director walked over to the craft truck.

"How's life after HUAC?" asked Zinnemann.

Michael wiggled his hand and said, "So, so." He looked at the craft worker. "Black coffee, please."

"It would be great for everyone if McCarthy and his bunch went back to D.C. where they could blow smoke up each other's asses," said the director.

The craft worker filled a cup and handed it to the producer.

"Thanks." Michael turned to Zinnemann. "I understand you're up to direct that James Jones book for Columbia."

Fred gave the producer a surprised look. "They said you never miss a thing. Yeah, that's the plan."

"Have you considered Sinatra?"

Fred shrugged. "Sinatra is a song and dance guy."

Michael leaned close in a conspiratorial manner. "Between you and me, he is having problems with his voice. He's looking for something dramatic to change his image."

Fred grinned. "Well, Sinatra sure doesn't have the build for the boxer."

Michael sipped his coffee. "The boxer has a friend, the Italian guy. Sinatra could certainly play a wop."

Zinnemann laughed. "Good point."

Michael looked at the director. "I'll be straight. I need this, Fred."

Michael didn't say anything about the call from the Gambino family. His expression told Zinnemann all he needed.

The director was silent for a moment, then said, "I'll see that Sinatra gets considered."

"Thanks."

A man in a brown suit carrying a briefcase walked up to the producer and director. "Mr. McGuire?"

Michael turned to the man. "Yes?"

The man thrust an envelope in the producer's hand. "You've been served." He hurried across the street and disappeared down Hyperion.

Michael opened the envelope and read its contents, his expression darkening. "It appears that my wife would like a divorce."

* * *

Lee May Sing took the train to San Diego. It had been years since she had visited the city. The train rocked gently as it traveled south that morning. Lee May had a seat on the west side of the car. The sun gleamed off the Pacific as the waves rolled gently into the shore.

Lee May had brought a book, but she preferred to observe the scenery as it passed by. So much had been built up since her last trip before the war. She watched as surfers caught the waves in San Clemente. A mother played with her two children in the sand. A pair of young lovers sat on a bright beach towel and only had eyes for each other. A group of boys rode their bikes down the frontage road adjacent to the tracks.

Lee May Sing was dressed in black slacks and a red silk blouse. She wore a black beret that obscured her face. A pair of sunglasses further disguised her. She smoked a cigarette and stared out the window.

"Excuse me, are you Lee May Sing?" asked a young man.

Lee May turned. The man looked to be in his twenties and was well dressed.

"Yes."

The man stood in the aisle and grinned ear to ear. "I knew it. My fraternity brothers aren't going to believe this." He thrust a USC baseball program at the actress. "Would you mind giving me your autograph?"

Lee May took the program and glanced at it for a moment, frowning.

"I'm sorry. That's all I've got, but if you'd sign it. It would mean a lot," said the young man, trying to cover his embarrassment over handing the actress a sports program to sign.

Lee Ann reached into her purse and removed a pen. She was accustomed to autograph seekers and made sure she always had a pen handy. She looked up at the young man. "To whom should I make it out?"

"Chedder—no. Please sign it 'To Chet'."

Lee May signed the program and handed it back to the young man. He stared at the autograph and read it, "To Chet, my biggest fan. Best wishes, Lee May Sing." He smiled. "Thank you. I loved you in the *Evil Dr. Ming* movies. My favorite is *Death Ray from Mongo*."

Lee May used an index finger and slid her sunglasses down slightly. "You like that?"

"Yes."

"How about *Mission from Shanghai...Passage to Marseille*?

The young man thought a moment and then shook his head. "I don't know those movies. Were you in them?"

"H-m-m. How about, *The Good Earth*?"

The young man slapped his leg. "I know that one. That's my mother's favorite. She dragged me to see it three times when they re-released it during the war. You were in that?"

"I wasn't."

"Oh." The young man wasn't sure what to say.

Lee May pushed her sunglasses back up on her nose. "Well, I'm glad you enjoyed *Death Ray from Mongo*."

"Yes ma'am," the young man stammered. "Thank you." The fan turned and walked back to his seat clutching the sports program.

Lee May turned and looked out at the ocean and smiled to herself. She always thought it humorous when people sought her autograph. She was the daughter of a restaurant owner. She was the granddaughter of a cook from Canton who had been orphaned when he was ten. He had traveled to *Gum Saan* during the California gold rush with nothing more than a wok. If only they knew of her humble origins.

Lee May purchased a bouquet from the flower stand outside the station. She then hailed a cab, climbed in, and gave the driver the address.

"Sure thing, lady," said the cabbie. He hit the meter and pulled away from the curb.

The cab headed west from downtown toward Point Loma. Traffic was light, and they reached the destination in fifteen minutes. The cabbie stopped the car and turned back to his passenger. "You want me to wait?"

"Please, if you will."

"I've got to keep the meter running."

"That's be fine."

Lee May Sing got out of the cab. She stood at the top of a long sloping hill that overlooked San Diego Bay, one dotted with hundreds of tombstones. Lee May took out the map of Rosecrans National Cemetery and glanced at it. The spot she sought was not far away. Lee May replaced the map in her purse and headed off down the slope. After a moment, she slowed and began checking the markers.

A middle-aged man in a uniform placed a fresh bouquet of flowers on a grave that sat under a tall pine tree. The marker read *Chu San 1884-1951*. The officer stood up as Lee May approached the grave. He had a weathered face and piercing blue eyes. He forced an uneasy smile when he saw the bouquet in Lee May's hand.

"I can get another glass."

"No, that's fine." Lee May laid her bouquet on top of the grave.

The officer extended his hand. "I'm Major Reisman. Chu San provided a big help to us fighting the Japanese during the war. That's why she is buried here."

"I know, she spoke of you."

Major Reisman shifted his weight on his feet and adjusted his tie. "I come out here every so often and put flowers on her grave."

"That is very nice. Chu San would like that."

"Did you know her in China? She had a quite a dress business in Nanking before the war from what I understand."

Lee May shook her head. "No. Chu San worked for my grandfather. She was the friend of the man who saved my grandfather's life and set him up with his first restaurant. It was many years ago."

"I remember Chu San telling me she had spent a number of years in Los Angeles before returning to China."

Lee Sing smiled. "Yes. Chu San rarely left Chinatown, except to go to the movies with me. We'd go to the Million Dollar Theater on Broadway."

Major Reisman looked at the woman standing across the grave from him and finally recognized Lee May. "You're—"

"Yes."

"I'm sorry. I didn't recognize you."

"There is no need to apologize, Major. Chu San had no family. She would be very proud what you did to get her buried here."

The officer blushed and was at a loss for words. "It wasn't that much," he stammered.

"It was more than enough for a young girl from western China. I'm sorry I wasn't here for her funeral. We were shooting in New York at the time."

Major Reisman bid Lee May goodbye and left. The actress stood at the grave for a long moment. Lee May Sing finally turned and walked to the cab. She took the next train back to Los Angeles. The entire trip had taken just over six hours.

Lee May was tired when she arrived home, and the maid inquired if she was hungry. The actress then realized she had only eaten an orange for lunch. Lee May thanked the maid and declined dinner. The day had taken everything out of her. Lee May changed and crawled into bed.

As she lay under the covers, she thought of her family. Her grandfather was dead. Her mother and father were dead. Chu San was dead. Lee May Sing realized that she would have no one to mourn her after she died.

She rolled over and cried herself to sleep that night.

# 13

# *The Square*

The picketers arrived at Pershing Square around nine that morning. There were less than forty people when they started. Many held placards and signs that said *Justice for Chavez Ravine* and *Support Elysian Heights*. They marched and chanted "Justice now." One of the marchers brought a guitar. He began playing Woody Guthrie's, *This Land*, and the others joined in singing. By noon, dozens more had joined the picket line. The square was packed with spectators listening to the speakers who called out the Board of Supervisors and City Council for their actions.

Bill Parker's boys in blue converged upon Pershing Square like the landing at Normandy. They rolled up in dozens of patrol cars and took positions around the park perimeter. Captain George Mathis stepped out of his car. He was a tall and lean man pushing sixty who had come up through the ranks when Jim Davis was chief.

Mathis glanced to either side of him. The police stood at attention. He gave the signal. The phalanx of police marched two steps forward in unison and removed their batons. They leaned forward and began clacking their batons on the concrete. The picketers stopped marching. The people stopped singing. The crowd stared at the police. The cops continued to clack their batons in a cacophony of rhythm. Then suddenly, they stopped.

Silence filled Pershing Square. The protestors stood frozen. The silence was shattered. Captain Mathis blew his whistle, and the police charged the crowd. Pandemonium and chaos broke out as the hundreds of spectators and picketers scrambled to flee and found every exit blocked by an advancing line of blue slicing the air with their batons.

The cops cracked heads. They beat, battered, and boke bones of anyone who got in the way. The women, children, and elderly were given no quarter. Mayhem ruled. Captain Mathis had ordered his men to clear the square. LAPD accomplished the mission in under two minutes. By the time the lines of blue met in the middle, every civilian was either lying on the ground or had fled the area.

Blood spattered the concrete and dirt. Dozens moaned in pain. Their entreaties for help were met with further beatings, cuffing, and subsequently being tossed in the back of one of two police wagons that had pulled up and parked.

Sergeant Henry Bowers walked up to Captain Mathis. "Mission accomplished, sir."

Mathis gave Bowers a nod.

"We have forty-eight arrests. Six of those are injured and require transport to a hospital. Two others are DOA, sir."

"What about our men, sergeant?" Mathis barked.

"No injuries."

"Excellent work. These Reds obviously resisted arrest," said Mathis.

"Sir, I'm not sure—"

Captain Mathis turned and fixed his stare upon the sergeant. "Not sure of what, Sergeant? This is clearly an illegal gathering of communists and pachuco gangs."

"Sir, Rabbi Meyer was one of the picketers."

Mathis bounced on the balls of his feet. "Another commie Jew who joined his fellow travelers in an illegal gathering. How did you dispose of the good rabbi?"

"We let him go, sir."

Mathis rocked on his heels and did a slow burn.

"He is a rabbi, sir. It doesn't make for good headlines."

The captain's eyes widened. "Your job is to arrest criminals, not worry about headlines, Sergeant."

"Yes, sir." Sergeant Bowers saluted the captain and hastily made his departure.

Lieutenant Lee "Dutch" Houghlot walked over Mathis. Houghlot was the captain's right-hand man. "Everything looks in order."

"Make sure all are processed downtown first."

Dutch tilted his head. "What about the injured?"

"You have your orders, Dutch." The captain gave a salute. He walked to his car, got in, and the cruiser pulled away.

The lieutenant scratched his jaw and then turned to the policemen. "Alright, everybody gets processed before any transfers. Captain's orders!"

The cops kicked, shoved, and threw the arrested into the buses. Those that couldn't walk were dragged and then tossed onto the floor, which was soon covered with blood. Two cops slammed the doors shut, and the buses took off.

A man lay on the floor groaning and bleeding. His head had a gaping wound where a police baton had cracked open his skull. One of the shackled prisoners attempted to assist the injured man.

"Hang in there, EZ," said the shackled man. He looked up at the cop riding shotgun. "This man needs a doctor."

The cop turned around. "You're all going downtown first." The cop turned back.

"Pendejo," sneered the shackled man.

The cop got up and unlocked the gate to the rear. He pulled his club and jammed it into the shackled man's chest, knocking the wind out of him. The cop stared at the other prisoners. "Anybody else care to say something?"

Silence.

"I thought so." The cop returned to the front of the bus, locked the gate, and took his seat. "Fuckin' beaners," he said to the driver as he fished out a smoke and lit it.

* * *

The telephone rang, and Angela answered it. Forty minutes later, she rushed into Los Angeles County Hospital. Carmen was already there with the children.

"What happened?"

Carmen hugged her sister-in-law. Her eyes were filled with tears. "I don't know. EZ went to the demonstration. The cops arrested him and brought him here. They won't tell me anything."

"Do you know how badly EZ is injured?"

Carmen fought back more tears and shook her head.

Angela gave her a hug and then marched over to the nurses' station. "Can you please tell me which room Ezekiel Camacho is in?"

The nurse working the desk appeared to be in her forties and had a kind face. She glanced at the register and looked up at Angela. "He is in intensive care and is not allowed to have any visitors, miss."

"Can you tell me what happened to him?"

"Dr. Weisberg would be the one who could give that information."

Angela thanked the nurse and went back to sit down with Carmen and the children. She squeezed Letty's hand. "Everything is going to be all right."

A half hour later, a man in a white lab coat walked up. "I am Dr. Weisberg."

Carmen sprang to her feet. "I'm Carmen, EZ's wife." She indicated with her hand to Angela. "This is EZ's sister, Angela."

"Well, I have good news. Ezekiel pulled through. The surgery went well. He is going to need time to recover. He may have some memory lapses."

Carmen gave the doctor a quizzical look. "What kind of surgery? What happened to EZ?"

"You husband had a concussion. His brain swelled, and we had to operate to relieve the pressure."

Angela looked directly at the doctor. "Is my brother going to recover completely?"

Doctor Weisberg's eyes shifted to the floor and then up at the young woman. "His injury was severe. We will have to wait and see."

Carmen placed her hand on the doctor's arm. "Please…tell me."

Doctor Weisberg removed his glasses. He wiped them on his lab coat and then put them back on. "Your husband suffered a severe blow to the head. Let's just pray that he heals from his injury."

"You're not telling me what could happen," retorted Carmen.

The doctor sighed. "The brain is a very tricky organ. We don't know much about it…" He saw the two women weren't going to budge and nodded his head. "Worst case, your husband could be blind or not be able to walk or speak properly."

Carmen wiped her tears and gave the doctor a look of determination. "That will not happen to my Ezekiel."

"I hope you're right." With that, the doctor turned and walked down the hospital corridor.

_14_

# **The Deposition**

Michael and his attorney, Tim Cosgrove, entered the conference room. Both men were dressed in navy blue suits. Cosgrove was in his forties and was a graduate of Stanford Law. They were followed by a female stenographer. The woman looked to be in her late thirties and was wearing a brown skirt and white blouse. Her dark hair was pinned back, giving her the appearance of a matron schoolteacher.

Laurel sat at the table with her attorney, Marvin Blumenthal. The attorney stood up. He was wearing a white shirt, a black tie, and black slacks. The tassels of his Tzitzit hung down on either side. A Yarmulke sat on his head. He was short and clean shaven with a chubby face that sported a double chin.

"Thank you for coming," greeted Blumenthal.

The stenographer took a seat at the far end of the table.

Laurel sat silent as Michael and his attorney sat down on the opposite side of the table. She had worn a gray suit and looked straight ahead. Since leaving their residence with Nicholas, Laurel had refused to talk directly to Michael. Between the film's schedule and those of the attorneys, it had taken nearly six months to find a mutually acceptable date.

Michael was aware that Laurel had taken an apartment in Santa Monica and that Nicholas was well cared for by a nanny when he came home from school. Jack Warner had held up greenlighting Michael's next project on the excuse that the studio wanted to see how well _Federal_

*Squad* did. The picture wasn't slated to be released until that fall. Now that he was an independent producer, Michael found himself pitching projects to the other studios and juggling meetings while he waited for his film to be released. Michael loved his son and wasn't going to let him go without a fight.

Blumenthal looked at the seated parties. "I'm glad we could finally all come together on this." His gaze flitted over to Michael. "I'm a big fan of your films, Mr. McGuire."

"Thank you."

Blumenthal sat down next to Laurel. "Now, I won't waste any more of your time. The purpose of this meeting is to make a list and set the perimeters for your divorce."

"What type of list?" Michael asked.

Tim Cosgrove leaned close and whispered. "Let me handle this."

Michael waved him off and gave the opposing attorney a look that said, "Well?"

Blumenthal was momentarily caught off guard by Michael's directness. "Yes, well, obviously there will be a list of property and personal item—"

Michael looked directly at Laurel. "Laurel can have the house and the entire furnishings," he said, interrupting the attorney.

Cosgrove rolled his eyes and remained silent.

Blumenthal smiled. "Wonderful."

"I want my son," said Michael.

"You can't have him," Laurel replied.

Seeing that things were quickly escalating, Tim Cosgrove chuckled, "Well, it seems that we have something to discuss then."

Blumenthal was suddenly silent.

Michael stared at his wife. There were a million things he wanted to say but couldn't. He allowed a smile to fill his face and said, "Yes, I believe that is a subject we should discuss."

Blumenthal looked across the table at the movie producer. "I believe my client is adamant on that particular issue."

Cosgrove frowned. "Sole custody with no visitation rights, what the hell kind of deal is that?"

Blumenthal glanced at his legal opposition. "A rather generous one." The attorney saw the bewildered look on his colleague's face. "I see your client hasn't informed you of his previous occupation."

"Mr. McGuire once owned the *El Capitan*, a restaurant that was patronized by the mayor and sheriff and many of the city's finest people," Cosgrove replied.

Blumenthal waved the attorney off. "Please keep the studio bio for the boys in the press. I'll be brief. We have an eyewitness to a meeting that Michael McGuire had with a Max Greenberg at the *El Serape* restaurant during the fall of 1919."

Cosgrove glanced at Michael, who sat silent and expressionless. He turned back to Blumenthal.

"You've got to be kidding. My client meets some guy forty years ago and that's your argument?"

Blumenthal placed his hands on the table and folded his hands together. "Maxie Greenburg ran the rackets in Boyle Heights. Your client wanted Maxie's territory. They met at the *El Serape*. We have a witness to that meeting. After the police conveniently killed Max Greenberg, Michael McGuire took over his operation."

"Those are some bold accusations. Besides, what my client did back then should not reflect on his ability to be a good father."

Blumenthal looked directly at Michael. "Mr. McGuire might be a movie producer, but he was once a bootlegger who ordered people killed. That is not the type of person the court will look kindly on when granting custody to a young, impressionable boy."

Cosgrove glanced over at Michael, who continued to remain silent. "I'd like a word with my client alone."

Blumenthal opened his arms wide. "Certainly." He turned to the stenographer. "We'll take a five-minute break."

Cosgrove got up. "Come on."

Michael followed the attorney out of the conference room and office and into the marble corridor.

"What the hell is going on in there?" asked Cosgrove.

"He's right."

"That's years ago. The guy is bluffing about the witness. Even if he isn't, who gives a damn? You're a successful producer who's been making movies for years."

Michael wasn't surprised Laurel had told the attorney about his past. Blumenthal had obviously done a thorough job and dug up a witness. He sighed, "I don't want Nicholas dragged through this."

"Nicholas only has to testify to the judge regarding his life at home with you."

"The press will be all over the kid."

Cosgrove tugged on his earlobe. "Let me talk to Blumenthal."

Michael waved the attorney off. "Give her what she wants."

Cosgrove shot Michael a look of disbelief. "You'll be giving up any rights to see Nicholas."

"I know…"

* * *

Michael sat in the dark of his large home in Los Feliz. He sipped twenty-year-old scotch and thought about the deposition Blumenthal had conducted. He didn't have a picture in production which gave him time.

Michael knew that his grandfather, Sean, had been a hard man, a man of violence when he had been transgressed upon. Sean had raised Michael in his mold. Michael had killed his first man when he was sixteen. The man was a paid killer hired by the oil combine to assassinate Sean. Killing the man had little effect upon Michael. Later, he killed dozens of Germans during the war. Blumenthal digging up the past was not good. If certain people discovered the attorney's tactics, they might take exception to this. That would not be good for Michael.

A line had been crossed in Blumenthal's office. Laurel had gone too far. She and the attorney would have to be dealt with. Michael was barely seven when Sean McGuire looked at him and said, "Never lay hands on a man, curse him, or steal from him. If someone doesn't return that behavior to you, kill him." Michael had taken Sean's words to heart and lived by them. Those who did business with Michael never worried; they knew his word was solid. Dealing with the attorney was simple. Laurel would require a certain amount of finesse.

Michael drank his scotch and mulled over his options. Little did he know one would present itself to him shortly and send him on an entirely different path.

# 15

# *The Card Game*

James Hagen sat with his cards close to his chest. He was in a high stakes game with Tony Adronis and some of the fellas. They were playing at Tony's Tahoe cabin. Hagen had been constantly moving the last ten months on his Pullman car. He stayed with Tony's family at their home in Vegas. He traveled to Arizona and resided for a few weeks at a hotel in Phoenix owned by the Bonanno family. Now he was a guest at Tony's Tahoe retreat. The Feds had failed to find Hagen. He didn't like being on the run, but things could be worse. Now he was in a game and there was well over eighty grand on the table.

Tony was the table's dealer. He looked over at Hagen and said, "Hey, we heard Frank got that picture. You can tell your buddy, McGuire, it's noted and appreciated."

Hagen smiled. "Mike's a solid guy. He'll be glad to hear that." He glanced at his cards. He was holding a ten, jack, and queen of diamonds and a jack of hearts and two of spades. There were only three players betting at this point, Tony's attorney, Abe Saperstein, Bobby "Lips" Mantranga, and Hagen. The other players had long dropped out. Bobby Lips had obtained his nickname due to his method of cutting off the lips and tongues of those who had crossed Tony.

"I'll meet your thousand and raise another three," said Hagen as he tossed the additional chips into the pot.

Matranga sighed and tossed his cards on the table. "This is getting too rich for my blood." He had a pair of queens.

The rest of the fellas laughed and kidded Bobby Lips for not having the balls to stay in the game with a pair of queens.

Saperstein kept a stone face as he met Hagen's raise.

"Cards, gentlemen?" Tony asked.

"I'll take one," said Saperstein.

Hagen tossed the jack of hearts and two of spades and said, "I'll take two."

Tony dealt the cards to the men.

Saperstein picked up his card.

Hagen caught the tell. The attorney's eye twitched ever so slightly. Hagen picked up the cards he had been dealt.

Saperstein looked at his opponent and said, "I raise you five." The attorney tossed in the chips.

Hagen smiled. "I'll meet that and raise you ten more, Abe."

The attorney bristled. He thought for sure Hagen would've pulled out or at least called. The game had been going on for nearly nine hours. Saperstein was up by at least twenty grand and was feeling good about his hand. He figured he would end the match here and now. He glanced at Tony. "You've got some paper?"

Tony arched an eyebrow. "What'daya got to write an IOU, Abe?"

The attorney frowned.

"Get the man a piece of paper and pen," said Tony.

One of the observers quickly produced just that. The attorney took them and quickly wrote something on the paper and tossed it on the table.

"That's a letter with my signature giving you ownership of my radio station. That's worth at least a hundred grand."

"That station is in TJ, Abe," Tony joked. "What the fuck is Jimmy gonna do with that?"

Hagen never blinked. "I'll take the bet."

"That's a hundred fuckin' grand plus the pot," retorted Tony.

"I know," Hagen replied in a monotone voice.

Tony shrugged his shoulders. "All right, let's see your cards."

Saperstein laid his hand down. "Four Aces. Read 'em and weep." He began to reach for the pot.

But then Hagen showed his hand. He had gotten an eight and nine of diamonds to add to his hand.

"*Minchia*, a straight flush!" Tony exclaimed.

The other fellas slapped their knees, raise eyebrows and commented on Hagen's hand. Saperstein sat back in his chair a stunned and beaten man. The gang congratulated Hagen on his win.

"So, what you gonna do with a Mexican radio station?" asked Tony.

"Play fucking records," Hagen shot back.

Tom Hollister entered the room. He walked over to Hagen, bent down, and whispered in his ear. Hagen looked at the fixer. "You sure of that?"

Hollister nodded his head.

Hagen rubbed his hands together and chuckled. "It's been a very good day, fellas, but I've got to get back home now. Thanks for the game."

Los Angeles Tribune Headline – April 14th, 1952

## Allied Aircraft CEO Exonerated

James Hagen, CEO of Allied Aircraft, was exonerated in federal court. Judge Joshua Landis dismissed all charges against Hagen. "This has been a travesty of justice that I am very happy to see come to a conclusion," said Walter Cheney, Hagen's attorney. "My client has been harassed by the federal government for over a year. We are thankful to Judge Landis for seeing the light and making a decision on the behalf of justice." Hagen did not respond to reporters' questions, instead merely offering, "I'm glad it is all over and I can get back to doing what I do best: making airplanes."

# 16

# *The Taft Building*

Marvin Blumenthal's office was on the ninth floor of the Taft Building. The building was named after A.Z. Taft Jr., who purchased the Hollywood Memorial Church, tore it down, and put up the first high-rise building in the city. It primarily housed lawyers who couldn't afford a Beverly Hills address and agents whose clients worked on poverty row. A quick study of the building's register and a few hours surveillance gave Michael everything he required.

Murray Hunt was an agent who had a small office on the fifth floor at the back of the building. Michael knew Hunt worked from hunger and had no secretary or assistant. His was truly a one-man operation. Hunt left his office promptly at six. Blumenthal worked late and was a man of ritual. He would work until six-thirty and then take a dinner break that lasted approximately thirty minutes. He would return and work until nine and then go home. He was usually one of the last people to leave the building.

Michael had his plan. This one was a solid as it got. At 6:15, Michael pulled in and parked his car in the lot behind the Taft building. He entered from the rear and took the stairs up to Hunt's office. The well-dressed man carrying a briefcase didn't attract any attention. Reaching Hunt's office, Michael jimmied the lock and was inside in less than thirty seconds. He quietly closed the door and set the briefcase on the lone desk. Michael opened the case and took out a pair of men's coveralls. The logo *Hollywood Maintenance* was sewn on the back.

Michael quickly removed his Fedora and tie and slipped on the coveralls, zipping them up. He took a hat from the pocket of the coveralls and put that on his head, making sure it was pulled down and obscuring his face. He then removed a crowbar from the briefcase, stuffed it inside the coveralls, and silently exited the office. There was a supply closet on that floor down the hall from Hunt's office. Michael jimmied the lock on the supply closet and took a cart holding a large waste basket, broom, and feather duster and closed the door.

Michael checked his watch. It was now 6:30 p.m. He pushed the cart to the elevator and hit the button. The door opened. Blumenthal stood with another man in the elevator. Michael deftly positioned the cart in front of him and lowered his head when he saw the occupants.

"Going down," said the man standing next to Blumenthal.

"Sorry, need the next floor up," said Michael, coughing in his hand.

The door closed. A minute later, the doors opened, and the elevator was empty. Michael got it with the cart. He knew he had thirty minutes to complete the job and be out of the building. Michael was surprised that Blumenthal didn't bother to lock his office door. He quickly cased the place and located his file in the attorney's desk. Michael read Blumenthal's notes. He had done his work and located one of the waitresses that worked at *El Serape*. That was their eyewitness. Michael jotted down the woman's address and phone number and returned the file to its place. He then quietly exited Blumenthal's office and walked back to the elevator where he had left the cart.

Michael used the crowbar to pry open the elevator doors. He glanced into the shaft. It was as black as night. Next, he checked his watch. It nearly seven. Five minutes later, the attorney emerged from the elevator next to the one with the open door. He glanced at the opened door and frowned. Michael stepped from the shadows.

Los Angeles Tribune Headline – April 18, 1952

## Attorney dies in freak accident

Attorney Marvin Blumenthal died in freak accident last night when he fell into one of the elevator shafts at the Taft building. Inspectors are unsure how Mr. Blumenthal could have made such a mistake. "There is no record of any maintenance being done on the elevators," said Wayne Remick, the building manager. "It is a very tragic accident." Blumenthal was once a member of the of the firm O'Brian, Meyer, and Lansing but left under a cloud when he was investigated for improprieties. Even though Blumenthal was eventually cleared, he never regained his reputation as a top litigator. Services will be held at Wilshire Boulevard Temple next Tuesday at 9 a.m.

Michael sat in his office at Warner's and read the paper. He wasn't sure how to deal with Laurel. Michael loved her but hated the fact that she had taken Nicholas away. A point had to be made. He just wasn't sure of how to make it. The intercom buzzed.

"A Mr. Hagen is on line one," said the secretary.

"Thanks."

Michael picked up the telephone. "Pogue Mahone Pictures."

"Hey, buddy," greeted Hagen.

"Congratulations. I was going to call you, but I had some things to take care of first."

"Yeah, guess I don't have to look over my shoulder anymore. I heard you were having some trouble on the home front."

"I'm working on it."

"Maybe I can help. How would you like to run a radio station?"

"What?"

"Yeah, I won a fuckin' radio station in a card game. I don't know the first damn thing about running it. You're Mr. Showbiz. You run the damn thing. Come on down to my place in Ensenada next weekend and we'll talk. I've got a bungalow at the Riviera del Pacifico."

"Jimmy, I've got my hands full here."

"Yeah, I heard. Royal dumped you. Fuck 'em, Michael. They're an ungrateful bunch. Come down to Mexico. It's been a long time. It'll do you good."

Hagen hung up before Michael could respond. It had indeed been a long time since the two men had seen each other.

Michael leaned back in his chair and mulled over Hagen's offer of managing a radio station. The proposition sounded like it could be fun, and he certainly could use the money. Michael knew the man he wanted to handle the music programing. An idea also began to form regarding Nicholas and Laurel.

# *Rock Bottom*

Ezekiel struggled to get out of bed. It had been months since he came home from the hospital but he still couldn't walk without a cane due to a loss of equilibrium. He continued to experience excruciating headaches. Ezekiel had lost his job at the cannery. The money from their home in Chavez Ravine was gone. What the doctors didn't take, the lawyers did. Ezekiel didn't have to do jail time, but he was an invalid due to injuries received courtesy of LAPD.

Angela was now the primary support for the family. They had moved into a small two-bedroom bungalow in Boyle Heights. Carmen took in laundry and cared for Ezekiel and the children while Angela worked. There was little money except for necessities.

Ezekiel sat up on the edge of the bed. He could hear the radio in the kitchen playing and Carmen singing along as she hung clothes on the line outside. He didn't want to bother her; he was determined to get up and dress himself without assistance.

Ezekiel slowly stood up. The two walking canes were leaning against the wall in the far corner. Ezekiel took a step. Then he took another. White hot pain shot up his spine. Drops of sweat beaded his forehead. Ezekiel took another step. Two more and he would reach his walking canes. He stood waiting to get the strength to take another step. His temples pounded. The room spun. He took another step and lost consciousness. Ezekiel hit the floor with a hard thud.

Carmen walked into the bedroom and saw her husband lying on the floor. She bent down and wrapped her arms around Ezekiel. Though she was just over a hundred pounds, Carmen got Ezekiel up and into the bathroom.

"Where...oh," said Ezekiel.

"What were you doing?" Carmen demanded as she wiped Ezekiel's face with a cold washcloth.

"I was going to get dressed."

"Call me next time," Carmen admonished her husband.

Ezekiel remained silent.

Carmen helped him dress and got his canes. Ezekiel didn't come outside. Carmen left to continue hanging the clothes. She didn't sing. Ezekiel sat brooding in the bedroom as the disc jockey on the radio announced the song by Jackie somebody and his Delta Cats.

* * *

The network didn't renew the *Courier from Hong Kong*. Lee May Sing was forty-five and unemployed. The fatigue had continued after she had returned to California. Lee May attributed it to adjusting to the different time zone. When she passed out after getting out of the shower and found herself on the tile floor a half hour later, Lee May finally went to see a doctor at Cedars.

Lee May dressed after the doctor finished his examination. She had been referred to an oncologist by her GP. Lee May glanced at her watch, seeing it was just after twelve. She could still make lunch with her mahjong ladies. Lee May dressed and then knocked softly on Dr. Freeman's door, and entered. The doctor gestured to a chair, and Lee May took a seat.

"So, what have you found, doctor, that a middle-aged actress requires more sleep?" Lee May Sing asked glibly.

Dr. Freeman was a thirty-nine-year-old medical genius. He knew more about the human pulmonary system than just about anyone outside of Walter Reed Medical. He had graduated magna cum laude from John Hopkins. He could spot an anomaly in a patient's blood a mile away. The doctor smiled.

"How are you feeling?"

"Better today. That was a pretty thorough exam you put me through."

"Yes, well, we want to be sure." The doctor paused, and an uncomfortable silence filled the room. "When are you expected back at work?"

Lee May Sing grinned. "Not for another five months." She lied. Lee May had no picture lined up.

Doctor Freeman looked directly at Lee May. "Miss Sing, I'm going to be blunt. You won't be able to return to work. You have leukemia. It is already in an advanced state."

Lee May Sing's palms and mouth went dry. "What can I do?"

"We can begin radiation treatment, which could help."

Lee May Sing folded her hands on her lap. "I will also be direct, doctor. How much time do I have?"

Doctor Freeman glanced down at his desk. He always found it difficult to tell a patient they were mortal and their time had run out. "A year, maybe less."

"And if I were to go through the radiation treatment?"

"That depends. If we're lucky, four, five years, possibly more."

Lee May Sing took all of this in and never took her eyes off the doctor. "So, what you are telling me, is that if I don't have the treatment, I have a year to live. If I go through with the treatment, I will be sick and there is no guarantee that I won't die in a year anyway."

The doctor forced a smile. "The treatment could give you more time, Miss Sing."

"What would my quality of life be?"

Dr. Freeman gave Lee may Sing a perplexed look. "What do you mean? You would be alive."

"Would I be able to work?"

The doctor shook his head. "No, you will not be able to work during your treatment. You would be too weak. Afterwards, we will have to see."

"Would I be able to go out, go dancing, swim in the ocean, or ride my horse?"

Doctor Freedman sat up in his chair. "I'm afraid your life is going to change from this point on."

"Then my answer is no."

The doctor frowned. "Don't be rash. Think about this, Miss Sing. This is a very important decision."

Lee May Sing stood. "I don't need to. I choose to continue my life in the same manner I have since I could walk."

"I wouldn't advise that."

Lee May Sing gave the doctor a demure look. "Because that may kill me?"

"It certainly won't help you."

Lee May Sing batted her eyes and gave the doctor a sexy smile. "You have no idea the therapeutic wonders dancing at the Trocadero can have."

The actress exited the office. Lee May Sing did not have lunch with her mahjong ladies that afternoon. She got in her car and drove down Wilshire Blvd. Lee May turned on the radio. The band rocked.

The singer shouted, "Yes, it's great. Everybody likes my—"

Lee May quickly changed the station to one playing classical music. After a moment, she turned the radio off. Lee May drove home and had lunch alone on the patio overlooking the garden.

* * *

The recording session at Royal hadn't led to additional gigs for Cosmo. The Feds had come down on the studios and mandated their divestment of vertical integration. In layman's terms it meant they had to sell their theater chains, which was a major source of revenue for the studios. One of the first fatalities was the musicians. The studios no longer offered contracts to them. They were hired on a strictly "as needed" basis. The only players who were called were those on a producer's rolodex. Cosmo didn't know any producers, so his phone didn't ring.

The clubs that had booked big bands ten years ago were all but gone. Three and four-man combos were the thing. People weren't coming to dance. They wanted to experience the music. Bop hit.

"Sounds like a bunch of cats tunin' up," Cosmo observed when the conversation at the union hall came around to the new style of jazz.

Cosmo spent many days sitting at the union hall and playing cards. He hoped for a gig and waited. Occasionally a one-nighter came up. Fridays and Saturdays were generally better. Somebody was usually having a rent party and needed a band.

Eddie Ryan, a bass player who had once played with Count Basie, looked up from his newspaper and chuckled. "You're just sore cause they ain't playin' swing no more." Ryan was older than Cosmo and had played Europe.

"Damn straight. Shit, I had a good thing going 'fore the war."

Bobby Blake, a drummer, laughed. Bobby was two hundred-fifty pounds of man who laid down a beat like a metronome. "You mean that drugstore you turned into a club? Hell, the laws would'a shut your ass down if'n you hadn't been drafted."

Cosmo frowned. He knew what Bobby said was true. Cosmo had taken over a shop in Little Tokyo when the Japanese were evacuated and turned it into a nightclub.

Something caught Cosmo's ear. "Hey, Henry, turn up the radio."

Henry Hawkins, the union steward, stood behind the desk. He turned at adjusted the volume on the radio. The piano player was driving the song.

Cosmo got up and walked over to the counter to listen. This wasn't like Jordon's *Tympani Five*. The song had a solid groove that the boppers lacked. It was raw. It was powerful. Cosmo realized this was something entirely new.

"That was Jackie Breston and his Delta Cats with *Rocket 88*. You heard it first on KDAY radio, L.A. Coming up next, the Clovers and *One Mint Julip!*" the DJ exclaimed with an over-caffeinated rat-a-tat precision.

"Now that is something," remarked Cosmo.

"Sure is. We just ain't sure what it is," Bobby laughed.

Cosmo had enough. He looked at the heavyset man sitting in the chair. "What the fuck would you know, Bobbie? You're just a drummer."

Eddie and some of the other musicians chuckled. Cosmo tipped his hat to Henry and marched for the door.

Bobby hurled a "Fuck you!" at Cosmo.

He didn't respond. Cosmo had the song in his head. He wanted to go home and practice playing *Rocket 88* before the melody slipped away.

# 18

# South of the Border

Getting rid of lawyer Blumenthal's witness was easy. Michael had the studio art department make up an official certificate congratulating Delores Sanchez on her win in the *California Sweepstakes*. Michael included three hundred dollars and a plane ticket to Miami along with a bogus First Place certificate. The retired waitress was gone the following day. Dealing with Laurel would take greater finesse.

Michael picked up Nicholas from school at noon on Friday. The boy was happy to see his father and even happier to be taken out of class early. Michael explained to the principal that he had custody of Nicholas that weekend and had to leave early for a business meeting. The principal was impressed to meet the movie producer. He released Nicholas to his father and they left. Michael knew he had three hours before Laurel would discover he had taken their son.

The Riviera del Pacifico sat on the beach. Clumps of grass dotted the sand leading to the ocean. Hagen greeted Michael and Nicholas with a broad smile. "My place may be a little cramped. Let me call the front desk and get you a suite."

"No need. Nicholas will not be staying the night."

Hagen smiled. "Well, I hope you're planning on remaining."

"I'll have to see. I let the front desk know that if Laurel calls, they are to put her through to your room. I hope you don't mind."

"No."

The two men took Nicholas to the beach and watched the young boy play in the warm waters of Baja. There was a message from Laurel waiting for Michael at the front desk when they returned to the hotel. The note simply said, *I am on my way.* The clerk informed Michael that the call had come about thirty minutes previous. Michael looked at his watch. He had just about three hours before Laurel would arrive.

Michael, Jimmy, and Nicholas had dinner in the hotel's restaurant. Hagen once again offered Michael the radio station to manage.

"I don't have time to deal with a radio station," said Hagen.

Hagen made a face. "I don't know a damn thing about music outside of Sinatra. Besides I've got to focus running Allied. The government is cutting budgets."

"Eisenhower is a military man. Why would he cut production?"

Hagen smiled. "He cuts our production and moves the contract to Boeing. It's called *sharing the wealth.* The government gets its planes, and another part of the country gets an infusion of cash. The point is to stay ahead of the game. That's why we're working on rockets."

"Rockets?"

"That's the future, buddy. The Feds have Werner Von Braun working for them. We've got to develop one before the Russkies. They already have the bomb."

Michael looked at his friend. "Jaysus, Jimmy. We both know the government is more corrupt than we ever were on our best day."

Hagen flashed a smile and gave a nod. "I get carried away sometimes."

Nicholas watched his father and Jimmy talk business, sports, and cars, the talk of men. The young boy was entranced. It was a different world from the one lived with his mother. This was the first time Michael had taken him on a trip alone. Michael treated him as an equal, not as a child. His father and Jimmy conversed without asking Nicholas to leave the room, a common practice of his mother when she was with her ladies discussing feminine issues.

After dinner, Michael excused himself and Nicholas. "We are going to wait for his mother in the lobby."

Hagen gave a nod. "What about the radio station?"

"Let me think about it."

"Certainly."

"I'll call you next week."

Hagen looked at Michael. "Are you sure you don't want me to stay, for moral support?

Michael grinned. "No. Thank you anyway."

The two men shook hands, and Hagen headed down the beach. Ten minutes later, Laurel entered the hotel's large lobby. Nicholas was seated in a chair reading a book. Michael rose to his feet when he saw Laurel. She rushed over to the young boy.

"Are you alright?"

Nicholas looked at his mother. "Oh yes. I had so much fun. Daddy took me swimming, and then we went to dinner. I got to meet Daddy's friend, Jimmy. I had steak. Daddy had lobster." He scratched his head. "I don't remember what Mr. Hagen had."

Laurel ran her hand down Nicholas's cheek. "Yes, well, sit right there. Mommy has to talk to Daddy."

Nicholas nodded and went back to his book.

The two parents stepped away from their son.

Laurel's eyes shot daggers. "You handled this perfectly, public place, our son within earshot," she hissed.

"I wanted to make a point."

"The same point you made with my lawyer?"

"I read the police called it an accident."

Laurel glared at Michael. "You made your point. Kidnapping my son isn't beneath you."

"Nicholas is my son too."

"Yes, he is, but he will not grow up in your world, with you to teach him."

"Don't play innocent. You knew what I was before you married me."

"I was naïve. I believed you ran a nightclub. I didn't think you killed people."

Michael remained silent.

"I'm taking our son and going back to Los Angeles," snapped Laurel.

"Just remember, you can't keep Nicholas from me."

Laurel stood silent for a moment, looking at her husband. "You're right. You have more muscle and pull than I do. You can take Nicholas any time you please. You know, Michael, I never thought it would be possible for me to hate you. Pity, you showed me how to tonight."

Laurel brushed past him.

Michael turned to face her. "Fine, take him. Nicholas will seek me out one day. Mark my words."

Laurel didn't reply. She simply took Nicholas by the hand and the mother and son walked away as Michael stood silent in the large lobby.

# 19

# *Border Radio*

Cosmo drove his Chevy down the dusty road. He could never understand why Mexico didn't improve their roads. He had been driving down this street for the last seven years and the only thing that changed about it was what Mother Nature had done. The car bounced and bobbed over ruts and potholes. There was nothing around for the last three miles. The road finally smoothed out and became asphalt for the final mile to the radio station.

XELA radio station was housed in the former home of Don Paso, a rancher who lost his property in a card game. The winner had sold off the cattle and set up a radio station in the house. That was 1934, the height of the gambling era in Tijuana. The station languished during the war years. It was a broadcasting just twelve hours a day when Michael took over management. He knew the only way to make the station viable was to broadcast like their competitors. That meant twenty-four hours a day, seven days a week. He also knew he needed something that the other stations weren't playing. Michael remembered Cosmo from the studio session and called him. The rest was history. Just like the El Capitan had operated, Michael put together a team that ran XELA like a well-greased machine.

Michael had a knack for spotting talent and put together a group of DJs. Cosmo came up with a playlist composed of primarily rhythm and blues, artists like Johnny Otis, Wynonie Harris, Roy Brown, and Little Willie John. The station took off. The music was hot and had a driving beat. A DJ in Cleveland had called it *rock'n'roll*. Cosmo had been playing rhythm and blues for years, only with larger outfits that featured horns and piano over the rhythm section. This new sound was stripped down with a wild electric guitar running the lead. This wasn't the sound of Charlie Christian. This was the sound of rebellion. Rock'n'roll hit America like a right-hook from Marciano. The country was never the same.

The real secret to the station's success lay in its transmitter and loose Mexican regulation. XELA was a Class A, 50,000-watt clear-channel station that used a non-directional antenna during their daytime broadcasts. The signal reached as far north as Los Angeles and east to the Imperial Valley. At night, the station switched to a three-tower array directional signal and boasted their power to 150,000 watts. On a cool, clear night, the broadcast could be heard as far north as Seattle and as far east as Denver. On the AM dial, XELA was king in the California southland.

The station carried a small staff. It was rare that more than two or three employees were ever there at the same time. A secretary worked the front desk from eight to five. An engineer worked an eight-to-eight shift. It was up to the individual DJs to hold down the fort after 8 p.m. Cosmo's show ran from 5 to 9p.m Monday through Friday. He was at first reluctant to leave L.A., but after a week of commuting, Cosmo moved to San Diego. It was a twenty-minute drive to the border from his house in Golden Hills and another twenty minutes from downtown TJ to the station. Cosmo would do his shift and be back in San Diego to make a gig. He had a small combo that played regularly at *Leroy's on Broadway* on Saturday nights. The bar sat two blocks west of Horton Plaza. Cosmo was living the life.

The white hacienda that housed XELA sat in the middle of a grassy field that covered some twenty acres. Four transmitter towers dotted the field, standing tall against the stark Baja background. Cosmo parked his car in the lot and entered the station. Two men in gray suits sat in the lobby. They were both in their forties, clean shaven, and held sullen expressions. The only real difference between the two was one was blond, and the other man had black hair. Brenda Williams, the station secretary, had just a moment to give Cosmo an eye warning him of the pair.

The two men stood. The darkhaired man stepped forward.

"I'm Special Agent Walker." He nodded to the blond man next to him. "This is my partner, Special Agent Timmons. Is there some place where we could talk in private?"

Cosmo had a run in with a pair of Feds before when he'd had his club. They had hired him to find Nicole Sullivan. The case went sideways, and the Feds turned out to be private dicks running a scam with Sullivan. One of them nearly killed Cosmo. He killed the dick instead. Nicole disappeared. The other dick went to prison. That was years ago.

Cosmo looked at the two men and asked in a calm, cool voice, "May I please see your badges?"

Timmons frowned. Walker gave him a look. Both held out their IDs.

"If you will follow me," said Cosmo.

The two agents followed him down the hall to his office. Cosmo set his briefcase on the desk and indicated to the two chairs. The agents remained standing. Cosmo nonchalantly took a seat behind his desk.

"What can I do for you, gentleman?"

"We're investigating the pay to play racket the record companies have going with radio stations," said Walker.

Cosmo flashed a friendly smile. "I'm really sorry, but you gentleman appeared to have lost your way. This is a Mexican station."

"Michael McGuire holds the license on the station," barked Timmons. "Last I looked, he was an American, and so are you."

"I'm glad you recognize that fact, Agent Timmons. You should also know that U.S. law doesn't govern this station. If you have any questions regarding the legality of the business XELA conducts, you should contact the company's attorney, Leo Stone."

Agent Walker scratched his jaw. "This is a very simple process, Mr. Turner. You either help us, or we can make your life complicated."

Timmons smirked. "It'd be a tragedy to get caught at the border with contraband. You ever see the inside of a Mexican jail?"

Cosmo stood and looked directly at the two agents. "I've seen the inside of enough of American jails."

Timmons chuckled. "I bet you have. Be a smart Negro and answer our questions."

Cosmo glanced at his watch. "I have a shift coming up, if you gentlemen will please excuse me. Brenda at the front desk will provide you with Mr. Stone's contact information."

Walker tipped his hat. "We'll be seeing you, Mr. Turner."

The two FBI agents exited the office.

"Fuck you too, Ofay," Cosmo replied under his breath. He looked at his hands. They were as still as concrete. Cosmo chuckled to himself, "Cool as ice, muthafucka."

Cosmo called Michael and told him about the agents' appearance. Michael took their names, thanked Cosmo, and hung up.

Cosmo hit the control booth energized. He spun tunes, took requests, and made dedications. He typed up a memo and posted it on the bulletin board.

# Notice to All Employees

If contacted by the FBI or any other police agency, refer all questions to the station's attorney. Do not engage in conversation. Be sure to inspect your vehicles, trunk, hood, and interior before crossing the border into the U.S.

Station Director XELA,
Cosmo Turner

"This is powerhouse ten-seventy on the dial, and we're coming up on the hour with Little Richard," said Cosmo into the microphone. He walked over and grabbed the sheet that held the latest news and tore it from the machine. The song ended, and Cosmo adjusted the mic.

"This is XELA News."

Cosmo hit a tape. The sound of clacking typewriters played in the background as he read the news. "NASA introduced the astronauts of the Mercury Program today. Best of luck to you, men. In other news, Hollywood actress Lee May Sing died this morning at Cedars Sinai. Miss Sing had been battling cancer for a number of years. Lee May was best known for her role in the *Evil Dr. Ming* series."

Cosmo played a commercial for Cosgrove Pontiac and then read the weather report. He played another commercial and then spun a record.

Cosmo grabbed his mic. "Here's one that's rockin' the charts, San Diego! My man, Ray Charles with *What'd I Say*."

Ray's keyboard kicked it.

Cosmo took a bottle of scotch from a drawer, poured himself a shot into a paper cup, and grooved on Ray Charles. He knew Michael would handle the Feds.

# 20

# *The Funeral*

Lee May Sing was wrong to believe no one would mourn her passing. Hundreds turned out for her service at Forrest Lawn. Lee May had kept her condition a secret. She had relented and gone through months of radiation treatment. She told Michael and a few other close friends that she was traveling to China to visit her relatives when she underwent radiation. Michael had been occupied with his divorce at the time. Work kept him busy getting the station up and running and trying to interest the studios in a western he had penned. He and Lee May would talk by phone, but it had been a long time since Michael had seen her in the flesh.

Lee May Sing had called Michael a little over a month before she died and asked him to come for lunch. He readily agreed and was shocked by the actress's appearance. On her best day, Lee May stood five foot five and weighed one hundred and twelve pounds. Now her frame had shrunk and she weighed barely eighty pounds. Michael hugged his friend gently and they had tea on the patio overlooking the beautiful garden.

"I'm going to die, Michael."

"Why…how long…?"

Lee May casually sipped her tea. "I didn't tell anyone. You are the first to know."

Michael gave Lee May a look of surprise.

"I have few friends, Michael. You are at the top of the list. I did not want to burden you with my medical issues. I will ask a favor, though."

"Anything."

"I wish to be cremated. I do not want one of those Hollywood spectacles like Valentino and Harlow. I would also like you to spread my ashes in the ocean by the El Capitan."

Michael gave Lee May a quizzical look.

"My father used to take me to the beach. We would sit and watch all the people going into your nightclub. It was so glamourous. Father would always say he was foolish for not remaining partners with you. I wanted to be a part of that world. It was your club that made me want to be a star."

"Guess I was a bad influence even back then." Michael gave a nod. "Don't worry, I will see to it."

"Thank you."

"Is there anything else?"

Lee May Sing smiled. "Yes, let's enjoy this day, Michael.

The actress took the producer's hand and gave it a squeeze. They sat and enjoyed a lunch of wanton soup and cucumber salad in the warm California sun.

Michael kept his word. When Lee May died, he had her body cremated and spread her ashes in the Pacific at sunset. He refused to allow his friend to slip away unnoticed by the industry she had worked in since she was a teenager. Michael was Irish, and the Irish enjoyed world class wakes. He arranged a celebration of Lee May Sing's life at Forest Lawn. Michael gave the eulogy. A dozen actors and directors got up to reminisce and tell anecdotes about the actress and times past.

Michael and some others went to the Tam O'Shanter after the services and continued their celebration of the actress. After the group broke up, Michael didn't care to go home to an empty house, so he drove to his grandfather's ranch.

The Oso Negro was once a prosperous ranch covering some fifteen hundred acres at one point. That was seventy-five years ago. Now the ranch amounted to a mere twelve acres. Dozens of expensive homes hidden behind long driveways, shrubs, and fences dotted the landscape where Sean's cattle had once grazed. Michael had used the ranch as a site for westerns in the thirties. The post-war folks wanted bigger, bolder, and in technicolor. Michael made movies involving duplicitous women and gumshoes who kept a bottle of rye in their desk drawers.

For a time, he had allowed the Camacho family, Falcon's grandchildren, the use the ranch. Falcon had been Sean's guide on his first cattle drive to Texas. Years ago, Michael received a set of keys to the house in the mail with a short note informing him that Olivia Camacho had died and thanking him for the use of the ranch. The note was signed by Angela Camacho. Michael hadn't bothered to pursue the matter. He put the keys in his desk drawer and forgot about the place. Making movies, dealing with a divorce, and running a radio station occupied every minute of his day. Now he returned to the home where he had come of age.

Michael drove up the long drive and parked his car. The adobe had been rebuilt over the years. Michael had made sure the place was kept up. The barn and corrals were a different matter. The cattle and horses had been sold off years ago. The structures were in various states of disrepair. The house was surprisingly cold inside. It had been shuttered for years. A cleaning lady came once a week to check on things and dust. A gardener made sure the family cemetery where Michael's aunt, grandmother, and great uncle were buried was tended.

Michael patted his arms together trying to warm himself. He took a bottle of scotch down from its hiding place in the kitchen. Sean had always kept a bottle secreted inside the China cabinet in a small hidden cupboard on the bottom shelf.

The liquor warmed his chilled body. Michael took the bottle and went outside to sit on the veranda. He was rapidly reaching the age when most men retired. But that was anathema to Michael. He had to work to keep the demons at bay. He missed his son. Nicholas was graduating from high school next year.

After the incident in Mexico, Laurel and Nicholas relocated to the bay area. Michael didn't pursue them. He knew he had made his point. Michael knew Nicholas would seek him out when he was ready. He would teach Nicholas the ways of the world, as Sean had taught him. Laurel could only keep Nicholas innocent for so long. He was a McGuire first and foremost.

Michael took another swig of the bottle. The sky was a stunning blend of red, orange, and blue. The sun was just above the horizon. Michael remembered when Sean would take him riding in the hills. His grandfather was a hard man and raised his grandson to be a hard man. Michael had killed men. He killed bootleggers. He killed cops. He killed Germans. He had no regrets over the killings. They had it coming. Laurel came from a different world. She never forgave Michael for being a killer of men.

Michael took another long pull from the bottle. Lee May Sing was gone. She was Walter Sing's daughter. Walter was the son of Lee Sing, the man who became Sean's partner in real estate holdings in Chinatown. Lee May was the final link to the glory days of Sean McGuire and the Oso Negro. She was also a woman Michael had admired and loved. He finished the bottle. Michael wished he had a gun. When he was a young boy, the cowboys would toss their empties into the air and shoot them. Michael tossed the empty into the trash, locked up the house, and drove home. He had visited enough ghosts for the day.

# 21

# *The Eviction*

Captain Mathis and dozens of officers converged on Chavez Ravine. A fleet of bulldozers followed them. The media was there by the dozens to document the proceedings. Lookie-loos gathered and gawked as the lawmen removed the few remaining residents who refused to leave.

For two years the area had resembled more of a ghost town than the vibrant community it once was. Barely two dozen families held out against the Housing Authority,

The new mayor of Los Angeles wasn't going to allow a bunch of *wetbacks* to flaunt orders to remove themselves from the area. He had been elected on an anti-socialist platform. Nothing reeked more of socialism than Elysian Heights. The voters vetoed the project. The elite were elated. The city bought back Chavez Ravine from the Feds for pennies on the dollar and then turned around and traded it to Walter O'Malley for his park downtown. It was the greatest swindle on the citizens since the 1915 annexation of the valley. For five years the people fought. The mayor finally decided the time had arrived to end the debate. The reckoning for the remaining residents occurred on a beautiful Friday morning in May.

LAPD encountered little resistance. Most complied; they quickly gathered up a few belongings before the police escorted them to their vehicles. Flashbulbs blasted. Pictures were snapped as the residents were led away. Murmurs rose from the group of gawkers.

Ezekiel stood among the group. He wore an old Fedora pulled down to obscure his face. Many of the voyeurs were white. They had come to see the law get tough on the Mexicans. They weren't disappointed. Doors were kicked it. Tents were torn down. Possessions were smashed. Then the cops came to 1771 Malvina Ave.

The home belonged to Manuel Arechiga and his wife, Abrana. The family wasn't the most vocal in their protest to the city's use of eminent domain, but they were the most determined. The family had gathered inside their small home. The sheriff's deputies kicked in the door and roughly escorted the family from the house. The daughter, Aurora, had to be carried by four deputies as she kicked and screamed. Flash-blubs popped. Furniture got trashed. This was theater at its best.

Then the bulldozers moved in. The machines mashed dozens of homes. The residents had been removed. The gawkers had gone. The police had dispersed.

Ezekiel remained. He watched as the big yellow machines destroyed everything in their path. In less than an hour, every evidence of his old neighborhood was gone. Ezekiel turned away. It took him some time to make it down the hill. He didn't need a cane any longer, but his right leg had a decided limp.

Ezekiel had never fully recovered from the injuries inflicted by the LAPD. He continued to have terrible headaches, and his equilibrium was not the best. He would get dizzy and have to stop and rest before continuing to walk.

Angela had been the main support of the family for months now. It had been tough when she lost her job when the agency's director moved to the bay area. Angela and Carmen took in laundry, sewed, and took whatever work they could find. The six lived in a tiny apartment in Echo Park. Johnny was in third grade. Lucy was in sixth, and Letty was in her last year of junior high school. Angela eventually got a job as a clerk for the school district. Carmen found work as a checker at Cardenas Market in Silver Lake. Ezekiel had abdicated his role as pater familia. He brooded and his anger and discontent grew.

Tom Mendoza was waiting for Ezekiel when he reached the street. Ezekiel limped over and got in the pristine blue and white '57 Chevy. Mendoza was dressed in tan pleated slacks and a white t-shirt. He looked at Ezekiel. "See enough?"

"No," Ezekiel responded in a sullen tone of voice.

Mendoza grabbed the pack of Lucky's sitting on the dash, shook out a smoke, and lit it. "Come on, vato. The city won. Game over." He exhaled a cloud of smoke and gestured toward the windshield. "Look at this shit. There ain't nothing left. Why you want to come back here?"

"It was my home," Ezekiel seethed.

"Yeah, it was mine too. Not anymore."

Ezekiel glared at Mendoza. "You sound like Carmen and my kid sister."

Mendoza grinned and nodded his head. "Yeah, well, maybe you should listen to them, especially since they wear the pants in the family."

Ezekiel smashed his fist into Mendoza's face. The cigarette fell on the seat. Blood spattered the window. Mendoza fought back. Ezekiel fought like a wild animal. Mendoza struggled against Ezekiel's raining blows. He kicked hard with his right leg and caught Ezekiel in the chest. The car door flew open, and Ezekiel fell out onto the ground.

Mendoza wiped the blood from his mouth and spit out the window. He looked down to see the cigarette had burned a hole in the car's front seat and cursed. He glanced out the open door at Ezekiel who was struggling to get to his feet.

"Fuck you, EZ!"

Mendoza pulled the door shut. He gunned the engine and sped away.

Ezekiel struggled to his feet. He brushed himself off and began walking toward Sunset. It was painful walking and took Ezekiel nearly thirty minutes to reach the bus stop. By the time he made it back to the apartment, he was tired. He laid down on the bed and stared at the ceiling.

Someone had to pay. His parents would still be alive if they hadn't been forced to move. He wouldn't have been injured by the police if there hadn't been the evictions. The city had betrayed the residents of Chavez Ravine. Someone had to pay. Ezekiel lay on the bed and embraced his anger.

Carmen and Angela didn't say anything about the evictions that night at dinner. They knew Ezekiel had gone to watch. The conversation was kept to school and what the children were doing. Ezekiel didn't say much. When he finished his dinner, he took his chair outside and smoked his cigarette on the small porch. The two women were too tired to deal with one of Ezekiel's rages and left him be. Even the radio was kept off most of the time for fear of some broadcast upsetting Ezekiel. He was no longer the breadwinner, but Ezekiel continued to cast a long, dark shadow over the family.

Weeks passed after Chavez Ravine had been cleared. Ezekiel continued to take the bus down Sunset and walk to his old neighborhood. He watched the bulldozers change the topography of land. Crews knocked down the ridge separating the Sulfur and Cemetery ravines and filled them in, burying Palo Verde Elementary School in the process.

Ezekiel would take the bus back home and brood each evening. Carmen didn't know what to do. There was no money for doctors. She knew the man she married had vanished. She had tried to get Ezekiel involved with other groups, even going so far as inviting Tom Mendoza for dinner. Nothing worked. Ezekiel remained sullen and silent. Tom stopped coming around. Carmen attempted to find out why, but Ezekiel told her to mind her business.

She and Angela fell into the routine of keeping their conversations short while at home. The only joy for both women now came from their children. Carmen hoped it was just a matter of time before Ezekiel would snap out of it and become his old self. Angela knew it was only a matter of time before Ezekiel would explode, but she kept her thoughts to herself. She and Carmen went to work, kept the house, and strived to maintain a tranquil environment in their home. Neither woman knew a day of reckoning was fast approaching.

# 22

# Top of the Charts

Chubby Checker's *Twist* and *Pony Time* were double barrel hits on the charts. The former chicken-plucker was swinging the nation and XELA was rocking the southern California airwaves. Rock'n'roll was king. A pair of Jewish teenagers had made it happen with *Hound Dog,* one of the biggest hits for a heavy-set black lesbian singer. The Negroes had landed in America's living room. There were rumblings in the street. Wonder bread and *Ozzie and Harriet* ruled in suburbia. Storm clouds were moving in, and few saw them coming.

Cosmo leaned into the mic. "That was the Mar-Keys with *Last Night* on the big XL, radio ten-seventy on your dial. Comin' up next is Jackie Wilson with *Lonely Teardrops.*" He lit a Lucky as the record spun and exhaled a cloud of smoke.

Brenda Williams showed a man into the studio and quickly departed. The man was thirty, white, had a great haircut, and was dressed in a sharp sharkskin suit.

Cosmo got up from his seat and smiled. "My man, Murray."

Murray held an LP out to Cosmo. The cover was blank white. "It's the big man's greatest hits. It's coming out this fall. In time for the Christmas trade. There's a bonus in there as always, my man."

Cosmo chuckled as he removed an envelope from the record jacket and slipped it inside his coat pocket. The album had an orange label with the name *Parkway.* "XELA thanks you." He held up a finger and grabbed the mic. "O-o-o-h-h-h yeah, Mr. Reet Petite, Jackie Wilson."

He hit a button. A tape played. "Jose Gonzales is alive, alive!" exclaimed a woman's voice. Cosmo hit another switch on the console. A tape played a car commercial. Cosmo watched the clock and then spoke into the mic.

"XELA, XL radio ten-seventy and we're rocking with the hit that's blasting the nation, people! You know what I'm talkin' 'bout. Oh yeah, Big Daddy is bringing it on to you!"

Big Daddy was the nom de plume Cosmo worked under on the radio. It fit the man who stood five foot seven in his stocking feet well.

The record spun.

Murray smiled. "It's nice doing business with you, Cosmo."

Cosmo gave the A&R rep a grin. "That's Big Daddy to you."

Murray laughed. He pointed to the record and exited the studio.

Cosmo sat down behind the console and adjusted the mic. "We've got the man whose showin' you how to shake it, boys and girls. This is a bona fide hit that's startin' a dance craze across the nation that's the new sensation without imitation. Now all you cats and kittens out there better get hip, cause its *Pony Time!*"

The song spun on the turntable.

Cosmo took the envelope out and counted it, twenty-two-hundred-dollar bills. He queued up another record before leaving the studio.

Cosmo quickly walked down the hall to Michael's office. He knelt down and dialed the combination on the floor safe under the desk, opened it, and dropped the envelope inside. He closed the door, making sure to spin the dial. Cosmo quickly retraced his steps and hit the second turntable just as the song faded. Sam Cooke began to sing about what a wonderful world it would be. Cosmo's cigarette had gone out. He lit another, sat back in his chair, and exhaled a perfect smoke ring. Life was good.

The Feds had backed off on their payola investigation. After Cosmo called Michael McGuire, neither he nor anyone else at the station heard from Special Agents Timmons and Walker again. Cosmo knew Michael was tight with James Hagen, the real station owner. He knew Hagen had connections and wasn't someone you wanted to cross.

XELA's operation ran smoothly. It was a Mexican station, after all. It made it harder for federal authorities to enforce American law outside the country's border. While the Harris Committee gave Dick Clark a pass and then crucified Alan Freed, there was little it could do about business conducted south of the border.

Michael had declared, "What happens in TJ stays in TJ." Cosmo was the face of the station and ran the daily operations. For his services, he received a cut of the payola. The money was deposited in a Mexican bank. Michael then transferred the cash to a business account, and from there it went to a Canadian bank that was linked to Barclay's in England. A British holding company had the Barclay account. The holding company was located in Gibraltar and was actually a shell company Michael had set up when he produced a film in England for Royal Studio. The cash made the circuit and came back clean.

Cosmo was not privy to the financial details of the business. He just knew every month he got five grand from Michael. Cosmo knew you didn't ask questions of men like Michael McGuire and James Hagen. You took your money and kept your mouth shut. That was fine with him.

The studio phone rang. Folks were always calling in with requests. Cosmo queued up another record, segued into it, and grabbed the phone.

"XL radio ten-seventy. What can Big Daddy do for you?"

There was a moment of silence on the line. Cosmo could hear *I'll be Seeing You* play in the background. A woman's voice said, "I know what you did."

"What?"

"I know what you did," the voice repeated. The song continued to play in the background and then the line went dead.

"Fuck you too, Momma," Cosmo hung up the phone.

Cosmo finished his shift. He drove straight home that evening. He couldn't place the female caller's voice, but he knew he'd heard it before. He stopped off for Chinese take-out. Cosmo ate his dinner and had a cold beer. He thought about the call. What did the caller mean? The payola? Smoking reefer? The skim he took booking the band? Cosmo knew he was guilty of many sins. He couldn't figure out what the caller's purpose was. He had a cigarette and then went to bed. The call bothered him for another day or two. But then a new week started. Cosmo didn't think about it any longer. There was wax to spin and money to be made.

* * *

Michael drove to San Diego. Hagen had called and wanted to meet. He had been rather obscure about the reason for the meeting. Michael didn't press him. He merely asked when. He didn't have a film in production, a meeting or even a script to complete. Michael didn't have much going on. The town that once considered him hot now shunned him like week-old fish. He was surprised when Hagen said they should meet at the Mission Bay Marina. He took the slip number down and promised to be there.

Michael was on time. A pristine 1929 Dawn-Cruiser named *Sirocco* sat in the slip. Hagen was sitting in a chair enjoying a beer when said Michael walked up.

"Permission to come aboard, Captain?" said Michael.

Hagen jumped to his feet and grinned. "Permission granted."

The two men shook hands.

Hagen gestured to the boat. "She looks familiar?"

"Yeah. The lady carried quite a few cases of Canadian scotch for us as I recall."

"How 'bout a beer?"

Michael plopped into one of the deck chairs. "Love one."

Hagen ducked inside and grabbed a cold beer from the cooler. He popped the can with the church-key that hung around his neck on a chain and handed it to Michael.

"Thanks." Michael eyed Hagen's casual attire of shorts and a half buttoned Hawaiian shirt that revealed a tanned chest. "Casual Monday?" he kidded.

"Yeah, something like that." Hagen tossed off the lines and climbed up to the wheel station and started the engine.

Michael was surprised they were leaving the dock. "If I'd known you were playing on going fishing, I'd have brought my gear."

Hagen smiled. "It's good to see you, buddy."

Michael hoisted his can toward his friend. Hagen guided the boat out of the bay. Once past the buoy, he opened the engine up. The boat sped across the calm water, like silk on glass.

Hagen looked at Michael. "She'll do 35 knots, easy. I've got a new engine in her." He cut back on the motor and they cruised for a while. They were a good two miles out when Hagen cut the engine. He climbed down and took a seat across from Michael.

Michael knew his friend was up to something. "Guess you wanted a private meeting."

Hagen took a pull on his beer and looked at Michael. "How's life been treating you?"

Michael wasn't sure how to answer the question. He gave Hagen a quizzical look and chuckled, "Fine…I guess."

Hagen waved him off. He leaned close and whispered in a conspiratorial fashion. "Mine's shit…but that's okay." He took another drink off his beer then wiped his mouth with the back of his hand. "You heard it first, partner. Allied is filing for chapter eleven."

"*What?*"

Hagen gave a nod of his head. "Convair beat us with their Atlas missile. NASA's using it for the Mercury program."

Michael gave Hagen a questioning look. "What about the planes?"

Hagen laughed. "Gone. I closed that division down when the Feds were crawling up my ass with their investigation. Put everything into R and D on the missile program. I bet the house on our rocket, but we were a good ten months behind schedule from the get-go. Allied has been bleeding red for the last four years."

"So that's it?" Michael asked, still not believing his friend's news.

Hagen downed the remainder of his beer and tossed the empty in a sack sitting on the deck. "That's all she wrote. I sold off the company park a year ago. Somebody told me they turned it into a trailer park." He held up his hands in mock surrender. "I admit, I lost on bundle at the tables and on the ponies. What the fuck was I supposed to do traveling on that damn train between Vegas, Reno, and bumfuck Arizona?" He held up a finger to make a point. "I *did* win the radio station, though. That's been a producer."

Michael nodded his head in agreement. "We've been lucky with XL, but even if the Harris committee didn't nail us, the labels will eventually wise up and refuse to pay."

Hagen ducked into the cab, grabbed a beer, and opened it. He sat back down in the chair. "What if we didn't have to worry about money anymore?"

Michael sat up and looked at Hagen. "What are you talking about?"

"When was the last time you made a movie? Five years ago," Hagen answered before Michael could. "You sold your place in Laughlin Park and have been living at your grandfather's ranch."

"I didn't need a big house."

Hagen waved Michael off. "Let me ask you, if you had to come up with a hundred grand today, cash, could you?"

Michael hesitated, then finally admitted, "Laying my hands on that kind of dough would be difficult. I got killed financing my last two films."

Hagen sat back. "There was a time when we had that and more, just by opening the safe at the club." He gestured to the boat. "This is home now, buddy. After the lawyers file, I'm broke. I know you've been depending on the station skim to pay the bills."

Michael arched an eyebrow. "I've got a couple irons in the fire."

Hagen shot Michael a look of disbelief. "Really?"

Michael shrugged his shoulders. "Well, one...possibly."

"What if you didn't have to worry about going around with your hat in your hand to some studio shmuck?" Hagen's eyes glistened with anticipation.

Michael set his beer down. "What are you talking about, Jimmy?"

Hagen reached over and patted Michael on the shoulder. "I'm going back into business, Michael. It'd be nice if you joined me."

Michael tugged on his ear. "I kinda figured it was something like that. When are your lawyers filing?"

Hagen turned away and looked out over the ocean, frowning in thought. "Four weeks...maybe five. Apparently, there's an inventory of assets and some other paperwork that needs to be completed." He turned back and fixed his eyes on Michael. "There's a place at the table for you if you want it."

Michael smiled. "Thank you. Have you thought this out, Jimmy? We're not spring chickens anymore. The last time we did this type of thing, we were in our twenties, and there were a lot fewer players in the game."

Hagen took a pull on his beer and smiled. "Fuck it. I don't want to die poor. I'm planning on bringing up a load of heroin from Mexico."

"The Rodriguez brothers?" Michael asked, referring to the family he and Hagen had done business with years ago. "Manny is a hothead. Miguel is somebody you can work with."

Hagen shook his head. "No. The deal is with Emilio Hernandez."

Michael shot Hagen a look of surprise. "El Indio?"

"You know him?"

"I know Hernandez is not friends with the Rodriguez brothers. I also know that he has a direct line to Mexico City and the heroin market."

Hagen looked surprised.

Michael shrugged his shoulders. "Research for a possible script."

Hagen arched an eyebrow.

"What about distribution?" Michael asked.

Hagen laughed. "So, you're interested?"

Michael kept a poker face.

Hagen held up his hands, palms forward. "Don't worry about the distribution. I've got that set up with Patty Bono."

Frank Bompensiero was the defacto boss in San Diego. Pat Bono was a soldier and top earner in his crew.

"What's our part then?"

"Three vehicles, twenty keys each. It lowers the chance of the entire shipment being confiscated. Hernandez's men will drive the product across the border. We keep one vehicle. The other two we ship to Chicago. We need to find a warehouse to store the vehicles and work out of. We also need a shell company to ship the vehicles under. You're good at setting up that sort of thing. We split one point three mil for our work."

"What if I decline?" Michael asked.

Hagen shrugged his shoulders. "You decline. I've got a shyster I can bring in to set up the shell company, but I don't trust those guys." Hagen made a gesture with his thumb from his chin. "Those bastards would sell their mother to the Arabs before going to jail. You, I know. And you don't talk."

Michael didn't say a word.

Jimmy took a pull from his beer and chuckled. "You can't change a tiger's stripes, Mike. We're both criminals at heart. We love the game."

"It's leopard's spots. You can't change a leopard's spots," Michael replied.

Hagen laughed and shook his head. "Leopard's spots...who makes up that stuff?"

Michael stood up and stared out at the ocean. A seagull swooped down from the sky. His head plunged under the water. A second later the bird was airborne with a fish trapped between its bill. Michael turned and looked at Hagen.

"I need to think about this."

"Fine. I've got to wait until the bankruptcy filing. Let the dust settle, so to speak. Is three months enough?"

Michael nodded his head.

"Good."

Hagen climbed up to the wheel and started the engine. Neither man spoke on the way back to the marina. They docked the boat, and Michael bid James Hagen goodbye.

Traffic was light driving back to Los Angeles. Michael pulled up to the adobe and sat for a moment. He had repaired the corral and barn since moving back. Neither had horses, but the place looked better after the face-lift.

Michael walked into the house. He took a Swanson's TV dinner from the refrigerator and slipped it into the oven. Forty-five minutes later, he was seated at the long table in the dining room eating turkey, mashed potatoes, and corn out of an aluminum tray. He opened a bottle of beer and took a sip. Michael thought about Hagen's offer.

Jack Warner had never kept his word. Michael's first film made money for the studio, but Warner had allowed Michael's contract to run out. Michael put his own money into his next two films. Both failed to make money due to lack of distribution. Michael had been reduced to hustling pitches and writing gigs. He had been in the business since Jolson sang, but nobody gave a damn. Jolson was dead, and the young Turks weren't interested. Michael knew he didn't have much going on. A look at his bank account confirmed that fact.

The deal Hagen proposed was risky. It was an all or nothing proposition. Michael preferred life on that level. There was only one thing that kept him from calling Hagen and signing on that evening.

# 23

# *Fire*

Carmen and Angela made dinner for the children. Ezekiel was not at home. He had taken to coming and going and spent most days watching the crews build the new stadium. The foreman ran Ezekiel off the site. He just moved to another hillside and watched as the neighborhood he had known all his life vanished. Sometimes he would stay out all night and drink.

Carmen was alarmed at first. She and Angela went to the police. LAPD took the information and filed it. Ezekiel eventually showed up. Carmen got mad and demanded to know where he had been. This angered Ezekiel. The beatings started. Carmen stopped asking. A friend told her of seeing Ezekiel sitting on the hillside at night drinking and cursing at the empty construction site below.

Carmen knew Ezekiel needed to see a doctor. Psychiatrists were expensive. Money was tight. Laissez-faire was the rule of the house. Carmen didn't question Ezekiel. He came and went as he pleased. After a while, Ezekiel became a ghost. When he was there, the women left him alone. When he wasn't, a calm filled to the apartment.

Dinner was a quiet affair. Johnny and the girls knew their mothers worked hard and tried not to bother them with the typical issues children usually did. They ate their dinner, cleaned the table, and washed the dishes. Carmen and Angela would sit out on the small porch and smoke cigarettes while watching the sunset. Sometimes, they would take the children down to the lake and would get a shaved ice for dessert.

It was a quiet home. It was a house without a man. After dinner that night, Angela checked the children's homework. When she was finished, Angela went outside to sit with Carmen. The children watched TV on the small black & white portable Angela had purchased at a garage sale.

Angela held out a beer to Carmen, who waved her off.

"No thanks. I'm putting on weight."

Angela laughed. "You look fine." She sat down on the porch and popped the cap off the bottle. She placed the opener next to the railing and tipped the bottle towards Carmen.

"What are we doin', Angie?"

Angela gave Carmen a quizzical look. "What'd you mean?"

"We go to work, come home, fix dinner. Maybe have an hour or two before we have to go to bed, and then we do it all over again."

"That's life."

Carmen sat up. "That's not Ezekiel's life. That's not a man's life. They come, they go, and if a woman says anything, she gets the back of the man's hand. It isn't fair."

Angela took Carmen's hand. "Life has never been fair for women. We bear the children and care for them and have to care for the men as well." She shrugged her shoulders. "It is not fair, but if we didn't do the work, it wouldn't get done."

Carmen nodded her head. "In my next life, I want a pair of balls," she laughed.

Angela made a face. "Not me. Men are lame. They're responsible for the shitty way things are. No, I wouldn't want to be a man."

Carmen leaned back. "Yeah, you're right. Men are dogs. They're only interested in two things: coochie and beer."

The two women laughed. "Well, neither coochies in this house are getting any attention," said Angela.

"It isn't fair," groaned Carmen.

The two women laughed again. Carmen and Angela continued talking. Letty got up and sat near the open front door and listened. She thought her aunt and mother were the bravest women she knew and enjoyed listening to their conversation. They spoke of rights for women and music and movies. Leticia loved to listen and learn about the secrets of life from her mother and aunt.

* * *

Ezekiel sat on the hillside drinking a two-dollar bottle of rye. The stadium construction site was below. His old neighborhood had vanished. The soft rolling hillsides had been flattened. A near finished stadium stood in its place. It made no sense to Ezekiel why so many lives had been destroyed. His own life no longer made sense to him. He was no longer in control. He walked with a limp. He had severe headaches. The liquor helped numb the pain. Carmen and Angela only reminded Ezekiel of his failures, so he stayed away and drank. He was angry and felt he no longer had any place or purpose.

A stray dog trotted past the construction site. He was a husky looking mutt who could take care of himself. The dog stopped. He raised a leg and peed on a stack of lumber and insulation material and then trotted off, disappearing into the night. Ezekiel grinned, got up, and walked over to the construction site. He unzipped his pants and urinated on the lumber as well. Finished, he zipped up.

"Hey!" shouted a man's voice.

Ezekiel turned. A security guard raced toward him.

"What the hell are you doing? You ain't supposed to be here!" the guard shouted.

Ezekiel panicked and dropped the bottle of rye. It shattered, and the alcohol splattered across the lumber and insulation material.

The guard was middle-aged and thirty pounds over-weight, but he came on strong. "Don't move, buddy."

Frightened, Ezekiel swung and caught the guard hard on the side of his head. The man went down and didn't move.

"Hey."

Ezekiel bent down and checked the man's pulse. The guard was alive, merely knocked cold.

"Not moving so fast now, aye gringo."

Ezekiel grabbed the pack of Luckys in the guard's shirt pocket. He patted his pockets and fished out a pack of matches. Ezekiel lit a smoke and tossed the match. Suddenly, the lumber and a stack of insulation material caught fire. Ezekiel jumped back. He removed his jacket and tried to beat out the flames. The fire spread. Ezekiel saw it was pointless. Embers had set another stack of lumber on fire. The flames rose. The heat became intense.

Ezekiel grabbed the unconscious guard and dragged him away from the fire. Sirens could be heard in the distance. Ezekiel's eyes darted to the fire and then down to the unconscious guard. The man was safe. Ezekiel hurried away as quickly as he could.

24

# *The Interrogation*

The cops came to Cardenas Market the next morning. The guard had survived. He described Ezekiel. It didn't take the police long to figure out who had been responsible for the fire. The cops cuffed Carmen, took her downtown, and grilled her. Business as usual for Mexicans in the City of Angels.

Detective Frank Worton was a short man with a thick moustache. He stood to the side of the table in the interview room. He was dressed in a brown suit and smoked Luckys. His partner, Phil Howser, was taller, clean shaven, and wore a blue suit and stood directly in front of Carmen, who was cuffed to the table.

"How about you make it easy for everybody and just tell us where your husband is?" suggested Howser.

Carmen looked at the two detectives. "I don't know where Ezekiel is. I already told that to the policemen who brought me down here."

Worton leaned close and eyeballed Carmen up and down, making sure he lingered on her breasts. "You mean to tell me that with a hot tamale like you waiting at home, your husband stays out all night? What is he, some kinda fag? Is that it, your husband's a fudge packer?" The detective rocked back on his heels and gave the woman a wolfish smile. "Maybe you need a real man, sweetheart."

Howser frowned. "Cut the crap," he admonished his partner.

Carmen looked up with pleading eyes at the slender detective. "What has Ezekiel done?"

140

Warton took a drag off his cigarette. He flicked the butt on the floor and ground it out with the toe of his Florsheim wingtips. Howser glanced at his partner and then looked at Carmen.

"Your husband attacked a security guard at the stadium construction site. Then he set fire to the place."

Carmen gasped. "EZ would never do that. There must be some mistake."

"No mistake, sweetheart. Your man sucker punched the guard and started the fire. The guard gave us a very good description. Looks like Ezekiel had been warned off the site a number of times before," said Warton.

Tears filled Carmen's eyes. "EZ has never been the same after he was beaten by the police. He needs medical help."

Warton glanced at the file and then looked at Carmen. "You're going to try and blame Ezekiel's criminal behavior on the fact he was arrested while taking part in a riot? Good luck, sister."

"When was the last time you saw your husband?" asked Howser.

Carmen had to think. "Four...no five days ago."

Warton gave the woman a surprised look. "Your husband goes missing for nearly a week and you don't file a missing person's report? Either you're screwing around, or he's a homo. Which is it?"

Carmen wiped her tears and looked at the short detective with hateful eyes. "We filed a report before. The police did nothing."

The two detectives looked at each other.

"You know withholding evidence is a felony. That's aiding and abetting. The dykes at Sybil Brand are gonna love you, sweetheart," Warton said.

Howser gave his partner a look. They both stepped out of the interview room and left Carmen sitting there for half an hour. Howser returned alone and unlocked the cuffs.

"I'm going to give you a break. I believe you haven't seen your husband."

Carmen rubbed her wrists and remained silent.

"If he shows up, calls, or even sends you a postcard, we want to know."

Carmen nodded her head.

"You're free to go."

Carmen got up and exited the interview room. She wanted to go home and wash off the stink of the interview room. Carmen knew, though, that no matter how hard she scrubbed she would never get rid of the foul feeling of being at the mercy of two men who wanted Ezekiel.

# 25

# *The Decision*

Ezekiel was asleep in an alley. A passing mutt woke him up when he licked the face of the slumbering man. Ezekiel smiled, patted the dog, and sat up. The canine looked at the man and then turned and made his way over to an overturned garbage can and began rooting for food.

Ezekiel considered his state. His clothes were dirty, and he couldn't remember how he got there. He did remember a man charging him and then a fire. Everything was a blur. He stood up and brushed himself off. He checked his pockets and found them empty.

It was a long walk to the apartment. Ezekiel thought about stopping at Cardenas Market but then decided against it. He knew it would only start an argument with Carmen.

Ezekiel pulled his battered Fedora down and started up the street. It was early, and many of the shops hadn't opened yet. Ezekiel tried to remember what shift Carmen had that day, but he couldn't. He couldn't remember how long he had been gone from the home. A shopkeeper was just opening his store and extending the awning over the shop window as Ezekiel passed. He smiled and gave a nod.

An alley ran down the back of the apartments. Ezekiel didn't want to face Carmen if she was home, so he took the alley. He would slip in through the back door and grab something to eat, a clean shirt and head right out. Two young boys who looked no older than ten rode their bikes down the alley. One of the boys stopped. Ezekiel recognized the boy from the neighborhood, but he couldn't remember his name.

"Hey man, the cops are looking for you," said the boy.

"What for?" asked Ezekiel.

The boy shrugged his shoulders and pedaled after his friend, who had continued down the alley.

Ezekiel cautiously made his way down the alley to the back of his unit and tried the door. Carmen had forgotten to lock it. Ezekiel silently slipped in the apartment and closed the door behind him.

No one was home. Ezekiel walked over to the window, careful not to make any noise, and peered out the corner of the shade. A patrol car was parked across the street.

"Shit," Ezekiel whispered to himself. He tried to remember what had happened the previous night. All he could recall was a man racing toward him and then some kind of fire. He didn't know how the fire had started. It was just there. Ezekiel was glad that Carmen and the children were not home. He let the shade go and stepped back.

Ezekiel went into the bathroom and took off his clothes. He quickly washed up and put on a clean t-shirt, flannel shirt, khakis, and shoes. He grabbed the jacket hanging on the rack by the back door and slipped it on. Ezekiel then went into the kitchen and checked the cupboard next to the stove and removed a tin coffee can. He opened the lid and took out a wad of cash and some change from the tin. Ezekiel took half of the bills and stuffed them into his pants pocket and replaced the can in the cupboard. He grabbed two oranges from a bowl on the table and a package of flour tortillas from the cupboard and stuffed the items into his jacket pocket. Ezekiel slipped on his Fedora, silently opened the door and retraced his steps through the alley.

There was a bus stop just up one block. Nobody recognized him while Ezekiel stood at the stop. Five minutes later, a bus pulled up. Ezekiel didn't care which direction the bus was going, just as long as it got him away from Echo Park. He dropped some coins in the box and took a seat. The bus pulled away and headed east.

This alarmed Ezekiel. He didn't want to ask the driver or anyone about the route, so as not to draw attention. He hoped the bus would not end up downtown. Ezekiel smiled when he saw the bus go north and then turn east toward Glendale. Glendale was a quiet community. There were a lot fewer cops in Glendale than downtown. He sat back and enjoyed the ride. If the law was after him, Ezekiel decided he had no intentions of returning home. He would call Carmen later after he found a safe haven.

\* \* \*

Michael took the first flight out that morning for San Francisco. He rented a car at the airport and drove down to Mountain View. The city had begun as a stagecoach station between San Francisco and San Jose shortly after gold was discovered in California. Now it was home for employees in the aero-space industry and Christian book publishing. It was clean, small, and a decidedly conservative community compared to San Francisco, which lay thirty-nine miles to the north.

The house was a Craftsman and located on Loreto St. Michael parked a few houses up and on the opposite side of the street so he had a good view of the home. He checked his watch, seeing it was seven-thirty. A minute later, a late model Thunderbird pulled up to the curb and honked its horn. The driver was a well-dressed teenager. The front door opened and Nicholas raced out. He was dressed in tan slacks and a navy-blue blazer and carried a load of books. He jumped into the T-bird. and the car sped away.

"Sonofabitch," Michael said quietly to himself. He had barely gotten a glimpse of his son. He closed his eyes and tried to keep a mental picture of the teenager he had just witnessed running across the front yard. Michael wondered who that young man was. Did anyone teach Nicholas to play ball or shoot a gun? Both were skills Michael excelled at. He had been a star football star at USC, and only his grandfather matched Michael for being as swift and deadly when handling a firearm.

Michael removed a flask from his coat pocket. He took a short swig and returned the flask to its former place. A few minutes later, Laurel emerged from the house. She opened the garage door and then pulled out the Winter Green MG.

Michael sat up and watched as Laurel got out of the car and closed the garage door.

"What the hell?" Michael said to himself, bewildered at Laurel's choice of vehicle. "Damn Brit cars aren't worth a tinker's fart."

Laurel got into the sports car. Even though it was cool, the roof was down. She tied a scarf around her head, checked herself in the mirror, and then pulled out of the drive and headed down the street in Michael's direction. He ducked down as the car passed, then quickly sat up. He used the rearview mirror to watch as the green sports car disappeared when it turned right on the next block.

It was apparent that both Laurel and Nicholas had moved on. It had been nearly a decade since Michael had been a part of their life. He sat for a moment before starting the engine. Michael drove to the airport and took the next flight back to Los Angeles.

It was still light out when the plane landed at LAX. Michael got his car and drove out to the Oso Negro. He pulled up the long drive and parked. Michael walked down to the family cemetery where his grandmother, aunt, and grand uncle were buried. There used to be a creek that ran through the property, but that had dried up when the Army Engineer Corps cemented up the Los Angeles River. Later, the city declared that family cemeteries were illegal. The bodies had to be dug up and transferred to a local cemetery. That was price of progress the Osos Negro had to pay. The bodies were gone, but the headstones remained.

Michael kicked the dirt with the toe of his shoe. He looked out across the open field that stretched behind the adobe. He could almost see the cowboys bringing the calves up from the field for branding. A jet flew overhead, its turbines roaring like thunder. The moment was broken. Michael turned and walked back to the adobe. He went inside and placed a call to Hagen.

"Hello?"

"I'm in," Michael said.

# 26

# *The Reporter*

Los Angeles Tribune Headline – Morning Edition – March 12, 1962

## Stadium arsonist remains at large

### Howard Silver

Police have identified Ezekiel Camacho as the arsonist who set fire to the construction site at the new stadium. The incident included an attack upon the site's security guard, Melvin Cabot. According to residents of the area, Camacho hung out regularly at the site and had been run off by previously by workers. "We're lucky," said Philip Lipmann, one of the stadium's engineers. "It could have been much worse. We're still on schedule. Mayor Poulson remarked, "It is a sad day when pachuco gang members attempt to destroy our new stadium that is meant for all Los Angeles residents."

Howard Silver was seated at his desk smoking a cigarette and regaling a fresh-faced copyboy with a tale about the old days. Silver had worked for Tribune for over thirty years. He was a man who had comfortably slipped into middle-age, enjoyed what he did, and took joy in telling a good story. Harry Chapman walked up. Seeing the "Old Man," as Chapman was referred to by the staff, the copyboy vanished like a fart in a hurricane. The newspaper owner pushed his spectacles back on his nose and looked at Silver.

"I want a follow-up on the arsonist," barked Chapman.

Silver gave a questioning look. "I checked with LAPD. They still don't have the man."

"Find out who this Camacho is. Who are his friends? Where does he work? The way to root out a fugitive is to put the heat on. I want the heat on Camacho."

"Yes, sir," said Silver.

"Well, why are you sitting there?"

Howard Sliver grabbed his coat and hat and made a hasty exit.

Los Angeles Tribune Headline – Morning Edition – April 16, 1962

## Arsonist continues to elude police

### Howard Silver

Ezekiel Camacho, the man police have accused of attacking a security guard and setting fire to Dodger Stadium, remains at large. Camacho was arrested along with two dozen Mexicans when they started a riot at Pershing Square. He has been unemployed since. Camacho's wife, Carmen, is the sole support of the family. Camacho's great-grandfather was Falcon, an Indian who worked for Sean McGuire, the grandfather of movie producer, Michael McGuire. Both McGuires have had run-ins of with the authorities. Michael was once linked to the gang responsible for the Point Magu Massacre, which claimed the lives of two policemen. He was also considered an uncooperative witness by HUAC. Ezekiel Camacho was the beneficiary of the McGuire family largess. A family whose wealth and power were built upon blood, booze, and B movies. It is no wonder the hot-blooded Mexican took the law into his own hands in an attempt to destroy the stadium. No stone should be left unturned in apprehending this criminal and bringing him to justice.

# 27

# *A Plan*

The Tribune kept up the heat on Ezekiel Camacho the next few days. Nothing. They did a follow-up on Michael McGuire that just straddled libel. Still nothing. Ezekiel Camacho had disappeared.

Michael ignored the article. He knew the game being played. He arranged a meeting with Angela and Carmen. They hadn't heard from Ezekiel in weeks. Michael realized it was old grudges that were driving the press. The Tribune was pro baseball, pro-Dodgers, and pro-stadium all the way.

The paper also had carried on a long feud with the McGuire family going back to the 1880s when the first land boom hit the city. Sean partnered with Lee Sing, the owner of the Golden Dragon Restaurant. He had stood against the 1882 *Exclusion Act*, which barred most Chinese from entering the U.S., owning property, bringing a wife to the U.S., and just about every other civil right that every white man took for granted. Sean McGuire had hired Blacks, Indians, and Mexicans to work on his ranch. The oligarchy didn't truck with such ideas. The McGuires might have had money, but they had always been outsiders to Los Angeles society.

The Tribune wanted access to the actors in Michael's films. When he was successful, the paper laid-off the yellow journalism and gave Michael's movies decent reviews. Michael hadn't made a successful film in years. The gloves came off, and the paper played hardball.

Michael knew the dust would settle soon. If Ezekiel was caught, the paper would focus on him. If he eluded the authorities, the newspaper would find something else to write about. The public didn't have a long memory.

Hagen wasn't pleased. He suggested taking out Silver. Michael nixed the plan. He pointed out that killing a reporter would only serve to bring more attention to an ancient incident and them.

Michael and Hagen had found a warehouse in Long Beach that served their purposes. It was in an older section of town and wasn't known for its high police presence. Michael used an old movie script as the basis to create a production company. He set up an escrow account in a bank in the Dominican Republic. The money would start there and then go through a series of transfers and eventually end up in a pair of numbered Swiss accounts. Hagen couldn't understand why the money had to remain in Switzerland. Michael explained that since they were both essentially broke, it would send a red flag to the IRS if either of them suddenly had a fat American bank account. Hagen grumbled but agreed.

"We're doing this one time?" Michael asked.

He and Hagen were seated at a table in the bar at Anthony's Star of the Sea on the Embarcadero. The question had not been discussed up until that point.

Hagen shook his head. "This could be a regular thing if we do it right."

Michael was silent for a moment. "We don't want to end up spending our retirement in prison."

"All I'm saying is, keep an open mind."

The waitress soon brought over their drinks. She was twenty-something and had the face of an angel and a body you could bounce a quarter off of. Hagen smiled big and handed the women his Diner's

Club Card. Michael grabbed the card away from the waitress and handed her a crisp Benjamin.

"Run a tab, please. My friend's not paying tonight."

"Of course." The waitress set the drinks down and headed off to another table.

Michael picked up his glass and tipped it toward Hagen. "It's a cash world from here on out, my friend. No more credit cards, no more personal checks."

Hagen leaned back in his chair. "We tried straight for a while. It was a good run while it lasted."

Michael chuckled. "Neither of us have ever played it straight, Jimmy...ever."

Hagen laughed, picked up his glass, and tipped it toward Michael. "To outlaw ways."

Michael lifted his glass, and the two men toasted.

They kept a low profile. The lawyers hadn't yet declared Chapter Eleven for Allied Aircraft. Michael and Hagen knew there was the possibility that one or both of them were being tailed by the Feds. That only made it more exciting. It was like the old days during prohibition. The two men only spoke on pay phones or face to face. They met at large public places.

So far, the set-up only included them. Michael cautioned against hiring outside help on the first run. Hagen agreed. It was risker for them to deliver the vehicles themselves, but the chances of somebody messing up dropped dramatically. Both men knew that the greater the number of people involved in a criminal enterprise, the probability of something going wrong rose proportionately.

Sixty keys was heavy weight. It was enough to supply much of Southern California. Michael, always cautious, proposed that Jimmy wait before doing a second run. He wanted to make sure the Feds weren't watching. Hagen agreed but admitted that he wasn't sure if Emilio Hernandez would be as sensitive to their concerns. They agreed to present a unified front to Hernandez when they met him in Mazatlán.

Michael wanted to let Cosmo know that the station would most likely be shutting down. Hagen didn't care.

"Just make sure Turner doesn't say anything to the rest of the staff," said Hagen.

"Cosmo knows the score. I was the one to bring him on board, so we owe him a heads-up on closing up shop."

"You're a softy," Hagen laughed.

Cosmo was surprised when Michael called and asked him to meet for lunch at El Indio. Much like Michael's relationship with Hagen, he and Cosmo had kept theirs compartmentalized. Michael handled large matters at XELA and was rarely seen at the station. Cosmo took care of the day-to-day business. Both men were in on the skim from the labels. They had to compartmentalize, if the operation was to continue successfully.

Michael was standing near a table outside when Cosmo arrived. Michael liked the piano man. He found him interesting. Cosmo could be articulate, one minute expounding on the complexity of an Ellington performance and then instantly slip into a street arrogate that would baffle most white folks. Cosmo always dressed with style. That day, he was wearing a purple silk shirt with cream-colored pleated slacks and a black silk sports coat with two-tone wingtips.

"Whatdya' say, my good man?" Cosmo shook Michael's hand.

"Thanks for coming."

Cosmo eyed the restaurant and looked at Michael. "You down with the Mexican brothers food?" He smiled approvingly. "Who would've guessed a Beverly Hills cat like yourself?"

Michael frowned. "Please. The only people that live in Beverly Hills are Jews and homos."

Cosmo chuckled. "You sure aren't a pecker puffer or one of the chosen."

The two men went inside and ordered, then came back out to eat.

Michael took a bite of his taco and smiled blissfully.

"The Irish sure don't know what they're missing."

Cosmo gave him a look. "You the first Irish I know that's down with Mexican soul food."

"I was raised on biscuits, beans, and coffee," Michael replied.

"You ever been down south?" Cosmo took a bite of his taco.

"Texas, once. Once was enough. You?"

"No. Chicago was bad enough for a black man."

Cosmo wiped his mouth with a napkin and looked at Michael. "You didn't ask me here to discuss geography."

"No. You're right." Michael agreed.

*  *  *

The Los Angeles River started high in the Santa Susana Mountains and flowed down into Los Angeles County. The river stretched from Canoga Park at the west-end of the San Fernando Valley and ran just over fifty–one-miles to its mouth in Long Beach. Several tributaries once joined the free-flowing river. This frequently caused flooding and the destruction of bridges, rail tracks, and homes.

Before Mulholland's aqueduct, the river was the primary source of fresh water for Los Angeles. The Army Corps of Engineers attempted to tame the water. They walled up the river in a concrete channel. Most summers, it was no more than a few feet wide. Rainy winters could send water crashing through the channel like a raging monster carrying trees, cars, and anything else that came in its way.

Ezekiel had been living in the riverbed for the past few weeks. The tunnels provided a good hiding place, but he knew he couldn't stay there forever. He had called Carmen, but she hung up the phone as soon as Ezekiel said, "It's me." He read the newspapers and knew the police were looking for him. Ezekiel knew he needed a plan. He was a gimp on the run from the law.

The morning was warm. Ezekiel took off his clothes and washed them in the river. He placed his pants, shirt, and socks on the concrete to dry. He laid down next to them and closed his eyes.

*Ezekiel stood in an open area surround by hills and mountains. A beautiful brown stallion raced up him. It reared up and kicked its front hoofs in the air and then came over and nuzzled its head into Ezekiel's arm. A large bird appeared over-head, its wings outstretched, coasting on the gentle wind that blew across the hills. The bird landed on a large tree and suddenly changed into an Indian warrior.*

*"You can no longer remain," said the Indian sitting on the tree limb.*

*"What shall I do?" Ezekiel asked.*

*"The horse will guide you," the Indian replied.*

*"I cannot ride this horse."*

*The Indian smiled. "It is of no matter. The horse will guide you."*

*"What is your name?" asked Ezekiel*

*"Call me, Falcon."*

*The horse whinnied. Ezekiel glanced away. When he looked back, he saw the bird fly from its perch on the tree and soar high into the sky. He watched until it appeared to fly right into the sun. The rays blotted out the image of the bird, and it vanished. Ezekiel rubbed his eyes. The stallion had walked away and was standing some thirty feet up the road.*

*"Wait!" Ezekiel called out.*

*The horse snorted and stood there.*

*Ezekiel took a few steps toward the horse. The stallion trotted away.*

*"No, wait!" shouted Ezekiel.*

*The horse reared up and raced toward him. Ezekiel grabbed the animal's mane and pulled himself up. The horse took off at a gallop. Suddenly, they were airborne. Ezekiel looked down. He could see the river. The horse and rider sailed over the Sixth Street Bridge. A half dozen LAPD squad cars were parked on the bridge. A cop aimed his shotgun skyward toward Ezekiel and the stallion and fired. Ezekiel fell from the horse. It was all in slow motion as he fell toward the squad of police. He turned his head and saw the stallion gallop away in the sky. The cops and the bridge were coming up fast.*

Ezekiel suddenly sat up. He was breathing hard. He quickly gathered his clothes, put them on, and exited the riverbed. Ezekiel stood at the entrance to the 101. He was there only a few minutes when a truck pulling a trailer full of horses stopped.

"Climb in," said the driver.

Ezekiel quickly jumped in on the passenger side, and the truck rumbled onto the freeway. The driver looked to be in his fifties. He had a well-worn cowboy hat on his head and a thick gray moustache.

"Where you headed, friend?" asked the driver.

"Wherever you're going," Ezekiel replied.

The driver chuckled. He took a stick of tobacco from his red and white checkered shirt and offered it to Ezekiel, who declined. The driver bit off a chew and stuffed the remainder in his shirt pocket. He held out his hand.

"Al Moore. You can call me, Al."

Ezekiel shook the driver's hand. "Tom Trujillo."

"Glad to meet you, Tom."

"Where are you taking those horses?"

"We're going to Spahn Ranch. They're shooting a western up there, and they need some trick horses." Moore glanced over at EZ. "You any good with animals?"

"Yeah, sure." Ezekiel lied.

"Good, you can give me a hand with the horses."

Ezekiel smiled to himself and looked out the window as they left the city behind and headed into the mountains.

# 28

# *Ace of Hearts*

The *Ace of Hearts Gas & Casino* sat off of Boulder Highway three miles outside of Henderson, Nevada. The Ace, as it was more commonly known, pumped gas and had a roulette wheel, craps, three blackjack tables, and one for poker. Slots lined the perimeter of the room. The bar sat on the far side of the room. The entire club covered just under two thousand square feet.

What made the Ace unique besides its gas, gamble, and drink ambience was that it was owned by Della Rio. Della was a looker with a copper complexion and dark hair she wore short. She looked a dozen years younger than her current forty-four. More importantly, Della had a mind for business and took her business seriously.

Back before the war, the Ace had been a gas station and diner with a few slot machines and a card table. It was a stop-off for truckers. The Ace was on its last legs at the time.

Della saw potential in the place when she bought the Ace in '49, shortly after arriving in Nevada. Della kept the gas pumps and lost the kitchen. She knocked out a few walls to add more card tables. Since there was no gaming commission at the time, Della could do as she pleased with the property. She made sure the right palms were greased. Nevada was wide open territory when it came to gambling, liquor, and whores.

By the time the commission was created, the Ace had been operating for years. It was grandfathered in along with all the other truck stops that carried slot machines. The Ace did not serve food. It did not have dancers, a band, or a floor show. The Ace had gambling and booze. The place was clean, well-lit, and offered a straight game and decent liquor. Tourists sometimes stopped and got gas. They generally didn't play the tables at the Ace. They came to see big casinos, not some pitstop with table and slots. The Ace was primarily frequented by truckers and the locals who wanted a place to gamble away from the tourists.

The Ace was not a swank casino, but nobody pulled a fast one. Dealers dealt straight. The wheel spun straight. The dice rolled straight. The drinks weren't watered down or mickied-up. Della ran a tight operation. She kept a small staff who were paid above what they would make at many of the downtown casinos. When she needed additional help, Della hired through a temp agency. Anyone caught dealing from the bottom or skimming the house was dealt with by Victor Vega, Della's enforcer and right-hand man. Victor de la Vega was twenty-seven and viewed Della as family.

Victor was fifteen when he acted as a lookout for Lamont Daniels, a wannabe gangster. Lamont planned to roll Della after she left the club. As Della walked to her car, Lamont stepped out of the shadows and demanded her purse. Della didn't argue. She demurely handed her red leather purse to Lamont. As he rummaged through it, Della pulled a .22 strapped to her garter and shot Lamont in the leg. The robber dropped the purse and his gun and hit the ground screaming. Victor stood and stared, too scared to run. Della walked over and smacked the teenager in the face.

"Pick up my purse and bring me that gun," she ordered.

Lamont rolled on the ground and screamed in pain.

"Go on now," said Della, still holding the pistol.

Victor quickly complied with the lady's demands.

"That dumbass put you up to this?" Della motioned with the pistol toward Lamont.

Victor nodded his head and held out the purse and pistol.

Della took the pistol. It was an old .44 that looked like it hadn't been used in some time. She snapped it open and dumped the shells on the ground, then tossed the gun away. Della looked at the teenager standing in front of her holding the red purse. He was skinny, and his clothes were tread-bare and filthy.

"Your momma would be ashamed of you."

Victor lowered his head. "I don't have a moms."

"What about your daddy?"

"I don't got one," Victor admitted quietly.

Lamont continued to cry.

Della kicked the robber. "Shut-up or I'll shoot your other leg." She looked at Victor. "Who's been taking care of you?"

Victor remained silent. His eyes shifted toward the thief on the ground.

Della arched an eyebrow. "This muthafucker isn't fit to take care of a dog." She frowned and flicked the pistol toward a sleek black Ford. "Get in the car."

Victor stood transfixed by the woman holding the gun.

"Get in. I won't shoot you."

Victor started toward the car, then stopped. "You won't take me to the cops?"

Della was losing her patience. "Get in the damn car."

Victor complied.

Della looked down at Lamont. "You need to get yourself another line of work. This one sure don't suit you."

"I'm gonna fuck you up, bitch!" cried Lamont; his right pants leg was soaked in blood.

"Not tonight."

Della got in the Ford, started the engine, and drove away.

Two weeks later, Lamont's body was found thirty miles outside of Vegas in the desert. He was sunburnt and barefoot. There was no evidence of foul play. There were tire tracks near the body that stretched for miles back to the roadway. Someone had taken Lamont for a drive and let him out to walk back to town. Lamont didn't make it. Vegas PD had better things to do than investigate the suspicious demise of a Negro petty thief. They filed it as an accidental death due to exposure.

Della took Victor under her wing. She housed him and sent him to school. When he graduated, Victor worked the club. He was no longer the scrawny teenager. Victor Vega was six foot of sculpted Mexican muscle. Della taught Victor how to dress, understated fine silk Italian suits that cost hundreds of dollars. She taught him how to handle his business the same way: quiet, efficient, and effective.

"The weakest man in the room is the one who draws attention to himself. Just because a man talks loudly and wears a chinchilla jacket doesn't make him strong," Della counseled Victor.

Della taught Victor how to build a strong intelligence network. He had carhops, waitresses, busboys, and bellhops on his payroll. These were the little people nobody noticed. These were the people that kept the town running.

Victor was the final word on business on the casino floor. Anyone who wanted to speak to Della had to pass through Victor first. He was happy working for Della. She had given him a life. Della was as close to a mother that Victor had ever known. Della paid him ten percent of the club's take. Victor had a crew that did side jobs, mostly jewelry heists and high-end B&E jobs. He kept that work separate from Della. He wasn't sure she would approve.

Della intrigued Victor. Not in a sexual manner, though. He had too much respect for the lady to ever think of her in that way. He wanted to know who the woman was who had taken him off the streets and given him a home. Della did not talk about her past. All that anybody knew about her was that she arrived in Vegas a few years after the war and purchased the Ace. Della knew the town and showed respect. She had kicked the mob twenty-five percent right from the start. Nobody bothered Della.

"Seventy-five percent of everything is better than a hundred percent of nothing," Della explained to Victor. "Everybody has to pay. Doesn't matter if you're working in a factory, farm, or school; everybody has to pay. The only people who don't pay are bankers and lawyers. They make up the rules."

Victor pressed Della once about her past. It was after the employee Christmas party a few years back. Della was seated in her office. Victor was finishing off two fingers of Patron. He smiled and set the glass down on the desk.

"Hell of a party, boss."

Della looked up from her books. "Yes, it was."

Victor shook his head. "How did you get so good at what you do?"

"Practice," Della cracked.

"You must've been what, twenty-eight, twenty-nine when you bought the Ace. How'd you know this was the place to build a business?"

"I didn't," Della replied.

"What did you do before you bought the Ace?"

Della gave Victor a cool look. "Nothing. I was nothing before I came to Nevada. I bought a failing business and turned it around. End of story."

Victor knew well enough to leave the subject of Della's past alone.

The morning sun was just creeping over the horizon when Della got to the club that day. The place was better than half full. All the tables were operating, and dozens of patrons pumped quarters into the slots. Della went straight to her office, which sat behind the bar. The room was small but impeccably decorated.

The bartender brought Della a coffee and exited. Della sat down behind her desk and removed the copy of the *Las Vegas Review-Journal* from her briefcase and spread it out on top of the desk. She enjoyed this part of the morning the best. Victor wouldn't be in until noon. She could read her newspaper in peace before doing the bank from the previous night's earnings.

Della sipped her coffee and perused the paper. There was an article about Jackie and the White House makeover. There was one on the Mercury program and one on the state water bill. Della read the paper religiously. A small article in the business section caught her eye.

Las Vegas Herald – May 10th, 1962.

## *Allied Aircraft declares bankruptcy*

### Ross Pitman

Allied Aircraft of San Diego has declared bankruptcy. The once thriving enterprise had fallen on hard times after the war. The company bet heavily on their missile program only to lose out to Convair. James Hagen, the company's owner, was present at the court filing. Hagen stated, "We gave it a good run, but our missile program proved to be too little, too late." It is reported that the company was in such bad shape that Hagen has been reduced to living on his boat. "It is always sad to see a business like Allied go down," observed Fred Standish, CEO of Las Vegas Aero-dynamics.

Della picked up the phone and dialed Victor's number.

"Hello?"

"I need you to come in early."

"Sure thing, Della. Everything okay?"

"Yes. I'll tell you when you get here."

Della hung up the telephone. She picked up the newspaper and stared at Pitman's article. A smile crept across Della's full lips, and she chuckled to herself.

# 29

# The Way of the World

A dark cloud hung over the Echo Park apartment. Carmen reproached herself for having hung up on Ezekiel. No one had seen or heard from him in weeks. Carmen drank heavily in the evenings. She began to miss work. Angela did what she could to pick up the slack. Letty helped with the cooking and watched Lucy and Johnny after school. The cops had stopped cruising the supermarket and apartment. The stadium had opened and the Dodgers played their first game and lost to Cincinnati, 6 to 3 in front of 52,564 fans. The days rolled on until Carmen decided she could wait no longer and had to do something.

Angie awoke one morning to find Carmen gone with Ezekiel's truck. She left a brief note on the kitchen table.

*Gone to find EZ. Take care of the girls.*
*C.*

Angie had no idea where Carmen could have gone off to. She didn't have time to think about it, though. Carmen was gone, and the children needed to get to school. Angela barely had time to get them out the door and grab the bus to her job. During her break, Angela made some calls. No one had heard or talked to Carmen. She finished out the day and went home.

Carmen wasn't there. She didn't come home that night or the night after that or the night after that. Angela went to the police. They took a report.

Angela quickly realized that she was now the sole support and caretaker of three children. She took on additional work typing up manuscripts, thesis, speeches, whatever district administration would funnel her to do over and above her usual work. On the weekends, Angela made sure she spent Sunday with the children. They would go to the movies, or Griffith Park, or take the bus to the beach and walk along the Venice boardwalk. Angela liked the beach and enjoyed all the strange and different people she saw there. She knew Carmen would object to the girls being in such a place. She knew Ezekiel would think these people strange and mock them. They weren't there anymore. Angela was, and she was determined to expose her nieces and son to people and things outside of their Echo Park neighborhood.

They had gone to Chinatown that Sunday. Angela and the children took the bus down to Union Station. Johnny loved the trains. They visited the shops on Olvera Street, then walked over to Chinatown. They had lunch at a small café and then walked back to Union Station, where they got the bus back home. Angela was thinking about how wonderful the day had been when she saw two policemen standing next to a cruiser parked in front of the apartments.

"Are you Angela Camacho?" asked one of the officers. He was lean and had close-cut blond hair and looked to be in his thirties. The other officer was shorter by three or four inches and had a stocky build.

"Yes," Angela replied, growing worried.

"Would you please come with us?" said the blond officer.

She glanced between the two of them. "What is this about?"

"If you would please come with us, we will explain."

The children looked at Angela. She gave Letty the key to the apartment. "Go home and wait for me."

Letty took the key but lingered.

"I'll be okay. There're enchiladas and beans in the refrigerator. If I'm not back before dinner, heat that up. Be a good girl for auntie."

Letty nodded. She took Johnny and Lucy by the hand and walked to the apartment.

Angela looked at the two officers. "What is this about? If you won't tell me, I'm not getting in the car with you."

The two cops looked at each other. The shorter officer shrugged his shoulders.

"There's been an accident, ma'am. Please come with us," said the blond cop.

Angela saw something in the policeman's eyes that made her blood turn cold. She got in the patrol car with the two officers and drove away. Neither man said a word.

"Please tell me what this is about," pleaded Angela.

The short officer was riding shotgun. He turned and looked at Angela. "I'm sorry ma'am, we aren't at liberty to discuss the case. We were only asked to pick you up and bring you into the station."

"What case?" Angela asked. She was met with silence. Angela sat back in the seat for the remainder of the ride.

The cruiser pulled into Parker Center. The two officers escorted Angela to the homicide department and left. Detective Brett Tinsley walked over to Angela. Tinsley was forty, twice divorced, and had worked homicide for the last twelve years. He wore a dark blue suit and had a face that showed he had seen it all.

"Miss Camacho, I'm Detective Tinsley." He nodded toward the man standing behind him. "This is my partner, Detective Greg Miller."

Miller was in his late thirties, wore a brown suit, and was smoking a cigarette.

"What is this about, detective?" Angela asked.

"We believe your sister-in-law, Carmen Camacho, was murdered two nights ago."

The air went out of Angela's body like a balloon. Detective Miller helped her to a chair.

"What…how?" Angela stammered.

"Her body was found in the women's room at a rest stop near El Cajon. She had been strangled."

Tears poured down Angela's face. She fought them back and regained her composure. "What was Carmen doing in El Cajon?"

The two detectives looked at each other.

"We were hoping you might be able to provide that information, Miss Camacho," said Tinsley.

"Carmen took off a month ago to look for my brother."

"Where was your brother?" asked Miller.

Angela looked at the two detectives dumbfounded. "You guys wanted to arrest EZ for starting a fire at the stadium. He ran. Carmen went to look for him."

Miller scratched his head, grimacing. "The stadium fire? That was a while back."

"Yes. Some of your co-workers interrogated Carmen. They weren't very nice."

Tinsley flicked his butt on the floor, ground it out with his shoe, and raised his eyebrows. "I'm sorry, Miss Camacho, we weren't privy to that information. The El Cajon police contacted us. They are handling the primary investigation."

"How do they know it's Carmen?" Angela asked anxiously.

"Her wallet was found next to the body. It had her driver's license in it. The truck she had been driving was parked outside."

"Do they have any suspects?"

The two detectives were silent.

"Anything you might be able to tell us could be helpful," Detective Miller finally said.

Angela glared at the two detectives. "The police beat my brother. They damaged his brain. They accused him of trying to burn the stadium down. He ran away. Carmen went to look for him. You say that Carmen is dead. That is all I know." Angela stood up. "Excuse me, I have to get back to my nieces and tell them their mother was murdered." Neither detective stopped her as she walked out of the room.

*  *  *

The Spahn Ranch was fifty-five acres of rugged country with a western movie set. There was nothing around the place for miles. It was rumored that William S. Hart had once owned the property. Shortly after the war, Lee and Ruth Reynolds purchased the land from Dr. Atkins, who had owned it since the late twenties. Lee built a few western sets to augment the trading-post shop he and Ruth ran. George Spahn purchased the property from the Reynolds in 1953. He added more sets and brought in horses. The place became a popular location to go riding and shoot westerns. After the war, the little box challenged the big screen. TV consumed product at a voracious level. Westerns were cheap to shoot. The viewers ate them up. *Gunsmoke*, *Bonanza*, *Wagon Train*, *Maverick*, and dozens of others played weekly on the small screen. Westerns were king on TV.

Ezekiel had become Tom Trujillo. He took to the horses, and they took to him. The horses sensed he wasn't threatening and allowed the man great latitude when he handled them. Al Moore was impressed.

The shoot they had worked on was a low budget western and only lasted nine days. When the production wrapped, Al offered Trujillo a ride back to Los Angeles and the offer of a job working the stables he had in Malibu.

Ezekiel thanked him but turned him down. He had no intention of returning to Los Angeles. The police wanted him. His wife didn't. He had money from the shoot. The production had outfitted him with two pairs of dungarees and some shirts and a nice cowboy hat. The head of crafts even left a cooler of food. Ezekiel bid the crew goodbye and remained at the ranch.

A week later, another film crew arrived. Ezekiel was hired as an assistant wrangler. They shot an episode of *Bonanza*. Ezekiel recognized Dan Blocker and Michael Landon. Three days later, they were gone.

Ezekiel enjoyed the work. His job was to tend to the horses at the ranch. He fed them, brushed them down, and cleaned their stalls. When a horse was needed on the set, Ezekiel would get it from the stable and bring it to the actor.

He handed the reins of a black stallion to Michael Landon. Ezekiel was surprised by how short the actor was.

Ezekiel rarely got headaches anymore. His focus was on the horses. There were rarely more than a few days between one production and another at the ranch. If the company didn't use horses, they would still put Tom Trujillo on the payroll. Hollywood was a small town and word of mouth quickly spread about the crazy Mexican who lived somewhere around the Spahn Ranch. No one knew for sure where he lived. A film crew would show up at the ranch, and Tom Trujillo would appear.

James Garner sat in his chair under a tree reading the Los Angeles Tribune. He was dressed in his Maverick outfit, sans the hat. The A.D. walked over to the actor.

"It'll be just another few minutes, Mr. Garner."

Garner looked up from the newspaper and smiled. "I'm ready when you are."

The A.D. tipped his cap and hurried back to where the crew was setting up the shot in front of a barn. Garner returned to his newspaper.

Ezekiel watched the crew work. Garner looked up. "You're the wrangler that lives up here?"

Ezekiel nodded his head.

"Beautiful country must be nice."

"It is."

The A.D. hustled over to the actor. "We're ready, Mr. Garner."

Garner stood and picked up his hat, which was sitting on a table, and slipped it on. "Gotta go to work." He smiled at Ezekiel and walked over to where the director was standing.

Ezekiel looked down at the sports page that sat in the actor's chair. There was a large photo of a Dodger's player being called out at home with the headline: *Dodgers lose to the Cardinals.*

Ezekiel picked up the paper and opened it. Inside was another photo of the stadium with a headline: *50,000 Pack Dodger Stadium.* A cold sweat broke over his body. He dropped the newspaper and hurried away. Tom Trujillo was absent the rest of the day. He was absent when the crew left the following day. The headaches returned. Ezekiel didn't want to be around people when he had headaches. He had trouble speaking properly and would sometimes stutter.

Ezekiel had built a small cabin for himself from odds and ends he had found at the ranch. It was nothing more than two small rooms, but it had a wooden floor and kept him out of the elements. He had built a tub to hold water, which he would lug from the ranch in five-gallon bottles left by the craft trucks.

When the headaches came, Ezekiel retreated to his cabin and remained until they passed. They persisted. Ezekiel soaked his head in the tub. He drank tequila. Nothing helped. After three days, Ezekiel crept out of his cabin and walked east into the desert. The hot sun beat down on him. He had taken no water with him. Ezekiel continued to walk. The headache increased. It felt like a vice tightening on his skull. Ezekiel tramped on across rock and through the thick sand. He continued walking until the blazing heat knocked him to the ground, like a giant swatting a fly. He lay on the hot sand. He could go no further. He smiled and thought of the time when he was young and rode his bike down the long dirt road in front of the family home.

"You alive, pilgrim?" asked a man's voice.

Ezekiel felt cool water being splashed on his face, and he slowly pried open his eyes. A man dressed in some type of robe knelt next to him. He had long brown hair and a long beard and looked to be somewhere between the age of thirty and sixty. The man poured some more water on Ezekiel's face.

"Yes," Ezekiel whispered.

The long-haired man helped him up. He gave Ezekiel a canteen. "Easy."

Ezekiel took a sip. The water hurt his parched throat at first and then soothed it as it went down. He took another sip and handed the canteen back to the man. "Thank you."

"What the hell are you doing all the way out here?" asked the man.

"I have bad headaches," said Ezekiel.

The man nodded. He reached into a leather pouch strapped to the belt around the robe. The man removed some type of dried root and handed it to Ezekiel. "This is should take care of your head."

Ezekiel ate the roots. The man sat down next to Ezekiel.

"I'm Bernard."

"Tom Trujillo"

The two men shook hands.

"I come out here to meditate and collect shrooms."

Ezekiel gave the man a questioning look.

"Mushrooms...Peyote. That's what you just ate, brother."

Ezekiel's eye widened.

"How'd you feel?" asked Bernard.

Ezekiel shrugged his shoulders. "Okay. My headache isn't as bad as it was."

Bernard smiled. "Give it awhile."

Thirty minutes later, Ezekiel felt a warm buzz coursing through his body. Forty minutes later, Bernard's beard had turned a beautiful pink. An hour later, Ezekiel became a large bird and soared high over the desert.

"You from L.A.?" Bernard asked later that evening. The two men were seated around the fire pit in front of Ezekiel's cabin.

Ezekiel didn't answer.

Bernard looked at Ezekiel as if he was reading the man's mind. "Tom Trujillo isn't your name, is it?"

Ezekiel felt at peace. The trip was over. The painful headaches had vanished. He shook his head. "No, it's Ezekiel."

Bernard smiled. "Like the prophet. I found you in the desert. Karma put you there for a reason."

"I am the prophet of Spahn Ranch," Ezekiel laughed.

"Indeed, you are, brother. The god Ra told me to go out today and collect shrooms. I wasn't planning to, but when the gods call, you go. Me finding you was meant to be."

Ezekiel looked up at the stars. He hadn't felt this good in a long while. "It was meant to be," he said to himself.

# 30

# *School Days*

Cosmo could hear the ruckus as he walked down the hall at Hollywood High School. He opened the door to the band room. Thirty-two teenagers gabbed, chewed gum, buzzed the room with paper planes, and created a general cacophony. Cosmo set his briefcase down on the desk and faced the class.

"Ladies and gentlemen, please take your seats,"

The kids continued as if no one had said a word.

Cosmo reached into his coat pocket. He removed a stainless-steel whistle and blew hard. The shrill sound of the whistle filled the room. The talking stopped. All eyes were focused on the black teacher in the sharp-looking suit.

"Thank you," said Cosmo. He walked over to the blackboard and wrote his name on it.

"Hey, you Big Joe Turner's daddy?" cracked one of the kids.

The room erupted in laughter.

Cosmo wasn't sure which student made the comment, so he fixed the class with a cold look. "No, but I sure know who my mama was."

The class was surprised at the quick retort. They had never heard a teacher crack wise like that, especially a black teacher. Some kids chuckled, some stared in awe at the well-dressed man.

"Put down," cracked a kid with freckles and brown curly hair.

The class laughed.

Cosmo put up his arms in a stop gesture. "All right, all right. We had a laugh. I'm Mr. Turner. I'm your new music director. We've got a lot of work to cover. Those of you with more than five years on your instrument, please raise your hand."

The class was silent. No one raised a hand.

"Four?"

Two hands went up.

Cosmo gestured to the young lady with her hand raised. "Miss…?"

"Torres, Annette Torres. I've played the trumpet for four years, Mr. Turner."

"Excellent." He turned to the boy whose hand was raised. "And you, sir?"

"Dennis Peterson. I've played flute for almost four years, Mr. Turner."

"Skin flute," cracked a husky kid with brown hair.

"That will be enough, Mr.…."

The room went silent.

Cosmo walked over to the offender and gave the boy and look that shot icicles.

"Niedermeyer, Bob Niedermeyer," the teenager replied, shifting his eyes to the floor.

"What instrument do you play, Mr. Niedermeyer?"

"Saxophone, two years," the student replied.

"Might I inquire as to what type of saxophone you play?"

Bob shrugged his shoulders. "I don't know. My parents got it for me."

"Do you play, soprano, alto, tenor, or baritone saxophone?"

Bob gave Cosmo a goofy smile and replied, "Oh, alto."

"So, Mr. Robert Niedermeyer, player of the alto saxophone, would you like to get up in front of the class and demonstrate your skills for us today?"

Bob's face filled with fear. "Sir...Mr. Turner, you want me to get up and play for the class, now?"

"That was the general idea," Cosmo retorted. "How about hitting us with a little *Harlem Nocturne*? Or maybe you'd prefer something a bit mellower like *Sweet and Lovely* or something that swings, *Caledonia* perhaps?"

Bob swallowed hard. "I don't know those songs, Mr. Turner.'

Cosmo feigned shock. "And yet you joke about another player's skills? All of you, take out your notebooks and a pen."

The class quickly complied

Cosmo looked at the young faces. "Rule number one, a player will never disparage another player's skills. If you don't like how somebody plays, you don't run them down. A player who runs down other musicians is not secure in their skills and is probably not very skilled themselves."

Cosmo paused. The class was sat silent.

"Rule number two, and almost as important as rule number one. If the gig starts at seven and you're supposed to be there by six, if you show up on time, you're late. Drummers, you get there before anybody."

There was a groan.

"That's real, Lucille. Being a player is not easy. It takes work."

A young girl raised her hand.

"Yes?"

"Bernice Knowles, Mr. Turner. Junior, I played trumpet two years."

"Congratulations, Bernice. What is your question?"

"How long does it take to be a player—like you, I mean? My daddy told me about how you had a real cool club and band before the war and all."

This started mummers throughout.

Cosmo smiled. "Your daddy has good taste."

A group "Ah-h-h" went up from the class.

"It takes a lifetime. Any serious player practices every day and plays out whenever they can."

Groans and grumbles came from the students.

Cosmo looked at the young faces. "A player is a cat who puts a six-hundred-dollar instrument in an eight-hundred-dollar car and drives fifty miles to a gig that pays twenty-five bucks."

A boy with thick glasses raised his hand. Cosmo gestured for him to ask his question.

"Ralph Langstrom, sir. Is this material going to be on a test?"

Cosmo frowned. "Everything we talk about in this class is going to be on the test, Mr. Langstrom,"

There was another general groan.

Cosmo knew he had to get the students on his side. He walked over to the piano and sat down. He began playing a Beethoven piano sonata and segued into a boogie-woogie beat. His fingers glided across the keys and he sang, *Chicken Shack Boogie*. When he was done, the class was stunned silent. You could hear a fly fart in the room.

Cosmo stood and began to write on the blackboard. He gave the students notes on musical theory and history.

Bernice raised her hand. "Mr. Turner, are we going to play any today?"

"No."

Cosmo put up a hand, cutting off the class. "With the exception of a few, none of you are ready to play." He went around the classroom and passed out charts.

A heavy-set kid studied at the chart. "Hey, this ain't in the book."

Cosmo looked at the boy. "Very observant, Mr..."

"Bill Fetterman."

"Most of what you will be playing this year will not be in *the book*. This number is called *Rockin' at Midnight* and was composed by a piano man by the name of Roy Brown. Mr. Brown cut his record for a producer by the name of Cosimo Matassa. This was in New Orleans, which all good musical students should know is the birthplace of American music."

The students listened to Cosmo intently as he lectured them until the bell rang.

"Learn your parts. We will run through this number at the top of class Wednesday," Cosmo said as the students shuffled out of the room.

After four periods of band, Cosmo was beat. He drove home that afternoon feeling like he had gone ten rounds with Archie Moore. He shed his jacket, walked into the kitchen, and grabbed a cold beer from the refrigerator. Cosmo popped the top and plopped down on the couch. He had no idea teaching could be so hard.

When Michael had informed him of XELA's demise, he offered to help. Cosmo longed to move back to Los Angeles. He was pushing forty-three and had gotten accustomed to a steady paycheck. Playing clubs didn't offer that. Music was all Cosmo knew or had ever done. He had saved much of his skim money and had a tidy sum in a safe deposit box. Cosmo asked Michael if he might recommend him for a teaching position. A week later, Cosmo got a call from LAUSD administration. They offered him a job as band director at Hollywood High School. Cosmo believed he had fallen in clover. The salary wasn't anything like what he got at the radio station, but it was steady.

Cosmo took a pull off of his beer and wondered if he had made a mistake accepting the job. It wasn't like playing the clubs. There was nothing in the world like playing a packed house. He took another pull on the bottle and decided he would give teaching a month and then decide if he would continue. He didn't want Michael to think he was ungrateful. Cosmo set the bottle on the end table and quickly fell asleep on the sofa.

# 31

# *The Run*

The lawyers filed their papers. Allied Aircraft was officially defunct. Hagen was a free man living on a boat. Michael had a script in development at Columbia, but he wasn't holding his breath. Dalton Trumbo may have broken the blacklist with *Spartacus*. Hollywood was well known for its amnesia. HUAC was nothing more than a bad memory for many. It was the sixties. Young Turks were taking over the studios, and Michael was from a bygone era.

Michael and Hagen traveled to Mexico separately. Neither wanted to take chances being tailed by the Feds. Michael drove to San Diego. He parked his car in a long-term lot and took the bus to the border, where he walked across. He grabbed a cab to the airport and got on a private plane that flew him to Guerro Negro.

The small town owes its being to an American billionaire. Daniel Ludwig founded the city of Guerrero Negro in 1957. He headquartered his company, Exportadora de Sal, there to take advantage of the huge salt deposits. The U.S. was experiencing a salt shortage at the time, and Guerrero Negro provided the perfect answer for an American capitalist. The company quickly became the world's largest salt mine, producing over seven million tons per year. The fact that the town also had a lagoon that was frequented by the local whale population proved an added benefit. Tourists came to go whale watching and see the mountains of salt along the beach.

The pilot landed on the beach. Michael got out and walked to Rudy's Trading Post, a local watering hole. A driver was already waiting for him. Michael got in the Mercedes and was driven to one of the stately homes that dotted the hills overlooking the small town. Emilio Hernandez greeted him at the door. He was in his fifties. Hernandez had a medium build, dark hair speckled with gray, a moustache, and a friendly face, with brown eyes that glistened in the sunlight. *El Indio* certainly did not appear imposing.

"Please come in, Michael," said Emilio.

Hernandez led Michael into a large living room with a spectacular view of the salt mine and lagoon. Patty Bono was seated on a long leather sofa. Bono was shorter than Michael. He had a round face, receding hairline, and was a good thirty pounds overweight. Bono's looks belayed his nickname of *Patty Two-Two*, for his preference of employing a .22 pistol with a suppressor to dispatch rivals. Bono stood and shook Michael's hand.

"I really liked that movie, *Breakout*."

Emilio shook his head. "Oh no, Mike's best was *Pike's Gang*."

Patty waved Emilio off. "Ah-h you like that because it's a western in Mexico."

Emilio raised a brow. "So?"

"So? Pike and his gang killed all the Mexicans at the end."

"They were Huertistas," Emilio replied dismissively.

"I'm going to leave if you two don't stop arguing about my movies," Michael kidded.

Patty and Emilio chuckled. A valet entered the room pushing a liquor cart. He was in his twenties and wore black slacks and a white dinner jacket and black bowtie.

"Gentlemen, can I offer you a drink?" asked Emilio.

"Walker, rocks," said Patty.

"Just water, thank you," Michael replied.

Emilio fixed the drinks. "Jimmy will be here this afternoon. He's coming by boat." He handed the men their drinks then took a beer from the cooler on the cart and popped the cap. "Salude."

The three men toasted.

Emilio led Michael and Patty out onto a large balcony that overlooked the lagoon.

"Beautiful," remarked Michael.

"I am glad you're joining us, Michael. You showed respect to the family, and we never forget that," said Patty.

Emilio looked at Michael. "I understand you wish to proceed with caution."

Michael nodded. "I will be honest because I respect you both and don't want you to get any false impressions. When Jimmy approached me with this deal, I was surprised. We have both been out of the life for many years."

"You were a good earner, Michael." Patty held up a finger for emphasis. "And you never crossed the family. You always gave the Don a taste and when you decided to make movies instead of gin, you handed your operation over to him."

"For a price," Michael joked.

Patty laughed and shrugged his shoulders. "That is to be expected."

"I've set up the necessary companies and the banks to put the money through. We have a warehouse for the vehicles. I'm in on the maiden run and then I'm out."

Emilio and Patty gave Michael questioning looks.

"We were under the impression that you were in on this deal," said Patty.

"I am, but only one run. I've set up a system so Jimmy can handle everything himself. I would suggest waiting a minimum of three months before you send another shipment. I would also suggest you limit the use of the shell company to transfer funds to no more than twelve a year. It could arouse suspicions otherwise."

Emilio frowned. "We thought this was going to be a regular thing."

"How regular?" asked Michael.

"Monthly," Emilio replied.

Michael kept a straight face. "We should probably wait until Jimmy arrives."

Patty waved Michael off and indicated to himself and Emilio. "Frankly, we are interested *because* Jimmy told us you were a partner. There is plenty of money to be made here, Michael."

Michael smiled and nodded his head. "I appreciate your honesty and your generosity, but I'm on the first run, then out. I'm moving to Europe. The cash will help."

"What the fuck are you going to do in Europe that you can't do here?" asked Patty.

"Make movies," Michael replied matter-of-factly.

Emilio and Patty looked at each other. Neither had a response. After a moment, they broke into laughter.

"It looks like we will have Michael as a partner for the first run," Emilio laughed. "I like your movies too much."

Patty looked directly at Michael. "You will vouch for Jimmy?"

Michael gave Patty a quizzical look. "What do you mean, will I vouch for Jimmy? Jimmy's the one who brought this deal to me. Of course, I vouch for him."

Emilio tugged his ear. "Kennedy's kid brother has a hard-on for Jimmy. That's not good for business."

"Jimmy knows what he's doing."

Patty took a drink of his scotch. "You ran things back in the old days, Michael. We just believe you handle business better is all."

Michael looked at the two men and gave them a smile. "Thank you. Jimmy will do fine. You guys are going to make a lot of money."

"Yes, we are," laughed Patty.

Emilio slapped Michael on the back. "I like you, Amigo."

* * *

Michael and Hagen were crouched on a hill overlooking the San Ysidro border crossing. They both had their binoculars trained on the station. Emilo's men were driving three vehicles across, a Chevy Nova, a Ford Van, and a Dodge station wagon. The plan was for the drivers to make the crossing at various times, leave the vehicle at an Ace parking lot on Market Street, and walk away.

The run was a trainwreck. Emilio's men crossed the border at the same time, a vehicle in each lane. The Nova and Van were stopped by the agents. The Dodge got waved through. Michael and Jimmy watched the entire episode unfold from their vantage point.

"Sonofabitch, they were caught," cursed Michael.

Hagen stared through the binoculars as the Dodge crossed the border. He tracked the vehicle. After going a few blocks, the driver began slowing down. "What the fuck is he doing?"

"He's going to ditch the car," said Michael, already heading down the hill toward a beige Ford Galaxy.

The two men jumped in the car and took off. By the time they got down to the main drag, they saw the driver had ditched the wagon and was hot footing it back towards Tijuana.

"That asshole just took off and left the car," said Hagen, enraged.

Michael stopped the Galaxy just up from the Dodge. Hagen was ready to go after the driver. Michael grabbed his arm. "Forget him. Get the wagon. I'll follow you."

Hagen got in the Dodge. They drove to Filippi's on India St. and parked their cars. Patty Bono, who was waiting in the restaurant, came outside.

"What the fuck?" exclaimed Patty.

Michael frowned. "Don't say anything. Just get in your car and follow us to Long Beach."

"This better be fuckin' good." Patty walked to his Cadillac and got in.

The three cars pulled away, caught the freeway, and headed north. Two hours later, they drove into the warehouse. Hagen jumped out of the Dodge and closed the warehouse door. Patty got out of his car and gave Michael a quizzical look.

"What the fuck happened?" Patty asked.

"Two of the cars didn't make it. They all went through at the same time," said Michael.

"How the fuck that happen?" asked Patty.

Michael shook his head. "Somebody fucked up. Looks like it's on Emilio's side."

"I'll say somebody fucked up," growled Patty.

Hagen walked over to the two men and said, "Let's unload the wagon."

Patty frowned and shook his head. "No."

Michael and Hagen shot Patty a look.

"That car is going to Chicago," retorted Patty.

"What the fuck, Patty? Three cars were supposed to cross, and one made it. We get that one," said Hagen.

Patty gave Hagen a steely look. "Do you want to take that up with Sally G?" The name was in reference to Salvatore Giancana, the head of the Chicago family.

"No."

"Good. We ship the wagon tomorrow. As is, Sally ain't gonna be pleased he's only getting half a shipment."

Michael frowned. "Me and Michael sunk a lot of our dough into setting up this deal up. Now you're saying we don't get paid?"

Patty threw his arms up in the air and sighed. "We do another run. You get paid with that one."

Michael hadn't said a word. He looked at Hagen. He could see Jimmy was angry. Michael turned to Patty and said, "The system will need to be refined."

Patty smiled. "Good." He looked at Hagen. "Listen to your *paisan*."

Hagen silently nodded his head.

# 32

# *The Mission*

Victor Vega entered the phone booth with a fistful of change and laid it on the small counter. He glanced out the booth and watched a couple walk by. They were well-dressed, easy prey. Victor smiled. The couple was lucky. He was on a mission. Victor dropped the coins into a slot.

"Operator," said the voice on the other line.

Victor gave the operator the number.

"Please deposit eighty-five cents for the first three minutes, and I'll connect you."

Victor pumped the coins into the machine.

"Ace of Hearts," said Della.

"It's me,"

"So, what have you found out?"

"I don't have anything solid yet. This Hagen guy you wanted me to check out may be involved with some heavy people," said Victor.

"Find out what you can. He had a partner once, a movie producer, Michael McGuire."

"I'll check him out and get back to you." Victor hung up the phone. He let go of the cradle, pumped more money into the phone, and dialed a number.

"Ola," said a woman's voice.

"Hi, Betty, it's Victor Vega. Is Professor Norris available?"

"Let me see. Hold on one sec," the secretary replied.

A moment later, Professor Norris picked up the call.

"Victor, what can I do for you, son?"

"I'm putting together a book on the great film producers of the forties. There's one that I'm a bit short on information, Michael McGuire. If you could give me a hand on what he's doing now, I'd sure appreciate it."

"So, you're writing a book?"

"Working on one."

"I thought you were a business major."

"I was, but I always enjoyed your class on film history."

"Well, thank you, Vincent. I'll see what I can turn up on Mr. McGuire. You know he was a pretty big at one time. Give me your number, and I'll call you."

"I'll call you, Professor. I'm sort of on the move at the moment."

"You were always on the run."

"Yeah." Vincent spotted a single woman who looked to be in her twenties walk by. "I'll call you tomorrow." He hung up the telephone and exited the booth. It was just before sunset, and the evening now held a promise for Vincent Vega as he strolled casually following the young woman.

# 33

# *Me Familia*

Angela drove her Chevy Bel-Air down Franklin Avenue. The car was eight years old, but it was hers and paid for. Angela was now working as a script girl for Desilu Productions. A friend who was a carpenter at Paramount introduced Angela to a producer at Desliu, who hired her as a script assistant. The hours were long, but the pay was much better than her school district salary. Angela was mother to three children. The increased income gave her a new sense of accomplishment and freedom. She missed her brother, but Ezekiel had vanished. It had been months since Carmen's murder, and the police hadn't arrested a single suspect.

Detective Miller occasionally dropped by to talk to Angela. The El Cajon Sheriff's Department had done as little as possible. Carmen was just another dead wetback to them. Miller had an easy-going manner and was able to obtain the file from the El Cajon Sheriff's Department. The file was thin. Carmen had bought gas at the Standard Station on Broadway and Second around seven-thirty the evening of her death. She was seen at the Carousal Bar on Main Street later that night. No time was listed when she left the bar, just that someone named Noah Gittes, a navy serviceman, thought he had talked to her. The trail ended there.

Miller followed up on Gittes. He had been sent to some southeast Asian country called Vietnam. Miller felt sorry for Angela. There was little he could do. The case was colder than a Wyoming winter. Miller's visits became fewer. It had been two months since his last. Angela had resigned herself to the fact that no one would be caught and tried for Carmen's murder.

Angela rented a nice home on Finley. Letty and Lucy attended Hollywood High School. Angela depended on the girls to watch Johnny after school, as her hours were long at the studio. The show was *Taggart*. It was a one-hour detective series on CBS. Vince Taggart was a Palm Springs detective who each week got mixed up in murder, robbery, and mayhem. The crew filmed an episode in five days every week for twenty-eight weeks. The crew worked hard.

Angela was one of two females on the production. The men were protective of the ladies, but their talk was salty, and some loved to tell an off-color joke. Angela quickly learned to give as good as she got and not take any lip from the guys. They loved her.

Angela pulled the Chevy into the driveway. She grabbed the bag of groceries from the back seat and closed the door. Angela was going to make pasta and sausage for dinner. It was Johnny's favorite. The girls liked it too. As soon as Angela entered, she knew something was amiss. The piano in the corner was unattended. Johnny was seated on the floor watching TV. Lucy was in the kitchen getting things ready for dinner. Letty should have been practicing her piano lessons. Angela put the groceries down on the table.

"Where's Letty?"

Neither Lucy or Johnny answered. Angela turned off the TV. "Where is Letty?"

Suddenly the door to Letty's bedroom opened. A man in his twenties emerged. He was thin and pale and stuffed his t-shirt into his jeans. Letty followed. Her appearance was one of romantic dishevelment. She had a t-shirt and pants on. Angela noted her niece was missing a bra.

"Hi, Ange," said Letty.

Angela's expression was ice.

"This is Steve." Letty nodded toward the man. "He works at Wallach's Music and is a musician."

Angela arched an eyebrow. "Really, what do you play, Steve?"

"Drums," Steve replied flashing a smile.

"I suppose you were demonstrating your technique to my niece in the bedroom."

Steve was caught off guard by Angela's bluntness. He stammered, "Well, I was…what I meant was…"

Angela picked up the jacket that was hanging on the back of the chair and held it out. "I understand. You were just leaving, weren't you?"

Steve grabbed the jacket and made for the door.

"Ah-h-h, Steve?" Angela said calmly.

Steve turned. "Yes?"

"No, you may not see Leticia again. In fact, if I find out that you have even spoken to her, I will come down to Music City, cut your cajones, and cook them with the menudo."

Steve gave a nod and disappeared out the door like a ghost.

Angela turned and gave a cold look to Letty, who was pouting. "I know how this goes. You are seventeen and he's what, twenty-three, twenty-four?"

Letty stared daggers back at her aunt. "I wish it had been you instead of Momma who died!" The teenager stomped into her bedroom and slammed the door shut.

Angela looked up at the ceiling and counted to twelve. She glanced at Johnny and Lucy. "I'm sorry." Her eyes were filled with tears.

"Don't mind Letty, Auntie," said Lucy.

Angela hugged the two children.

Dinner was a tense affair. Letty sat silent. Angela didn't say much and picked at her spaghetti. Johnny talked about school. He talked about his friend, Jimmy Castro, getting a new Schwinn bike for his birthday. He talked about skateboarding. He talked about racing slot cars. Johnny kept the conversation going on his own. Lucy ate quietly and occasionally interjected a word or two.

After dinner, Angela went and sat outside on the patio while the girls cleaned up. Lucy and Johnny watched TV afterwards. Letty walked out to the patio and sat down. She brushed her hair back and looked at her aunt. "I'm—"

Angela placed her finger on Letty's lips.

"I know. I miss your mother too. I miss EZ. It's as if the world opened up and swallowed our family. I do know that I don't ever want to lose you or Lucy, me familia."

Tears welled in Letty's eyes. The two women hugged.

"I don't want to lose you, Auntie."

Angela wiped her eyes and smiled. "I also know you don't want to get pregnant. You've got your whole life ahead of you, Letty."

Letty nodded. "I know."

Angela gave her niece a feigned look of pain. "A drummer…"

Letty grinned sheepishly; her face was flush with embarrassment.

The two women sat for a while and didn't say anything.

"Do you think they will ever find Papa?" Letty asked, finally breaking the silence.

Angela glanced up at the stars for a moment and then looked at Letty. "I think EZ is gone, mija." She put her arm around the young girl and hugged her close. "That is why we have to stick together, you and me."

Angela and Letty sat on the patio for a little longer before they went back inside and closed the sliding glass door.

\* \* \*

It was Sunday. The sky was a pallet of black, orange, gold, and blue early that morning. Ezekiel, who was now called Golden Eagle, stood and chanted before a group of some two-dozen people. They were situated under a crude canopy made of driftwood and palm fronds.

Bernard and Ezekiel had become fast friends since their first meeting. Ezekiel continued to work at Spahn Ranch. During his off hours, he scrounged and collected useable items people had abandoned in the desert. He and Bernard had expanded his original encampment. Besides Ezekiel's cabin there was now had an old Air Stream trailer they had retrieved from the ranch when a Warner Bros. production abandoned it. The trailer was banged and battered, having been used in a stunt. That didn't matter to Ezekiel. He borrowed a truck and towed the trailer out to his encampment which Bernard had named *The Inner Peace Collective.*

All the walking had improved Ezekiel's leg. He still limped, but much of the pain was gone. The headaches had vanished as well. He and Bernard hunted for peyote and stored the mushrooms in glass jars. Bernard would come and go in his '54 Ford. Sometimes he would be gone for a day. Sometimes for a week. Bernard brought a small generator so the collective would have electricity. Ezekiel sunk some poles. Bernard strung lights and set up a P.A. system. They could blast music across the desert with the stereo system they had set up in one of the shacks.

Bernard was a former engineer and once taught at Cal Poly. One day, he looked out at the fresh faces of his class. He quietly closed his book and dismissed the students, telling them that they should use the time to improve their lives. Bernard got in his car and left the campus. A month later, he was living in a single bedroom apartment in Highland Park. He had shed his job, his house, and most worldly possessions. At sixty-three, Bernard figured he had enough saved to get him through until Social Security kicked in. He liked Ezekiel and saw someone who had be beaten by life and still sought a place in the community of people.

Ezekiel told Bernard about his great-grandfather, Falcon, and how he had fought the Mexicans who killed his people and led a cattle drive from Texas to California. They frequently ate peyote and tripped together. The mushrooms stopped Ezekiel's headaches. Ezekiel began to invite people out to the compound that he met while working at the ranch or out scavenging. He told them his ancestor had been a guide and that he could guide them to an inner peace. Those that came were given peyote. Some left and never returned. Others became followers of the man they referred to as Golden Eagle.

Bernard and two other men sat on a long bench and beat on wooden drums. Dozens of participants swayed in a state of nirvana consciousness. Golden Eagle ceased his chant. The drums stopped. The group let out a mighty collective "Om"

Golden Eagle picked up a bowl sitting on a scuffed wooden table that contained pealed orange sections. He walked among the assembled group and handed a piece to each saying, "Take of the fruit of life and become one." He then passed out small paper cups filled with Hawaiian Punch along with the admonition, "Drink the nectar of life and be one with the universe." Finally, he picked up a wooden bowl that contained peyote buttons and passed those out among the faithful, saying, "Seek the inner truth of your being and be reborn."

Bernard got up and hit a switch. The long string of lights that stretched from the canopy to two tall poles lit up. He walked over to an old bookcase holding a stereo system and turned it on. A TEAC reel to reel tape deck glowed and began turning. The Zombie's *She's Not There* blasted throughout the compound. The congregation got up and grooved with the music.

Ezekiel smiled at Bernard. "It's a good day."

Bernard glanced at the congregation, then looked at Ezekiel. "We could use more contributions." He rubbed his forefinger and thumb together.

Ezekiel lit a joint, took a long draw, and exhaled. "They will come, brother." He passed the joint to Bernard and gestured to the surrounding area. "Look at how we've grown."

Bernard exhaled and passed the joint onto one of the faithful. "Peace, brother."

The man took the joint and walked off toward a trio that was seated in lotus positions swaying to the rhythm of the music and sat down.

Bernard chuckled. "Well, it ain't St. Patrick's Cathedral, but it's a start."

Ezekiel put his arm around Bernard. "You gave me a purpose, Bernard. The church will come together. We are *familia*."

Bernard gave Ezekiel a warm smile. "Thank you, EZ. The wife and I never had kids. After Mary died, my job and everything else weren't important. I found you, and that was the first good thing that had happened to me in a long time. Just impatient, I guess."

Ezekiel glanced at the congregation that was now spread about the makeshift compound. "It's all good, brother. It's all good." He stared out across the desert. "I am staring to peak. I'm going to have a walkabout." Sometimes Ezekiel preferred to be alone when he tripped. He knew of an area that afforded shade and had a tent set up there away from the compound. Being alone allowed him to have an out of body experience where he became the Golden Eagle and soared high above the desert. Sometimes he would sail high above the earth with Falcon. They would fly and land upon a tree and Falcon would pass his wisdom onto Ezekiel.

Ezekiel walked over to the Air Stream and entered the trailer. A moment later, he emerged carrying a canteen. He turned to the group. "Peace."

Bernard waved. "Peace, brother." Some of the others waved as well and offered a salutation of "Peace." Others were lost in the music. Golden Eagle set out across the desert as the strains of the Riviera's *Californian Sun* faded in the distance.

* * *

Victor sat across from Della at Denny's Restaurant. It was two in the morning, and he had just driven in from L.A. He pulled a pack of Marlboros from his shirt pocket and lit one. Della reached over and snatched the cigarette from his lips and ground it out in the ashtray.

Victor frowned. "Hey."

"It's a bad habit, and it draws attention to you.

Victor gave Della a look that said, "What the hell?" He gestured to the others smoking in the restaurant.

Della ignored him. "What did you find out about James Hagen?"

The waitress came over and refilled Victor's coffee cup. He waited until the waitress left before answering.

"Hagen's in the life. He and McGuire hooked up with El Indio. They're bringing heroin in from TJ," Victor replied in a hushed tone of voice.

Della allowed a small smile to course across her lips. "Really?"

"My sources were vague. McGuire blew town some weeks back. I'm not sure where he went, but he's not in L.A. or San Diego."

Della's eyes lit up. "Hagen is working this alone?"

Victor shook his head. "No. He's partners with Patty Bono and El Indio. These are guys you don't fuck with. Bono is a made man. El Indio is a psycho."

Della was silent for a moment. Her dark eyes showed no fear. "So, this operation is relatively new?"

Victor shrugged. "Four, maybe five months up and running." said Victor.

"We are not going to take their drug trade," Della replied.

Victor smiled with relief.

"I want you to kill Bono. Make it look like Hagen was responsible."

Victor stared at Della in disbelief. "This is the mob you're taking on," he shot back in a whisper.

"You and your crew didn't seem too concerned about hitting Murray Rosen's place, and he's hooked up with Sam Rothstein," Della retorted with a dismissive wave.

Victor was silent. Della obviously knew about his crew and the heists.

Della remained cool. "Patty Bono is collateral damage, which is why it has to appear that Hagen is the responsible party."

"What about the movie producer? You aren't interested in him?

"He would be a bonus…but not important."

"Why don't I just take out Hagen?"

Della frowned. "No. I want him to feel fear."

"This type of thing could take time."

"I trust you will succeed."

Victor took out a cigarette and lit it. Della didn't stop him this time.

"If you want me to do this thing, then you must tell me why."

Della sipped her coffee and put the cup down. "Fair enough."

Della told Victor about the Point Magu Massacre and how a young man named Jimmy Grazzi killed a policeman named Harry Sullivan. How the cop had a daughter with a colored woman. She told him of how that girl, now a woman, crossed paths with James Hagen and how she discovered he was actually Jimmy Grazzi with a new face. She told

Victor of how Hagen had the woman's brother murdered and gave her
to the boss of a Mexican mob to do with as he pleased. She told how the
woman was forced to run grifts on wealthy gringos. She told him of how
the woman convinced the mob boss to allow her to run a grift in Dallas.
The woman nailed the mark. She sent the cash to the boss, changed her
name, and left Texas. The boss sent a man after the woman. She killed
the hired gun and sent the boss ten grand and a note. The note told the
boss that the money was for the loss of his gunman. It went on to say
that if the boss sent any others, they would be killed and he would not
receive any money. The boss declined to send any others after her. He
didn't have to pay the hitman, and he was ten grand richer. Business
was business.

"So, what's your name?" Victor asked when Della had finished her
story.

Della didn't bat an eyelash. "Della Rio."

Victor reached across the table and placed his hand on Della's. "If
you want me to do this, I need to know you trust me. You always said
we were family."

"Family...yes. People used to call me 'Cinnamon Carlyle' in my
singing days," Della replied matter-of-factly. She gave Victor her stage
name and withheld her real name of Nicole Sullivan.

Victor tilted his head and looked at Della, trying to see her as a
singer. "When was that?"

Della patted Victor's hand. "Before your time, during the war. Are
you going to do this thing for me?"

Victor exhaled a cloud of smoke and flashed a smile. "Yes."

Della sipped her coffee.

*34*

# *Cosmo's Blues*

Cosmo stopped by the Union Hall. You could've shot a canon and not hit a player. Cosmo got back in his Impala and cruised down Manchester Blvd. He stopped by the Pure Pleasure Lounge. The place was as dead as Lincoln. He stopped at a few other clubs, finding it was the same, few patrons and no band.

Cosmo drove home. He got a beer and sat out on his porch. He had recently purchased a Craftsman bungalow on Wilton Ave. The place was small but had a nice size backyard with a couple of orange trees. Cosmo liked to putter around in his yard. It gave him a sense of accomplishment.

Bubba Taylor dropped by. He played bass and was once in a group with Cosmo. He got out of his Plymouth and walked over to Cosmo, who was sitting on his porch. He was a large man with a jovial demeanor. He wore a blue suit and black Fedora. His hand practically encased Cosmo's slender fingers when they shook hands.

"Heard you moved. Nice place you got here."

Cosmo smiled. "Thanks." He got up, went in the house, retrieved a beer, and handed it to Bubba. The two men sat down on the porch and enjoyed the afternoon.

"How's teaching?" asked Bubba.

"It ain't the same as gigging, but I do like a regular paycheck," Cosmo replied with a casual shrug.

"I hear you," Bubba chuckled. "Shit, all them damn clubs have a jukebox now. Why pay a band when they can make money off the fuckin' box?"

Cosmo nodded his head. "I stopped by Pure Pleasure and Dupree's and a couple others, not a jam at one of 'em."

"Babe's & Ricky's still got it goin'."

Cosmo waved Bubba off. "That's Monday nights. I gotta be at work six-thirty on Tuesday."

"Havin' a job does cramp your style," Bubba acknowledged.

They sat there for a while and didn't say anything.

"You miss it...playin out?" Bubba finally asked, breaking the silence.

"Like a mutha. Teaching's a bitch. A few of the kids are worth it, but most..." Cosmo tossed his hand in the air. "I might as well be fartin' in the wind."

"There's that regular money," Bubba replied.

"Yeah. That's what's keeping my black ass there. I got a mortgage to pay, and you sho' can't do that gigging."

Bubba shook his head. "Face it, Cosmo, a player is fucked, no matter how he look at it. If he gigs, the money is short, the food lousy, and you're lucky if you ain't havin to sleep on the bus. If you get a straight job, you ain't got time to play. We fucked comin' and goin', brother."

Cosmo chuckled. "True." He finished his beer a stood up. "You want another?"

Bubba downed the rest of his bottle. "No, thanks. Gotta hit it. T. J. and me playing out Palm Springs tonight. Got to pick him up. Just wanted to come by and say 'hey'."

T.J. was in reference to T.J. Barnes, the R&B guitarist who had once played with Cosmo and went on to record with Jack McVea's band.

Bubba set the bottle down on the wicker table. The two men shook hands.

"Say, 'hey' to T.J."

"I will." Bubba looked at house and then smiled at his friend. "You got a nice place, Cosmo. You doin' alright."

Bubba got into his car. Cosmo waved and watched as the Plymouth disappeared down the street. It was nearly four. Cosmo felt like it was much later. He picked up the empties and went inside his house. Cosmo was now feeling more depressed than before. He showered and changed his clothes. There was one place Cosmo knew would be jamming that evening. He wondered if he still had the chops. It had been over a year since he had played any gig other than the music room at Hollywood High.

It was Saturday night. Cosmo looked sharp in his cream-colored suit and dark brown Fedora as he slid behind the wheel of his car and drove off.

Sophie's Cellar was a fire hazard waiting to happen. It was also one of the best kept secrets in L.A. The nightclub was a floor below street level on Florence Ave. It didn't even have a sign above the door leading down to the club. The place was a leftover from prohibition days.

Sophie paid the police, and they left her club alone. Sophie Wright had been a blues singer back when Bessie Smith was going strong. In the thirties, she quit the chitlin circuit and bought the club. Every black musician who played Los Angeles played at Sophie's. On any given night before the war, it was not uncommon to see Louis Armstrong jamming with Lester Gordon or Eubie Blake. After the war, Dizzy Gillespie had jammed with King Curtis and Art Blakey on Sophie's stage. A player's chops had to be hot to play Sophie's. One up, one down was a hard lesson many a performer learned. The audience did not tolerate second stringers.

Cosmo walked up to the door. Bald Barry, a six-foot four behemoth, was standing watch as Sophie's doorman. Barry smiled when he saw Cosmo.

"My man. Haven't seen you 'round since Moses was in high school."

"That was a couple of years after you graduated," Cosmo shot back.

The two men shook hands.

"What you up to, Cos?"

"Teaching band for L.A. schools."

"The road can be a hard mother. What happened to your disc jockey thing?"

"Station was sold. Man, who own it went bankrupt."

Bald Barry shook his head. "Damn, that can happen to a white man?"

"Apparently so."

"Shit. A nigga don't stand a chance."

Cosmo laid a fin in Barry's palm. "Take care brother."

"My man." Barry opened the door, and Cosmo descended the stairs.

The club was poorly lit. Neon lights ran the perimeter of the bar, and two neon palm trees sat on either side of the stage. Colored lights running along the front of the stage illuminated the band. A single spot was used to train on a player when they soloed. Any player was welcome on the stage. Those that could play remained. Triflers were off the bandstand after one number.

Cosmo allowed his eyes to adjust to the dim light. There were a couple of white boys on the stage, one on guitar and another on piano. They were playing with Jay McNeely, Clyde Stubblefield, and Red Callender. The place was packed. The band was rocking. The dance floor was jumping. Cosmo saw half a dozen players in the room that he knew.

Joe Harper spotted Cosmo and waved him over to his table. Joe played trombone. Seated next to him were two women. One was dressed in a low-cut red dress and was obviously Joe's girl. The other woman was dressed more conservatively in a green cotton dress with small purple flowers.

"Ladies, this is Cosmo Turner. Cosmo this is Nola and my gal, Denise."

Cosmo tipped his hat and took a seat next to Nola. "Pleased to meet you, ladies."

"You playing tonight?" Joe asked.

Cosmo shrugged his shoulders. "Who's the white cat on keys?"

Joe nodded toward the stage. "He, Leon Russell, outta Oklahoma. The cat playing guitar is Tommy Tedesco, session players."

Cosmo watched the piano player for a moment, then turned to Joe. "He bad for a white boy."

Joe Harper chuckled and gave a nod.

"You used to have a band back before the war, didn't you?" Nola asked.

Cosmo smiled sheepishly. "The Kings of Rhythm."

"Cosmo had a jumpin' outfit back in the day," added Joe.

Cosmo looked at Nola. "You don't look old enough to have frequented the clubs back then."

Nola smiled. "My brother saw you play. He really liked your band."

Cosmo spread a big smile and adjusted his tie. "Your brother has good taste."

Nola dipped her head. "Lonnie sure did.' She looked at Cosmo. "He died in the war."

"Oh, I'm sorry. Where'd he serve?"

"Africa."

"I was in Sicily and then Germany."

"You don't have a band now?"

Cosmo's eyes shot over to Joe Harper. The bone player was chatting it up with Denise.

"No. I teach band at Hollywood High now."

A look of recognition spread across Nola's face. "You used to be on the radio." She snapped her fingers trying to remember. "Big Daddy."

Cosmo grinned and held his hands up in mock surrender. "Guilty."

"I liked your show."

"You've got good taste, sister."

"You're not on the radio anymore?"

"No, just a teacher now."

A hand fell on Cosmo's shoulder. He looked up and was staring straight at Miles Davis.

"Say, how 'bout you and me show 'em how it's done?" suggested Miles.

Cosmo grinned. "Done."

The impromptu band finished their set.

Buddy Williams the M.C. took the mic. "Give it up for the band! Ain't those white boys something?"

The audience cheered loudly.

"We got something real special next. I ain't even sure what you're gonna hear, but put your hands together and give a big 'hurrah' for Mr. Miles Davis."

The crowd roared.

Cosmo followed Miles up on the stage. He was followed by Art Blakey and two other musicians he didn't know. Miles walked up to the mic.

"You all know Art Blakey and Cosmo Turner. Give them a warm welcome."

The crowd applauded.

"These other two cats I recently met out in Tennessee. Please welcome Jimi Hendrix and his bass player, Billy Cox."

The audience gave a tepid response. This crowd was waiting to see what the tall, lean, twenty-two-year-old and his buddy was going to do.

Miles turned to the band. "St. James Infirmary."

Miles Davis put the trumpet to his lips and blew. It was magic. The players locked like a Swiss watch. Miles took the first solo. The music that came from his horn was like melted butter. Cosmo took the second solo. His fingers danced across the keys kicking the dirge into a rumba and bringing it back again. Jimi took the final solo and burned the house down. Miles went into a note for note duel with the guitar player. They danced through the blues and bop. Each player seemed to instinctively know what the other was going to play before they did. Miles hit a high F on the horn and cascaded down. The band was right with him. When they ended the song, you could have heard a pin drop. Then the house erupted in loud applause and cheers.

"I guess the band passed the audition," said Miles.

The audience cheered louder.

The band played two more songs and then left the stage to more thunderous applause.

Cosmo thanked Miles and the other players and returned to the table. Joe and Denise were gone. Nola sat alone smiling at Cosmo as he took his seat.

"That was amazing," said Nola.

Cosmo chuckled. "Yeah, that was some fun."

"Say Cosmo, you playing Newport?" asked a voice.

Cosmo turned. Lionel Thornton, a bass player, stood next to Tiny Williams, a tenor saxman.

Cosmo got up and hugged both men and introduced them to Nola.

"No, just came down tonight to see some of you cats," said Cosmo.

Lionel shook his head. "You the man, Cosmo. You killed it, brother."

"Yeah," agreed Tiny.

"You playing tonight?" asked Cosmo.

"Naw. Heard you was teaching now," said Lionel.

"Yeah," Cosmo replied with a shrug.

Lionel gave Cosmo a pat on the shoulder. "Good for you. Kids need a teacher like you. You smoked 'em tonight. You still a player, Cosmo."

Lionel and Tiny headed over to the bar.

Cosmo looked at Nola. "How about we get out of here and go someplace quiet?"

Nola smiled. "I'd like that very much, Mr. Turner."

Cosmo took the lady's hand, and they made their way through the club and up the stairs. Cosmo put Nola's arm in his as they walked down Florence to his car. The music of the band playing at Sophie's drifted behind them.

# 35

# *Dinner with Sergio*

Michael watched the Movieola screen as the editor ran the reel. Eduardo Santorre, the editor, was thirty years younger than Michael. The two men were situated in a small room at Cinecitta Studios. The studios were founded in 1937 by Benito Mussolini and journalist, Luigi Freddie. Their stated purpose was to revive the Italian feature film industry, which had hit bottom by the early thirties. Founded under the slogan, *Il cinema è l'arma più forte*, "Cinema is the most powerful weapon," the fascist government mainly employed the studio as a factory to turn out propaganda films. The allies bombed the studios during the war. After the war, the studio were used as a refugee camp that housed some 3,000 displaced persons from such distant countries as Egypt, Poland, Iran, and China. Cinecitta made a comeback in the 50's and became known as *Hollywood on the Tiber*.

"We should cut when Jack gets out of the car and pulls his gun," said Eduardo in heavily accented English. He quickly cut the film and replayed it in the abbreviated from. "Faster, yes?"

"Faster, yes, but you lose the suspense," Michael replied. "Let's see the first version again."

Eduardo spliced the original footage back in and loaded it in the Movielola. There was a knock at the door. Michael and Eduardo turned. Standing in the doorway was a short, rotund man with a full beard and a happy looking face.

"Ciao," greeted the man.

Eduardo jumped up. "Sergio."

The two men hugged and spoke in rapid Italian. Michael's command of the language was rudimentary, and he was unable to keep up with the conversation. Eduardo turned to Michael.

"Michael, this is Sergio Leone. He is a director who much admires your work."

Michael shook Sergio's hand. The Italian director was effusive in his joy meeting Michael. He talked a mile a minute as he pumped Michael's hand.

"Sergio says, 'It is a great honor to meet Michael McGuire, a true master of the cinema.'"

Michael smiled sheepishly. "Please tell Mr. Leone that I was lucky to work with some very talented people."

Eduardo quickly translated. The director spoke again, his hands gesticulating as he did so.

"Sergio wants to know what your secret was for making so many good films. His favorite was *Guns at Dawn*."

Michael chuckled and looked at Sergio. "Never let the bosses tell you what to do with your film. Nobody knows a damn but you. Stay true to your vision."

Eduardo translated. Sergio roared with laughter.

"How long you will be in Rome?" asked Sergio.

"Until this movie is completed," Michael chuckled. "Here, show him the scene."

Eduardo said something to Sergio and then sat down at the Movieola and ran the scene the way it was originally cut.

"Please show him the shorter version," said Michael when the film finished.

Eduardo cut the film and ran it for Sergio. The heavy-set director frowned and said something in Italian.

Eduardo did not smile. He nodded his head and put back the original footage. Michael gave the editor a questioning look.

"Sergio said the mood was ruined. No suspense."

Michael grinned. "Don't take it too hard, Eduardo."

The editor ran the film again. Sergio nodded his head and gave a thumbs up. He said something to Eduardo.

"What is the title of your film?" said Eduardo.

"The Big Rip Off... ah-h *Strappare Grande*. It's about a robbery of a jewelry store."

Eduardo spoke Italian to the director, and Sergio replied talking a mile a minute.

"Sergio likes the title. He would like to invite you to dinner. He is working on a script for a western and would value your opinion," said the editor.

"Certainly. You will have to come along as my interpreter, Eduardo."

Eduardo's eyes lit up. He turned and said something to Sergio. The two men hugged. Sergio shook Michael's hand. "Ciao." He waved and was out the door.

"We are to meet Sergio at Peppone's at nine."

Michael looked perplexed.

"Your driver will know," Eduardo added quickly.

"Fine."

The two men turned and began watching the film on the Movieola screen.

Italians loved to eat, and Sergio was an Italian who loved to eat. His appetite was nearly as epic as his films. Ristorante Peppone's was located on Via Emila in the old part of Rome and was one of the oldest in the city. Michael sat across from Sergio with Eduardo sitting at the head in order to translate and keep the conversation going.

Sergio did the ordering. They had Insalata di Carciofi con Freschi, mentuccia e grana, Prosciutto di Parma con bufala, and Parmigiana con Carciofi fritti e bufala for a first course. This was followed by Spaghetti Cacio E Pepe, which was in turn followed with Saltimbocca alla Roma, Catoletta Alla Siciliana, Cotoletta alla Milanese, and Pollo alla griglia disossato, marinato alle erbe patate. This was finished off with fruit, Tiramisu, and espresso. Sergio was pleased to see that Michael enjoyed the espresso as much as the meal.

"My grandfather used to say, if you can't tar the road with the coffee, it's just brown water," Michael quipped.

Eduardo translated.

Sergio roared with laughter. "Americans have a way with words," he replied in heavily accented English.

"And you Italians have such a way with art. Even in the way you eat."

Eduardo translated, and Sergio laughed again. He fixed Michael with a serious expression.

The conversation continued with Eduardo translating.

"I would like to make a western, Michael. I am thinking of using Kurosawa's *Yojimbo* as the basis for the script."

"A gunman playing two families against each other," said Michael.

"Si." Sergio frowned. "I do not want to make the protagonist the typical American gunfighter."

Michael sipped his espresso and thought for a moment. "Don't give him a name. Make your gunfighter a man of mystery. You don't explain where he came from or who he is. He just shows up in the town."

"What would be his motivation for fighting the gangs?" Sergio asked.

Michael didn't need Eduardo to translate. He knew instinctively what the director was asking. Michael rubbed his forefinger and thumb together. "Dollars. He saves a family, but he is motivated solely by the money the gangs pay him. He should be the fastest gun and think nothing of killing a man."

Sergio leaned back in his chair, laughed, and rubbed his meaty hands together in glee. "Si, si. Uomo di mistero." He sat and thought a minute. "Dollari," he said over and over to himself.

"Yes," said Michael. He held up a handful of lira and made a mean looking face. "Dollari."

Sergio's eyes lit up. He jumped up and enthusiastically kissed Michael on his cheeks. "Graci. Graci."

# 36

# New Year's Eve

Victor took the long view. He knew knocking off Patty Bono could easily turn into a suicide mission. He hadn't questioned Della further after their meeting at Denny's. Victor returned to Los Angeles and set his sights on James Hagen. He set up survelience on Hagen's boat and was able to place a bug under the cabinet that held the radio. He could monitor any conversations that occured near the wheel and Hagan's side of them over the radio. Victor read everything he could about Hagen and Allied Aircraft. How a small company that once had a dozen employees grew to become a major manufacturer during the war years, only to fall on hard times. Hagan had succeeded in never being formally charged and thus staying out of prison, but Allied Aircraft went bankrupt.

Victor read what he could find about the Point Magu Massacre. He found the obtites Della told him about, Marcellus Monroe, Bennie Meyer, and Lester Beauchamp. He found Monroe's and Beauchamp's obits in the *Sentinel*, but nothing to connect them to Hagen. Same with Meyer, whose death had received scant mention in the *Tribune*. The deaths jibbed with Della's story. The connection to Hagen was tenuous at best.

Jasmes Hagen was an enigma. He was nobody when he purhased the small aircraft company in 1928. A year later, Allied won a contract to turn out planes for the U.S. postal service. Once the war came, Allied took off and soared before crashing in a tangled, bankrupted heap two decades later. Hagen was occassionally mentioned in the social and business pages but rarely photographed. His former wife had married a senator and now lived 3,000 miles away.

Victor did not see a connection between Hagen and the people Della told him about. He accepted that information of faith. Della was the closest thing he had as a mother. If she said Hagen needed to suffer, then so be it.

Victor studied the drug runs for months and knew them by heart. Two brown vans with the *Pollo Grande* insigna on the side crossed the border every three weeks like clockwork. The drivers left the vehicles at various locations in San Diego, usually a grocery store or where there was a large parking lot. Five minutes after they walked away, two other men would show up and drive the vans to a Long Beach warehouse.

Victor tailed the drivers on three different occasions. He even gained access to the warehouse disguised as a pizza delivery man. He was inside long enough to drop off three pies and get paid. It was enough. He saw a dozen men and assumed they were all armed. He saw Patty Bono sitting at a desk playing cards with Hagen and two other men. The mob boys never looked up at the slender Mexican in the jeans and sweatshirt delivering the pizzas.

Victor knew he couldn't do the job alone. He recruited two men from his crew. Eddie Valenzuela and Ronnie Zavala were criminals with a limited scope of the world. Victor kept it very simple. Steal the Pollo Grande trucks before the second team arrrived to drive them away. He did not tell them what the vans contained. He did not tell them about Patty Bono or James Hagen. Victor simply told them to steal the vans and meet him at a prearranged loation in Poway. Edddie and Ronnie took the job without question when Victor told them it would pay three grand each for the work.

According to the schedule Hagern's crew kept, their next run would be on December 31st. New Year's Eve was on a Tuesday that year. Hundreds of southern Californians flocked to Tijuana to celebrate. It was one of the busiest nights of the year at the crossing. The guards would be overworked and less likely to check every vehicle. Victor also knew that everytime there was a shipment, Patty Bono had dinner at Marechario's Pizza Parlor in El Cajon. It was small, quiet, and far from Chula Vista, Little Italy, and Long Beach.

Marechario's closed at six on New Year's Eve. That meant the run would be early. Victor had Eddie and Ronnie in position at ten that morning. They had to wait until nearly five when they spotted the two Pollo Grande vans.

This time, the vans did something unexpected. They split up. Eddie and Ronnie folllowed suit. They each took a van and folllowed it. The van Eddie was following drove into San Diego and parked in the Sears parking lot on University. Ronnie tailed the second van that drove into San Diego and parked at the Capri Theater. The driver got out and walked away.

Eddie Valuenzuela was out of the Dodge he boosted and raced to the van in the Sears lot. He jumped in and had the vehicle hotwired in no time. Eddie and the Pollo Grande van were gone in less than sixty seconds.

Ronnie wasn't as fortunate. The theater lot was full. The van had grabbed the last spot. Ronnie had to dump his car on a side street and hurriedly walk back to the theater. As he got to the van, the theater doors opened and the audience poured out into the lot. Ronnie was circumspect, hot wiring the engine. This cost him time. He had been spotted. A man in a leather jacket and a hat pulled down had approached the van just as the engine kicked over. The man kept his face obscured, but his eyes followed the vehicle as it pulled out of the parking lot.

Victor sat in a beige Ford he had boosted. The car was parked in the Home Federal parking lot that sat directly aross the street from Marechario's. He watched as Patty Bono ate his dinner. A man wearing an apron approached the table and spoke to Patty. Bono wiped his hands, got up, and followed the man. A long minute later, Patty rushed out of the restaurant and hurried to the phone booth on the corner.

Victor got out of his car and crossed the street. He was careful not to draw attention. He wore a hooded gray sweatshirt that hid his face. Patty's back was to him as Victor approached the phone booth. He could see Bono was agitated and spoke in a loud voice. Victor pulled the .22 pistol, kicked open the door, and fired two shots point blank at Patty, hitting him in the heart.

Patty collapsed to the floor. Victor stuck the gun in Patty's mouth and pulled the trigger. He then walked swiftly back to his car, got in and drove off.

He glanced at the rearview mirror and saw the man with the apron dash across the parking lot to the phone booth. Victor kept it under the speedlimit. The cops would be out in force tonight. Forty minutes later, Victor rendevoused with Eddie and Ronnie just outside of Poway. They met in an open field. A quick look at the two men told Victor who messed up.

"What happened?" Victor demanded.

Neither man replied. Ronnie glanced down at the ground and kicked the dirt with his feet. "I might have been spotted."

"Explain," snapped Victor.

Ronnie looked at Victor for a moment, then shifted his gaze away. "The driver left the van at some theater parking lot. Before I could get away, the movie let out. People were heading to their cars. There was a guy that could've been the driver."

"What did you do?"

Ronnie shrugged his shoulders. "Nothing. I drove off and came here."

As if appearing out of thin air, a gun flashed in Victor's hand and he fired. Ronnie's body slammed back against the van and collapsed to the ground. Eddie put up his hands and looked at Victor.

"Hey, man, nobody saw me."

Victor stuffed the gun in his belt. "If Ronnie was seen, the job is compromised. Help me put him in the van."

The two men picked up the body and tossed it into the back of the van. Victor retrieved a five-gallon container of gas and soaked the inside of the van. He lit a match and tossed it on Ronnie's body. The vehicle went up in flames.

Eddie glanced at Victor. "What's in the vans? They're empty?"

"Nothing." Victor quickly doused the second van and set it on fire.

Eddie put his hand on his head and gave Victor a look of disbelief. "We just stole two empty vans? What the fuck?"

Victor pulled the gun and shot Eddie. "You ask too many questions."

Eddie looked shocked. He tried to say something but collapsed to his knees before falling face-down on the ground.

Victor poured the remainder of the gasoline on Eddie's body and struck a match. Eddie went up in flames. Victor removed two .45's from the trunk of his car and opened it up on the two blazing vans. Metal blew, and glass shattered. He stood for a moment watching the vehicles burn, then got into his car and drove away. Victor stopped at a phonebooth in Santa Ana. It was nearly ten when he placed the call.

"It's me."

"How did it go?" asked Della Rio

"It went."

"Any problems?"

"No."

There was a moment of silence, then Della asked, "Are you okay?"

"I'm good. I'm heading back to L.A. I'll call when I have more news."

"Thank you."

Victor didn't say anything. He hung up the telephone, got back in his car, and drove to Los Angeles. He knew there could be no witnesses left after pulling the heist. They had left a wealth of heroin on the vans that went up in flames. He hoped it was worth it. Reliable thieves were hard to come by.

\* \* \*

James Hagen was hoping to bang a waitress from the Brown Derby. Her name was Catherine, and she was thirty, divorced, and had no kids. Cat, as Hagen referred to her, was just what the doctor ordered. Hagen had promised to take Cat to dinner and then out to dance at the Coconut Grove. He wanted to make sure he got more than just a handshake at the evening's end. They were in his suite at the Roosevelt when the incessant knock came on the door.

Hagen got up and slipped on a pair of pants. "This better be damn good," he growled through clenched teeth as he marched to the door and opened it.

Tony Donato, one of the crew, stood in the doorway.

Hagen shot Tony a peeved look, "What the fuck, Tony?"

The look on Tony's face told Hagen something was up. He stepped out into the hallway. "What's the problem?" Hagen asked in a hushed tone of voice.

"They got Patty."

Hagen looked at Tony with disbelief in his eyes. "What'da ya mean?"

"Patty's dead, Jimmy. They shot him outside Marechario's."

"Who shot him?"

"We don't know."

"Where's the shipment?"

"We don't know that either."

"Jesus fuckin' Chirst."

"Frank wants to know why you aren't at the warehouse tonight."

Hagen's eyes widened. His face filled with an incredulous expression. "It's fuckin' New Year's Eve. I thought Patty was down in Dago handling things. I was going out for the night."

"You thought wrong, Jimmy. Frank ain't happy. He sent me to get you."

Hagen gestured to his lack of clothes. "You head over to the warehouse. I'll be right behind you."

"Make it quick."

"Yeah." Hagen stepped inside and hurriedly got dressed.

"Hey, what's going on?" asked a surprised Catherine.

"Get dressed! Now!"

Catherine reluctantly got out of bed and began getting dressed. "Some New Year's."

"An emergency at work," Hagen replied off-handedly.

"I've heard that one before." Catherine grabbed her purse off the end table and marched out of the room.

Hagen picked up the phone and quickly dialed a number.

"Yes?" said a man's voice.

"Frank, it's me."

"No fuckin' names."

"Yeah, sorry. I just heard."

"Where the fuck are you?"

"The Roosevelt, I'm heading over to the warehouse right now."

The line went dead.

Thirty minutes later, James Hagen was standing in the Long Beach warehouse along with Tony Donato and the rest of the crew, which had now grown to two dozen.

"What the fuck happened?" Hagen demanded.

Bobby Ricci, a thin and wiry man, stubbed out his cigarette and looked at Hagen. "It was a pro hit. Pat took two to the heart and one in the mouth. Leon saw the guy who lifted the van at the Capri theater."

"Fuck. Check out Leon's story. Did anybody locate either of the vans yet?"

The crew stood silent.

"Find the fucking vans."

The telephone in the office rang. Hagen gave a look at Tony Donato, who hurried over to answer the call.

"This has to be handled subtly, no wild west shit," said Hagen.

Tony came back and whispered something in Hagen's ear. Hagen gave him a look of disbelief. "What the fuck? Are you fucking serious?"

Tony nodded, then shrugged his shoulders.

Hagen walked to the office, entered it, and closed the door behind him. He picked up the telephone and dialed a number.

"It's me."

"So, now you're gonna tell me that the goods went up in flames and that there's two dead mooks burnt to a fuckin' crisp lying next to the vans," said the voice on the other end. It was Frank B.

"Something like that," Hagen replied.

"And...?"

"We're working on it."

"You better find out and you better take care of it. This happened on your watch. It don't look good, Jimmy."

The line went dead.

Hagen hung up the receiver. He returned to the main area, where the crew waited.

"Tony, Paulie, Bobby, come on. I need you guys and your crews to hit the streets and find out what the fuck happened tonight. Ten grand to the man who brings back solid information."

The crew scrambled. A minute later, the warehouse was empty. Hagen drove back to the Roosevelt. It wasn't even midnight. The crowd in the Cinegrill was boisterous, and the band was swinging. Hagen went up to his suite. The shipment was lost, Patty was dead, and he didn't get laid. It was a banner New Year.

Hagen took off his jacket and tossed it on the back of the chair. He wished Michael was there. He would know what to do. Hagen picked up the phone and asked the operator to place a call to Rome and gave her the number. He made himself a drink while he waited. The operator called back and informed Hagen the call was ready to go through. Hagen sipped his scotch.

The line rang and rang, but no one answered it. Hagen finally hung up. He walked over to the window. Dozens of pedestrians were making merry along the boulevard. Hagen took a long sip of his scotch and gazed out the window.

"Happy fucking New Year."

* * *

Johnny Otis was playing the dinner show at a club on La Brea. Cosmo and Nola had a ringside table. Cosmo couldn't believe a woman like Nola would give him the time of day, let alone go out with him. Nola may have liked the blues, but she was a churchgoing lady and had real standards. Cosmo had spent most of his life chasing loose women and whiskey. That kind of behavior didn't play with Nola. She made that abundantly clear the first night they went out.

Cosmo toed the line. There was something about Nola that reminded him of his mother. She had died when Cosmo was twenty. He hadn't played a club since that night at Sophie's. It turned out that Nola had been dragged there by her friend, Denise. She loved music but felt that a lady should stay out of bars as a rule. Cosmo was a teacher. The work was hard, but he grew to enjoy working with the kids. He wasn't very spiritual. His mother had sent him to Catholic school. The nuns and the war beat whatever spirituality Cosmo may have ever had out of him. Nola didn't press him. Cosmo played in the church band, and that was enough for her. She knew Cosmo had a past. Nola was only interested in the present. Cosmo was a good man.

Johnny Otis gave Cosmo and Nola a nod. The band played a cool first set during dinner. Cosmo had steak and baked potato. Nola had salmon and rice. They shared a bottle of champagne.

"You're trying to get me drunk," Nola teased.

"You having a good time?" Cosmo asked.

Nola nodded her head and pushed her plate away. "I'm stuffed. That was delicious."

Cosmo placed a small velvet box in front of Nola. "Care for dessert?"

Nola stared in disbelief at the box. Her hands trembled slightly as she opened it. Inside was a beautiful engagement ring. Tears filled Nola's eyes.

"Well?" said Cosmo. "Will you marry me?"

Nola jumped up and hugged Cosmo, giving him a big kiss.

Cosmo feigned embarrassment. "People are looking, baby."

Nola regained her composure. She sat down and held out her hand. Cosmo slipped the ring on. It was on the larger side and easily slid on to Nola's slender finger.

"We'll get it sized," said Cosmo.

"It's beautiful, and yes I will marry you, Cosmo Turner."

Cosmo grinned from ear to ear.

Johnny Otis and the band returned for the second set and opened with *Caldonia*. The band jumped. Cosmo led Nola out to the dancefloor. The couple swung. Nola might have been a churchgoing lady, but she knew how to tear up a dancefloor. After the song, they returned to their table.

"You've made me the happiest man in town tonight, Nola."

The band counted down to midnight.

Nola reached over and hugged Cosmo close, giving him a long, passionate kiss. They broke away, and she looked into Cosmo's eyes. "Happy New Year, baby."

\* \* \*

Johnny Camacho and his best friend, Kenny Houghton, peered through the crack in the bedroom door at the group of teenagers in the living room. Letty had wanted to go to a New Year's party. That didn't play with her aunt. Angela suggested that Letty invite her friends to their home for a celebration that way sister Lucy could be there as well. Nearly two dozen teenagers stood talking and eating in the living room. Lucy sat with her friend Bertha Lopez in a corner eating chips and drinking Cokes.

"That Teresa Kramer sure has some big tits," whispered Kenny. "I'd sure like to squeeze them."

Johnny laughed. "Leche grande."

The two boys fell on the floor laughing.

The door opened, and Angela stood looking down at the boys who now registered shock at her presence.

"You two young men seem to be having a good time. Why don't you come out and join the rest of the kids?"

Kenny and Johnny exchanged glances and then shook their heads.

"That's okay, Ma," said Johnny.

"There's plenty to eat, and I'm sure your cousin won't mind."

"Kenny and I are going to watch *Lost Horizon*."

"Oh, I always liked that movie."

"We're cool, Ma."

"Yeah, thanks, Mrs. Camacho. We're cool," said Kenny.

"Quit spying on your cousins and their friends. It's not polite."

Angela disappeared, leaving the bedroom door wide open. A pair of older boys stared at Johnny and Kenny.

"Come on," said Johnny.

He and Kenny brushed past the two teenagers as they headed to the kitchen. The living room was segregated, with most of the girls on one side and the boys on the other. A short kid with glasses was manning the phonograph. He threw on a record. The song was up tempo but was nothing any of the other kids had heard before.

"Who's that?" asked a tall, skinny kid wearing brown chords and a red and white checkered shirt.

"The Beatles," replied the kid with the glasses.

"Never heard of them," said the checkered shirt.

"They're from England. And way bigger than Elvis."

The checkered shirt kid waved him off. "You're nuts. Nobody's bigger than Elvis. Not even the Four Seasons are as big as Elvis."

The short kid shrugged his shoulders. "That's what my dad says. He owns two music stores, so he must know something."

"Well, these guys sure don't sound better than Elvis," said the kid in corduroy.

The short kid held up the record jacket. "I like their hair."

"They look like girls. These guys must be homos."

The short kid frowned. "The Beatles are cool."

The kid in corduroy shook his head and walked away.

The song ended. The short kid picked up the needle and placed another record on the turntable. Martha and the Vandellas sang *Dancing in the Street*. Some of the girls danced while the boys stood in groups talking and gawking.

Johnny and Kenny filled their plates and returned to the bedroom, shutting the door behind them.

"Oh cool," said Johnny, noticing the film that just started on the TV.

"Oh man, *Invasion of the Body Snatchers*. That movie is totally bitchin'," said Kenny.

The two thirteen-year-olds sat on the floor and chowed down as they watched the movie.

"This is way better than Letty's dumb party," said Kenny.

Johnny grinned. "No kidding."

Kenny ate a big bite of his enchilada. "New Year's is pretty cool."

"Yeah," agreed Johnny.

The two boys ate their food and enjoyed the movie, certain that theirs was by far the best party going on.

There was a knock at the front door, and Angela answered it. A man stood on the porch. He was dressed in green slacks and a paisley shirt with a brown scarf around his neck.

"Hi, I'm Terry Kelcher, Sophie's father.

"Please, come in," said Angela.

Terry stepped into the large living room. He chuckled at the site of a segregated room of teenagers. He looked at Angela. "My hat is off to you for having to courage to throw one of these."

Angela smiled. "It's nothing. It keeps Letty and the others off the street and out of trouble. Would you like something to eat? There's plenty in the kitchen."

"Oh no, thank you. I've just come to collect Sophie. We're driving out to the desert for a sunrise meditation."

Angela gave Terry a questioning look. "That's nice."

"There's a shaman out by the Spahn Ranch, Golden Eagle. He leads a meditation group."

"A shaman?"

Terry nodded. "Golden Eagle is a holy man. We haven't been yet. Some of the people I work with have gone to his services and recommended it. I think it's good for Sophie to be exposed to alternative concepts."

Angela nodded her head.

Terry caught himself. "I do go on. Sophie said you work for Desilu?"

"Yes."

"I'm A&R for Columbia Records." Terry spotted his daughter and waved her over.

Sophie was a short brunette with skinny legs. "Hi, Daddy."

"You have a good time?"

Sophie nodded her head. "Letty's aunt is the best cook, way better than ours."

Angela blushed. "I'm glad you liked it."

Letty came over and stood next to Angela. "Thanks for coming, Sophie."

"How late is this going?" asked Terry.

"Eleven. My aunt wants her beauty sleep," Letty replied with a sly smile.

Angela feigned shock. "Why you…"

Letty laughed.

"Thanks again," said Sophie. "Happy New Year."

Letty and Sophie hugged. "Happy New Year."

Angela wished Terry a safe journey and a Happy New Year and opened the door for them. The father and daughter walked down the drive to their car. Angela closed the door. Letty had returned to the girl's side of the living room and was chatting it up with friends. The boys were huddled in two groups talking about sports and cars. The short kid with the glasses continued to maintain the record player. Some band was singing something totally unintelligible as far as Angela was concerned. The only words she could make out were *Louie, Louie.* Angela shook her head and headed back into the kitchen.

An hour later, the kids had all gone home. Letty and Lucy cleaned up the kitchen and living room. Johnny and Kenny had fallen asleep on the floor in the bedroom. Angela covered them with blankets, turned off the TV, and closed the door.

Lucy had crawled into bed after finishing her work.

Angela turned on the TV in the living room and collapsed on the sofa. The *Tonight Show* came on.

"It's three minutes," Angela called to Letty.

The teenager finished washing the glasses and dashed into the living room, plopping down next to her aunt.

Johnny Carson was talking to Woody Allen.

"Who's that?" asked Letty.

"I don't know, some comedian. He isn't very funny."

"Looks like a creep," said Letty.

The show went to a remote camera outside. There was the countdown. The band played *Auld Lang Syne.* Outside, firecrackers blasted like pop guns in the night.

Angela and Letty hugged.

"Happy New Year, Auntie."

"Happy New Year, Letty."

Both women got teary and brushed their eyes, laughing.

"Thanks for the party, Auntie."

Angela hugged her niece close and kissed her forehead. "You deserved it, mija."

# 37

# *Death of an Eagle*

Dozens came to the desert for Golden Eagle's sunrise meditation. Golden Eagle, however, was a no show. Ezekiel refused to leave the Air Stream until Bernard showed up. He hadn't arrived. Around seven, a police cruiser drove down the dirt road. This got many of the congregation scrambling for their cars and driving off. A few dozen of the devout remained.

The cop parked his black and white and got out.

Ezekiel stepped out of the trailer. His hair was long with a red scarf wrapped around as a headband. He had a moustache and looked nothing like he did when he lived in L.A.

"Are you Golden Eagle?" asked the cop.

"Yes."

"Do you know a Bernard Radcliff?

"Why do you ask?"

The cop gave the compound the quick once over, then turned his attention back on Ezekiel. "He said you were some kind of shaman."

"Yes, I know Bernard."

"Your buddy is dead."

"When did this happen?" Ezekiel asked, shocked at the news.

"Some yahoo ran a red light and t-boned your friend's car last night. He asked me to come out here and tell you. Well, I did." The cop indicated to the compound with his forefinger. "This here is government land. Ya'll are trespassing. You can't be livin' out here."

The cop walked back to the black and white, got in, and drove away.

Ezekiel stood silent for a moment. The others looked at him as if waiting for an answer. Ezekiel entered the trailer, and a moment later he exited. A canteen and back-pack were slung over his left shoulder. He looked at the few remaining people.

"Peace."

Ezekiel walked off into the desert. Bernard had been his friend. They had tripped and meditated together, sometimes for days. Bernard helped build the collective. Ezekiel kept hiking and ate some mushrooms. He had a bad trip. His first. He laid on a rock for hours screaming and crying, trying to fight off the thousands of translucent neon reptiles that were attacking him and attempting to suck his oxygen away. Falcon did not come for him. Ezekiel was lost. The sun was high as he continued to fight the monsters. He shut his eyes and hoped they would go away.

The sun was much lower when Ezekiel finally opened his eyes. The rays shot white light that temporarily blinded him. He held up his hand and tried to focus. He saw a large, tangled tree with a body lying at the foot. It was his body at the foot of the tree. An eagle was perched on a branch and gazed at the body. Then the bird flew away, soaring high toward the sun.

Ezekiel rubbed his eyes. The tree and body had vanished along with the eagle. Ezekiel realized he had an epiphany. Bernard had called him a shaman. That didn't actually make him one. Everyone who came to the Inner Peace Collective wanted something. Bernard wanted to belong to something and helped ignite the idea that became the collective. Some people came for answers to problems they had. Some came to hide from society. Some people came for the drugs. They all looked to Golden Eagle for an answer. Ezekiel realized that was his mistake. He had no answers. Golden Eagle had to die.

Ezekiel returned to the collective late that afternoon. All but three stragglers had vacated the area, a woman, man, and a teenage girl. They hung out near the fire-pit. The man and woman smoked cigarettes and were talking. Ezekiel entered his trailer without a word to the others. The woman and man eyed the trailer.

"Should we ask him?" asked the man who was dressed in green slacks, a paisley shirt, and brown scarf.

The skinny blonde next to him shook her head. "We'd better wait and give him some space."

The teenager rolled her eyes. "I don't believe this. You take me away from Letty's party so we can drive out here for some meditation bullshit. The Shaman walks off, and we sit around all day so you can talk to this guy, and now you aren't sure you want to?" The girl threw her hands up in disgust.

"Sophie, calm down. Golden Eagle just lost a very good friend," said Terry.

"You are such a wennier, Dad," said Sophie.

The blonde took a drag from her cigarette and exhaled. "How long are you going to wait, Terry?"

Terry Kelcher frowned. "Can it, Amber. When I need your advice, I'll ask for it. Brian Wilson said Golden Eagle was the real deal. I've got Streisand coming in for a session next week." He rolled his eyes. "If I can get Golden Eagle to come to the recording sessions and lead a meditation group, it just might mellow things out."

"Jesus, Daddy, then just ask the guy." Sophie gestured to the surroundings. "I'm sure he could use the money."

Terry adjusted his scarf and took a step forward.

Suddenly, there was a loud explosion. The Air Stream went up in a ball of flames. The trio was knocked down by the concussion.

"What happened?" Terry sat up. Seeing the trailer engulfed in flames, he got to his feet and stared dumfounded at the burning Air Stream.

Sophie stood and brushed herself off. "Well, that settles that."

Amber got up and combed the bits of wood out of her hair. "What?"

"We can't stay here, Amber," Sophie replied matter-of-factly. "Golden Eagle just blew up his trailer and him in it. The cops will be crawling all over this place."

Terry realized his daughter was correct. "Yeah, we'd better get back to L.A."

The trio scrambled to the black Lincoln Continental and sped away.

Ezekiel marched into the desert. He had gotten his bedroll and a few belongings and slipped out the back window. He left the gas on the stove running and a lit cigarette on the counter. Chemistry did the rest. The Air Stream exploded into a glorious fireball that shot some twenty feet skyward. Ezekiel was two hundred yards out when it blew. The cops could come back. They would find nothing. There were three witnesses that saw the trailer explode. Golden Eagle was dead. Ezekiel smiled to himself as he trotted off into the brush. It was a New Year.

* * *

Patty Bono was dead. That was certain. Hagen's crew had come up with bupkis. They had located the vans, but not Patty's shooter. The phone call came at six New Year's Day. The boss wanted to see Hagen.

Frank had a modest home in Pacific Beach, a primarily working class neighborhood. James Hagen was ten minutes early. You didn't make the boss wait. Hagen was greeted at the door by Tony Spilotro, who showed him to the den and left the room. A minute later, Frank entered. He was a short man with gray hair and wore glasses. He gestured to a chair, and Hagen sat down.

"What happened, Jimmy?"

"I told you, Frank, Patty went down to make sure the shipment crossed the border. He gets a call that the vans made it and has dinner at Marechario's and then drives back to the warehouse with the vans."

Frank nodded his head. "We checked it out. Emilio's man called Patty at five. Both vans made it across."

"What about the drivers?"

"They're clean, according to Emilio. One of them was his cousin."

"There was a five minute window from when Emilio's drivers parked the vans until our guys picked them up. It has to be an inside operation."

Frank shot an icy look at Hagen. "What have you got?"

Hagen shifted his eyes. "Nothing. The vans were torched, and so were the bodies. We think whoever did it took the heroin and killed his accomplices. It's gotta be an inside job."

"What're you, fuckin' Sherlock Holmes?" Frank barked.

"I've got a guy in the coroner's office. As soon as—"

"You don't think I got my own fuckin' guy at the fuckin' coroner's office?" Frank interrupted, cutting Hagen off. "The stiffs had no ID, and there ain't nothin' left of them except some fuckin' burnt bones. Both were shot in the heart, one to the head, same as Patty. It was a pro. I tend to agree with you, Jimmy. It was an inside job." Frank fixed Hagen with the cold look of a shark about to devour its prey. "You've got twenty-four hours to fix this."

"It's a holiday. How am I supposed to fix it in twenty-four hours?"

"That's right, it's a fuckin' holiday. Everybody'll be home watching the games. Should be easy to track people down. Don't disappointment me, Jimmy."

Frank exited the den. Tony Spilotro appeared and escorted Hagen to the front door.

"Happy New Year, Jimmy."

Hagen drove back to L.A. and put through a call to Michael. The operator told him there was no answer at the number. He tried twice more throughout the day and got the same result. He placed a call to Cinecitta Studios around three in the afternoon and got the switchboard. The operator explained in broken English that yes, Signore McGuire was working at the studio, but that the studio was closed. Hagen hung up. Time was running out. He called his crew. Nobody knew nothing. Nothing from nothing was nothing. Hagen looked at his watch. It was nearly nine p.m. He went to the front desk and sent a telegram to Michael in care of Cinecitta Studios.

James Hagen returned to his room, packed a few items in a leather satchel, grabbed a brown leather attaché case, and left the room. Michael kept a cream Ford Galaxy in a lot behind the Egyptian Theater. He took the stairs and went out the rear exit. Hagen kept to the alley as he made his way down the three blocks to the parking lot. He paid the attendant and got the car keys.

Hagen opened the trunk and lifted the rubber matt covering the wheel well. A brown attaché case like the other sat where he had left it. Hagen popped the locks and opened it just a crack. Stacks of one hundred dollars bills filled the case. Hagen closed the case and set its twin next to it. He covered them with the rubber matt and shut the trunk.

Hagen traveled west on Sunset, then south on La Brea, and then west again out Venice Blvd. He took PCH north and stopped at the site of the El Capitan. The place was owned by an order of priests. Hagen pulled into the parking lot. He sat in his car and looked at the former nightclub. It had been forty years since the gin flowed free and the roulette tables spun while the band played hot jazz in the building. Now it was a book repository. Hagen chuckled to himself. He opened the satchel sitting on the seat next to him. He removed an Arizona driver's license. It had his photo with the name 'James White' with a Phoenix address. He removed James Hagen's California driver's license from his wallet and replaced it with James White's Arizona license. He tore up the old license and let the pieces fly out the window with the evening breeze.

"So long, Mr. Hagen," said Jimmy Grazzi.

He started the Ford up and drove north. Jimmy Grazzi had become James Hagen, who had now become James White, Phoenix realtor. The car was registered to a shell company and wouldn't draw much interest.

The dice had come up snake-eyes for Jimmy with Patty Bono getting whacked and the shipment gone. Jimmy didn't have much of a back-up plan besides a cold car and trunk full of cash. He did know that coming up with nothing for Frank was unacceptable. He had two options. Face Frank's wrath, or run. Jimmy Grazzi ran.

# 38

# *La Dolce Vita*

Italy had been a breath of fresh air for Michael. His take from the second shipment had allowed him to finance *Strappare Grande*. The film opened on New Year's Day and was a hit. The Italians and French loved Michael's use of real locations and realistic lighting. He used the locations because they were cheaper than building sets. Michael used whatever lighting was available in order to keep the budget down. The shadows helped cover up the cheap sets he did use. Shooting without sound and looping it in post was a different process, but it allowed for dialogue flubs without a retake. The film and living expenses had burned through much of his nest egg.

Michael had rolled the dice and came up with sevens. He needed the film to make money. Michael was the talk of European cinema that holiday. He had spent Christmas with Sergio and his family. They had become fast friends, even though neither could speak the other's language very well.

Michael went to Paris the day after New Year's. He met fellow American ex-patriot, Jules Dassin. The director showed Michael a three-hour cut of *Topkapi*. Over dinner at a small restaurant in the Left Banke, Michael and Jules discussed the cuts the film needed.

"How do you like Europe?" Jules asked.

"It isn't Royal or Warner's, but they leave you alone."

Jules smiled and nodded his head. "Financing your own film was a bit risky. My hat is off to you."

"Look how long it took you to get this film, Jules. The bastards back home would just as soon see us dead."

Jules chuckled. "I won't argue that point, my friend. So, what's next, now that you're the toast of Europe?"

Michael took a sip of his water and set the glass down. "I've got a meeting with Sam Bronston next week."

Jules frowned. "I hear Sam is hurting financially. He's making some circus film with John Wayne that isn't going too well."

"I need outside financing for my project."

"What is it?"

"*Nanjing*. It's based on the life of someone I knew, or I should say my grandfather knew. A woman who came to the Golden Mountain as a child, returned home to build a business, and lost everything when the Japs invaded Nanjing. She escaped, returned stateside and aided the army with her knowledge of the Japanese positions."

Jules was quiet for a moment. "Sounds like a great story, but the studios aren't going to make a picture that's sympathetic to the Chinese. There's a Cold War going on. You and I are victims of that war."

Michael stood up. "Thank you for showing me your film, Jules."

Jules was taken aback by his friend's abrupt change of behavior. "Michael, please sit down."

Michael put on his overcoat. "Never tell an Irishman he's a victim of anything, Jules."

"Michael, it was meant as an observation of our common predicament. The studios fucked us. We got blacklisted."

"Just because some studio head won't hire you, doesn't make you a fucking victim, Jules. You fight back and do whatever it takes to make your film."

Michael tipped his hat and exited the restaurant. It started to rain. He hailed a cab. Michael brooded over Jules's remarks. Sean McGuire had taught his grandson years ago that a victim was a man who was wronged and did nothing about his situation. The players back home didn't want Michael to play? So be it. He took his game elsewhere and proved them wrong. Michael smiled to himself. *Strappare Grande* was a hit. He would find the money somehow for *Nanjing*. Michael McGuire was back.

The cab passed the Eiffel Tower. Lit up in the rain, it was a thing of beauty. Pedestrians dashed inside doorways. Michael sat back in the cab. It was the beginning of a New Year. He had beaten the odds.

Michael returned to Italy two days later. He had his meeting with Sam Bronston. Sam wasn't interested in *Nanjing* and wanted Michael to direct a sword and sandal epic. Michael declined. He shopped his project around, but found even in Europe there was little interest in a story with a female Chinese lead. Carlo Ponti suggested Michael take the project to England. David Lean had done well with *Bridge on the River Kawi*. Michael thanked Carlo and returned to his office at Cinecitta.

A telegram was sitting on his desk. It had taken nearly a week for Hagen's telegram to finally reach Michael.

Michael opened the envelope the message was brief, but direct. *I slipped, Joey.* Michael reacted as if the wind had just been knocked out of him and slowly sat down. He reread the message. It was a line from *Blind Alley*, one of Michael's early pictures. Two boys grow up poor. While stealing a crate from the back of a truck, Bobby slipped, got caught and sent to the reformatory, which set him on a life of crime. Joey gets away and ends up becoming a baseball coach. When their paths cross years later, the gangster tells his friend, "I slipped, Joey," to explain why he ended up a criminal.

It was Michael and Jimmy's code. If either was in trouble, they sent word with that line. Jimmy needed help. Michael knew he couldn't call. The telegram was a week old. Jimmy could be anywhere. Michael did know someone who knew someone who knew people that could help him. He slipped the telegram in his pocket and picked up the telephone.

# 39

# *The Drop*

Dominic Torelli walked into the Ace of Hearts and liked what he saw. Torelli was a *capo* for the Bonanno family. He was well dressed, and he came alone to check the place out.

Dominic sat down at the bar and ordered a scotch neat. He didn't miss a thing. The bartender poured freehand, and it was a perfect shot. His eyes scanned the room. It was a Wednesday night, and all the black-jack tables were in operation and nearly devoid of tourists. These were local folks with a penchant for gambling. Just the type of spot Dominic Torelli was looking for.

Dominic held out a business card to the bartender. "Please give this to the owner and tell her I'd like a minute of her time."

Blaine Richards had worked in Nevada clubs, joints, and casinos long enough to spot a made guy, even one dressed in a Bond Street suit. He took the card and exited through a door behind the bar. That told Torelli access to the boss's office was behind the bar. Dominic studied the area and realized the large aquarium behind the bar must be acting as a one-way mirror in the boss's office. From that position, the entire room could be viewed in privacy without the gamblers knowing they were being watched. Smart.

The bartender returned and motioned for Dominic to follow him. Della's office was well appointed but understated. Della stood when Blaine escorted the crime boss inside.

"Thank you, Blaine."

The bartender exited the room, closing the door behind him.

Della smiled and gestured to a cream-colored stuffed chair. "Please have a seat, Mr. Torelli."

Dominic noticed he had been correct. The aquarium was a one-way mirror from which Della could see the entire room. "Please, call me, Dom," he said, taking a seat.

"To what do I owe this pleasure?" Della asked.

"I'll get right to the point, Miss Rio. I like your place."

"So, do I. It's not for sale," Della replied.

Dominic smiled. "I don't want to buy your establishment. I merely want to use it, and for that use, you will be well compensated."

Della grinned back slyly. "And what am I to be well compensated for?"

"My business partners would use you club as a drop. We would leave money from our other business ventures here for safekeeping until it could be picked up later by one of our associates, usually within twenty-four hours. For that, you would be paid five grand a month. That's money off the books."

Della met Dominic's gaze with a cool look. "I'll take four points on the package you want to leave with me."

Dominic chuckled, "I'm sorry, but that is not possible."

Della folded her hands and looked directly at Dominic. "Mr. Torelli, you need my club as a drop. That is because it is located outside of the city, just off the main highway. It is also won't raise many eyebrows with the Feds or the local riff raff."

"Half a point," said Dominic.

"One and a half."

Dominic studied Della. "I heard you were a tough broad. Fine, I accept." He extended his hand, and Della shook it.

Victor was not happy when he heard that Della had made the deal.

"What were you thinking? They suspect us of hitting Hagen's drug operation," Victor cautioned.

They were alone in Della's office later that day. She shot Victor an icy look. "My house, my rules."

"Looks like it's Dominic Torelli's house."

Della raised a hand but then regained her composure. "If they suspected you killed one of their people, they would not offer us a deal. They would simply kill us and take what they want. They need the Ace, and they need me. If the place changes ownership, it will have to go through escrow. That means the Gaming Commission and new regs. They don't want that."

"I hope you're right." Victor replied before storming out of the office.

Della let him go. She realized the pressure was getting to him. She had not said a word about the fact that James Hagen had dropped off the map. He was on the run. Della knew as soon as Hagen popped up, he would be gunned down. The mob didn't take kindly to those who crossed them. Victor had performed well, making it appear that Hagen was the person behind the hit on Bono and the theft of the vans.

Hagen wasn't the problem any longer. Victor was. Della sadly realized that he was now a liability. That was unacceptable. Something needed to be done about Victor.

# 40

# *Ed Sullivan*

Michael met the man in a small café. A friend of Ennio Morricone had put Michael in touch with him. Ennio had once mentioned that he knew a flautist whose father was connected. Michael reached out to the composer through Sergio. He explained his need and the necessity for delicacy. Ennio made a call. Two days later, Ennio called Michael and told him where to meet the man.

It was a cool evening. Michael had been waiting for about ten minutes when a slender man in a brown suit and Fedora walked up and took a seat at the table. He was clean shaven and appeared to be in his sixties.

"I liked your westerns," said the man.

Michael grinned. "Thank you."

"What do you need?" asked the man.

"I have a friend I'm trying to locate. His name is Jimmy Grazzi. He also goes by James Hagen. Something has happened to him. I need to find out what and where he is."

"This friend, he works with friends of ours?"

"Yes."

"You would prefer that these friends were not aware of your inquiry?"

"Yes."

The man stood. "I will be in touch."

Michael was surprised. "That's it?"

The man looked at Michael. "You could make another western." With that, he tipped his hat and walked away.

Michael had been too preoccupied to notice the inside of the café had filled to near capacity. He finished his espresso, left some coins on the table, and walked over to a man in his twenties who was craning to see into the café through a window outside.

Michael tapped the young man on the shoulder. "What's going on?"

The man looked at Michael. "It's Ed Sullivan. The Beatles are on his show tonight. My girlfriend is crazy about them."

"Where's your girlfriend?"

The young man made a sad face and pointed inside the packed café.

"Good luck." Michael tipped his hat and walked down the boulevard.

* * *

Ezekiel had found an area with thick brush in the back country and built a hut, keeping mostly to himself. He would work at the ranch and help with the horse rentals when he needed money. Old man Spahn offered Ezekiel a cabin at the ranch in exchange for work. Ezekiel thanked him but turned him down. He preferred to live away from people.

The headaches had returned. The mushrooms offered some relief. Sometimes Ezekiel would trip for days in order to rid himself of the migraine. Life was simple. He had a lantern, sleeping bag, camping stove, and cooler. Most of his food, he caught or scavenged from the trash.

Ezekiel could not understand why Bernard had to die. He was his friend. Ezekiel had lost his wife. He was ashamed to face his children and sister. After Bernard died, Ezekiel felt adrift and sought solace in the wilds of Los Angeles County. Occasionally some hiker might come upon Ezekiel. Depending on his frame of mind, Ezekiel would either flee like a deer or engage the stranger and barter for something he had on his person. Stories of a wild holy man drifted down to Los Angeles. They were not taken seriously by most and relegated to the urban legends file.

Old man Spahn took sick, and Ezekiel worked and stayed on the ranch while the rancher recovered. Ezekiel would have preferred to remain out in the wild, but he wanted to help out the old man. Living in the wild, Ezekiel was rather lax on hygiene. His unkempt appearance was considered "colorful" by old man Spahn, as long as Ezekiel was down-wind. Ezekiel spent most of his time caring for the horses. Working meant Ezekiel couldn't trip, so he ate aspirin to stave off the headaches. He ate aspirin by the boatload, sometimes dry chewing four or five tablets at a time.

Ezekiel checked his knapsack after work that Sunday. The day had been slow, with only a few tourists coming out to ride the horses. He was down to just two aspirins. His head throbbed. Ezekiel was glad he would be leaving the ranch in the morning. He could return to his hut and enjoy some real relief the mushrooms offered. He popped the lid and gobbled down the last two pills dry. Ezekiel decided he would hitch a ride into town and pick up another bottle to get him through the night.

Don Shea, one of the workers on the ranch, gave Ezekiel a ride into town. The short man had insisted Ezekiel shower before he would allow him inside his car. The drugstore was just about to close when they drove up. Ezekiel hurried in and purchased a bottle of Excedrin Extra Strength aspirin and jumped back inside the car.

"Let's got get a drink," said Don.

"I don't know. I don't do so well with alcohol."

Don waved Ezekiel off and headed down the street. "It's Sunday, time to take it easy, brother."

The Black Sheep Tavern sat about a mile out of town. Don pulled into the parking lot and got out. He turned to Ezekiel and raised a brow. "You coming?"

Ezekiel sat for a moment and then reluctantly followed Don Shea into the bar.

The Black Sheep Tavern was a small roadhouse that catered to bikers and locals who weren't picky about the type of liquor they drank. The place was poorly lit, had a pool table with a tear in the felt, and a jukebox. It wasn't a busy night. Don ambled up to the bar. The black and white TV behind the bar was on.

"A Miller High Life and a shot of tequila for me and my friend."

Ezekiel shook his head. "That's okay. I'll just have a water, thank you."

The bartender quickly placed the beer and shot in front of Don. He placed a plastic glass with water in front of Ezekiel. "Water for Gabby Hayes."

Gabby Hayes was an actor who frequently appeared in Roy Rogers westerns. Ezekiel hated Roy Rogers westerns. He was a John Wayne man. He frowned as he picked up the glass, took a sip, and set it down.

"I'll be outside." Ezekiel marched out of the bar.

Don shrugged. He downed the shot, and took a pull on his beer.

Ezekiel paced back and forth outside. He popped open the bottle of aspirin and took a couple. The pills crunched between his teeth as he dry-swallowed them. Ezekiel noticed the flickering of a television coming through the window of a house just down the road. He shuffled over to the house. A family was sitting on a couch watching TV. The husband had his arm around the shoulder of his wife. A young boy sat on a chair. A teenage girl sat on the sofa next to her father.

Ezekiel stood outside and watched through the picture window. A band was on the TV. They had long hair and wore matching suits. The audience was going wild. Ezekiel couldn't hear the music. The boy turned and saw Ezekiel. The man suddenly jumped up. The woman quickly pulled the drapes shut. Ezekiel hobbled away as fast as he could.

The man raced outside. He picked up a rock and threw it at Ezekiel. "Get the hell outta here!"

The rock hit Ezekiel in the back of the head. He fell. Another rock hit him in the ribs. The man shouted profanities. Ezekiel struggled to get to his feet and hurried away as quickly as he was able to. He felt the back of his head. There was blood on his hand. It was a long walk back to the ranch, but Ezekiel wasn't going to wait for Don.

An hour later and miles down the road, Don spotted Ezekiel. He pulled over and honked his horn. Ezekiel got in the car and closed the door.

"I thought you were going to wait outside," said Miguel.

Ezekiel shrugged absently. "I got tired."

"And you were going to walk all the way back to the ranch?"

Ezekiel didn't answer.

Don chuckled. "Man, you should've stuck around. Ed Sullivan had the Beatles on his show."

Ezekiel mumbled something. He just wanted to get back to the ranch and soak his head in cold water and get some sleep. The image of the family reminded him of his own. He had failed as a father and as a husband. He wished he had some peyote so he could find Falcon and fly with him. Ezekiel leaned his head against the window and counted the fence posts as the car rumbled up the hill towards the ranch.

# 41

# *The Rehearsal*

Cosmo watched as Letty played the Brahms concerto beautifully. They were in the band room. Cosmo saw promise in the girl and offered to tutor her during seventh period. Letty had transferred to Cosmo's class the previous semester. She had been playing the piano for two years and was able to play stride like nobody's business. Cosmo marveled at the arbitrariness upon which art was bestowed. He thought Letty was a fine candidate for the district piano competition and offered to mentor her. Letty finished with a flourish and then broke into *Roll Over Beethoven*.

"All right, all right," said Cosmo.

Letty stopped playing, giving him a nervous look.

"That was good, but you need to put more emotion into your playing. You were executing the piece instead of playing it," said Cosmo.

Letty sighed loudly, "This is so boring."

Cosmo hid a smirk that threatened to creep across his lips. "It's what you need to play if you want to win this competition."

"Boring."

He gave Letty a pat on the shoulder. "I hear you, girl. Unfortunately, the people who judge these things want to hear music by dead white men, preferably from Germany and Austria. Let's try it one more time."

Letty frowned and then began playing the piece again. She made faces of extreme emotion whenever she reached a place in the music where it would fit. Her playing was superior. When she finished, she gave Cosmo a big grin.

"Very good, but leave the pantomime at the door." Cosmo glanced at the clock on the classroom wall. "It's four o'clock. Time to rock, Letty. It's Friday. Go home and enjoy the weekend."

Letty gave Cosmo a sheepish look as she removed a sheet of music from her folder and set it on the stand. "I was wondering if you would give me your opinion on something."

"Something you wrote?"

Letty smiled and then played a soulful intro before heading into the first verse of the song.

*Sitting by the window, watching the rain. It makes me remember all the pain you've put me through. You were a dog. You were a cur. I was the kitten you made purr...*

Letty rocked, she swayed, she was lost in the music.

Cosmo watched in astonishment.

Letty continued for two more verses. When she finished, she looked at Cosmo.

"You wrote that?" Cosmo asked, not bothering to hide his astonishment.

Letty grinned and nodded her head.

Cosmo looked at the chart and then at Letty. "How old are you?"

"Seventeen."

Cosmo studied Letty. "Girl, you have skills. How you come to write something like this? There's a lot of grown-up sadness in this song."

Letty looked at Cosmo. "My dad left us when I was a kid. He got beat up by the police and had mental issues. My mom was murdered two years ago. The cops never found the guy who did it."

Cosmo struggled to keep a straight face. "My Lord, girl."

Letty smiled. "My aunt takes care of me. She's the one who got me the piano lessons after Mommy died. She thought it would help me focus on something positive."

Cosmo gathered up some papers, placed them in his briefcase, and snapped it shut.

"Your aunt was right. You have a gift, Letty."

Letty gathered up her things and walked out of the classroom with Cosmo.

"What do you want to do after you graduate?" Cosmo asked as they walked to the parking lot.

Letty shook her head. "I don't know. I'd like to play in a band like you did, Mr. Turner."

Cosmo laughed sadly. "Set your goals a bit higher, Letty. You're a smart girl.""

Letty grinned, embarrassed. "Thanks. Have a nice weekend, Mr. Turner."

Letty turned and ran to catch the bus that had just pulled up to the stop.

Cosmo got in his car and drove home. He was glad it was Friday.

# 42

# *The Itch*

Della Rio had an itch. It was an itch she couldn't scratch. Victor had killed Patty Bono and destroyed James Hagen's drug business. Hagen had gotten away. The mob hadn't found him. It had been months since anyone had seen Hagen. This made Della uncomfortable. That meant Hagen had time to make inquiries himself. That kind of activity could prove fatal for Della.

Business was doing fine. The drop proved to be profitable. Della was clearing ten grand a week at that alone. She continued to kick twenty-five percent of her place to the mob. Life was good. Della didn't need Hagen crawling from under some rock and ruining everything.

Della didn't ask Victor about Hagen. Their relationship had changed. A détente had settled in since Patty Bono's murder. Victor did his thing at the club, but he kept his distance. He and Della didn't go for coffee at Denny's at 2 a.m. anymore. Victor kept all outside business away from the club and Della. He had seriously compartmentalized. Finding Hagen would have to be on Della's watch. If she asked Victor, it could spook him, and that wouldn't be good for business. Della decided to come at the problem of Victor and Hagen from a different angle.

Della made a call to Brother Kenneth. Brother Kenneth had grown up on the streets of Los Angeles. He was a self-educated man who could discuss the differences between Nietzsche and Sartre and slit a man's throat without hesitation when he was paid to do it. Brother Kenneth in an earlier life was Kenny Roberts of the *Rolling 60's* gang. He shot a rival gang member and did seven years. He discovered Yahweh and Islam in prison. When he was paroled, he renamed himself Brother Kenneth and resumed a life of crime. Prison had educated Brother Kenneth. He dressed conservatively like the Brothers of Islam, and would kill, but solely for profit.

Brother Kenneth had developed connections in prison. The connections put him to work. Brother Kenneth was lethal. He rarely traveled out of state. He knew the streets and neighborhoods of Los Angeles better than Rand McNally. Once Brother Kenneth set his sights on a target, that target was got.

Della had crossed paths with Brother Kenneth when he vacationed in Nevada. He had stopped for gas at the Ace and ended up having dinner with Della. The hitman liked the lady. He gave her his number and told her to call him if she ever required *special services*. Della had always carried her own water and handled her business. This one was too close to home and required the services and finesse of a man like Brother Kenneth.

Victor knew Della was up to something. She never said a word about Hagen's disappearance. The guy was like a ghost. Hagen was in L.A., and then he was gone. Victor couldn't put the word out on him on the street; people would want to know what his interest was in the man.

So, Victor decided to come at his problem from a different direction. He got every bit of info he could on Cinnamon Carlyle. He went to L.A. and spent hours in the library reading old newspapers. Victor discovered she had been a nightclub singer who had disappeared from the scene in 1943.

He read everything he could find in the papers about Hagen. He knew Hagen owned a radio station. Victor found an article about XELA among the newspaper archives. The article listed the disc jockeys working at the station at the time and their shifts. A quick reference with a Los Angeles and San Diego phonebook directory eliminated four of the seven listed in the piece. A call to San Diego got him a woman who told him that Screamin' Jim was now Happy Jim on a station in Denver and that if Victor should locate the S.O.B. he should tell Happy Jim that he was five months late on his child support. On the second call, Victor was informed the man sought had died the previous winter.

That now left only one Los Angeles number.

That Saturday morning, Cosmo got up early. He washed his car and drove to the nursery. He was putting in a new bed of flowers in the front yard when the phone rang.

He let it ring. It was Saturday, and he was busy in his garden. He was digging a hole for a new rose bush when the phone rang again. Cosmo continued to ignore the call. He found it ironic how for years he had chased gigs and skirts every moment of his waking day. Now he'd rather work in his garden. The house was nearly paid off. Cosmo had used his payola cash to pay down the mortgage. He had Nola, and she had a decent job as a secretary at Metropolitan Life downtown. Life was good.

Cosmo placed the rosebush in the hole and filled it with potting soil and dirt, finally packing it down with his shovel. The phone stopped ringing.

Nola drove up in her little green '60 Falcon. She got out and opened the trunk. Cosmo set the shovel down and walked over to Nola and gave her a big hug.

"Hey, baby."

Nola kissed Cosmo on the cheek. "Want to give me a hand with the groceries?"

Nola picked up a bag. Cosmo picked up two. They carried them into the house and set them down on the kitchen counter.

"You need my help?" Cosmo asked.

Nola was already putting up the groceries. "No, I can handle this. Go on and finish up with your flowers."

Cosmo smiled and headed outside. He dug another hole for a bed of carnations. They were his mother's favorite flower. She said they reminded her of snowballs. The phone rang again.

"Hey, Nola, can you get that?" Cosmo called out.

Nola walked over and answered the phone in the kitchen.

"Hello?"

"May I speak to Cosmo?" said a man's voice.

"May I ask who's calling?"

"Please, I would like to speak to Cosmo."

Nola cupped the receiver and called out, "Cosmo, some man wants to talk to you."

Cosmo frowned. He wanted to finish up getting the flowers in. "Get his number."

Nola lifted the receiver back to her ear. "Could I please have your number?"

"I'll call back in one hour. Please tell him Cinnamon Carlyle needs his help."

The line went dead.

Nola relayed the message to Cosmo when he came in the house a few minutes later. She did not inquire as to who Cinnamon Carlyle was or the purpose of the call. Nola trusted Cosmo. He thanked her for the information and said little else, only inquiring what restaurant Nola wanted to dine at that evening.

The phone rang an hour later. Cosmo answered.

"Hello?"

"Cosmo Turner?"

"Speaking."

"Cinnamon is in need of your help."

"What type of help?"

"Cinnamon needs to reach James Hagen. I understand you once worked for him at XELA. I was wondering if you might be able to assist me in locating Mr. Hagen?"

"Please tell Miss Carlyle that I'm sorry. I haven't been in touch with Mr. Hagen in years. I have no idea of his whereabouts or how to get in touch with him."

"Mr. Hagen had a partner, a Michael McGuire. Would you happen to know how I might reach him?"

That confirmed that Nicole Sullivan was alive. Obviously, she had briefed the caller on Cosmo's involvement with her, but hadn't used her real name.

"I'm sorry, Mr..."

"Smith. Let's just say I watch out for Miss Carlyle's interests."

"Well, Mr. Smith. I'm sorry but I haven't had any contact with Mr. McGuire either in years. Please give Miss Carlyle my regards and let her know I am no longer a source for information or interested in her business."

Cosmo hung up the phone. He slowly removed his hand from the receiver. It wasn't shaking. Nola walked into the den where Cosmo had taken the call. He looked up at the woman standing in the doorway.

"I know you have a past, being a player and all. I just have one question. Are you in any trouble?"

"No."

Nola walked over to the chair where Cosmo was sitting and sat down in his lap and kissed him.

Cosmo was silent for a moment and then said, "You are correct, Nola. I have a past and was mixed up with people who didn't always walk a straight line. I cut corners, too. The man these folks are looking for is the type that if he don't want to be found, there's a reason. I'm not gonna get up in the man's business. Now where do you want to eat tonight?"

Nola smiled. She hugged Cosmo and kissed him long and hard. "I love you, baby."

\* \* \*

Brother Kenneth sat in the passenger seat of the white Ford. Marvin Gilmore, a very large black man with a clean-shaven head, sat behind the wheel. They watched Victor slam the phone down. They were set up on a corner off of Western. The payphone Victor had made his call from was outside a TV repair shop on Western. Marvin turned and looked at Brother Kenneth.

"What you want to do?"

Brother Kenneth kept his gaze on Victor. "Let's give him some rope. See where the man takes us."

Victor got in his Chevy and drove off. Marvin put the Ford into gear and followed.

# *43*

# *Arrivederci Roma*

Ennio called Michael and told him to be at the same café at six. Michael arrived ten minutes early and took a seat. The sun was setting, and the sky was a mix of purple, orange, and red. The dinner crowd hadn't arrived yet. The man walked up and took a seat across from Michael's Neither said a word until the man ordered his espresso and the waiter walked back inside the cafe.

"Your friend has disappeared." said the man.

"What do you mean?" asked Michael.

"Our friends in America tell us that one of their people was murdered, and they believe your friend was responsible."

The waiter returned with the espresso. He set the cup and saucer down and departed.

"Do they have proof?"

The man's expression turned serious. "You know as well as I do, in that business, proof is often hard to obtain."

"How long has he been missing?"

The man shrugged his shoulders, "Two, three months."

"Do you have any information that might be useful in locating my friend?"

The man took a sip of his espresso and set the cup down. "Your friend is not in any of the cities he stayed in when your government was seeking him. He is not in Kansas, Cleveland, New Orleans, or New York either."

Michael gave the man a questioning look.

"Trust me on this. He has most likely left the country. It would be the smart move." The man shrugged his shoulders. "He will turn up one day. Or not."

"I know Jimmy. He was crazy, but not that crazy. This was supposed to be his final stake."

"Who knows? Some men get greedy."

"Jimmy isn't stupid."

The man allowed a slight smile to slip across his lips. "I admire your loyalty. That is hard to come by."

"We fought in the trenches in the war."

The man arched an eyebrow.

"The first one," said Michael.

The man nodded his head. "Ah-h-h, that explains it. I will give you my opinion on the matter, for what it's worth. If you friend remained, he most likely is still in California. A man on the run will stay where he knows the terrain and offers him a quick escape. California does both. I could be wrong, but I doubt it."

Michael looked hard at the man sitting at the next table. "Did you share your thoughts with the people you talked to?"

"No."

"Why are you doing this?"

"A friend of yours asked a friend of mine to do this favor for you. I hope I was able to."

Michael's expression warmed. "Yes."

"Good. Good luck then." The man stood and tossed some coins on the table. "My thoughts." He offered a friendly smile. "Those were strictly for you."

Michael gave a nod. "Thank you."

"Others will come to the same conclusion eventually. Arrivederci."

The man tipped his hat and walked away. The waiter came over and asked Michael if he wanted anything. Michael shook his head. When he looked down the boulevard again, the man was gone.

# 44

# *The Haight*

Jimmy Grazzi looked out the window of his room in a Haight Ashbury tenement. When he ran, he had a new identity as James White from Phoenix. He didn't have a new face like before, though. Jimmy grew a beard and let his hair grow long. He had tried to reach Michael but wasn't successful. Jimmy knew if he showed his face in any of the places where he hid from the Feds, he'd be found. He knew it was the smart move to stay out of major cities.

San Francisco was different. Jimmy Grazzi was an unknown in the city. He also knew Michael's name carried certain weight in the city because of his grandfather, Sean. Jimmy initially hid out inland around Solvang. He had stayed in roadside motels, changing residence every few days or so. That quickly got old. Jimmy needed a place where he could move around and not be easily spotted. That meant a big city. San Francisco was the best option.

Jimmy smiled to himself as he watched kids panhandling in the street below. People in the neighborhood thought he was a professor or a writer. Jimmy did nothing to discourage such notions. He kept to himself and primarily ventured out in the evenings. Even then, Jimmy was careful to leave a torn matchbook in the door jam, as a precaution to warn him if anyone had entered his room while he was away. It had come to this, sixty-eight years old, on the run with a case full of cash and little to spend it on.

Jimmy had first checked into the Cartwright Hotel when he hit town, but after a few days there, he thought it better to find less conspicuous digs. He found a decent room that served his needs in the Haight.

The denizens of the district were working class and artists. People came and went, so a newcomer didn't stand out.

Jimmy bought a second suitcase and divided the money up. He stashed one case in a locker at the bus station and kept the other in his room. He wrapped a chain around it and padlocked the case to the floor in the closet. It wasn't theft proof, but it would deter most. Jimmy would occasionally venture out in the morning. It was generally just to run to the corner market or grab an espresso at the coffeehouse across the street. He could keep an eye on his building while he enjoyed a morning coffee and read the *Examiner*.

Jimmy wished he could talk to Michael. He would have a plan. Michael always had a plan. Jimmy thought it too risky to attempt contacting him after the first telegraph failed. He didn't want any of his dirt affecting Michael's life in Italy.

He decided to try and reach Michael in a different manner. He knew Cosmo lived in Los Angeles, so he found Cosmo's address in the phone book and sent him a post card with the picture of Mark Twain. On the back was the message, *M: Coldest summer, Joey. belle vie, rank, division, horseman, tower, church, tag, decimal, precarious, much. Out.*

It was addressed to Cosmo. Jimmy took the train to Sacramento, mailed it from there, and returned on the next train. He knew the message would mean nothing to Cosmo, but he hoped that Turner was in contact with Michael. Michael would understand the message.

# 45

# *The Recital*

Letty walked out onto the stage of the Hollywood Palladium as cool as an autumn breeze and nailed the Brahms concerto. She played flawlessly.

Cosmo sat in the first row, watching his student execute the piece like it was no more difficult than playing scales. Angela, Johnny, and Lucy were seated in the tenth row. Johnny was bored. Lucy sat quietly. Angela was enthralled. She turned her head and saw what looked like a homeless man standing in the doorway. He had long, scraggily hair and a beard. There was something familiar about him. Angela turned her attention back to Letty. When she looked back, the man was gone.

The performance received a standing ovation. Cosmo leaned close to Nola and whispered, "The gods touched that girl."

Letty was the last to perform that day. The other students lined up with her on stage. Harold Griffin, the District Head, came out and applauded the students as he walked over to the podium on the far-right side.

"I would like to thank each and every one of these fine students for sharing their talent with us today," said Griffin proudly.

The audience resumed their seats. Griffin looked at the table of judges sitting in front of the stage. A man handed him an envelope.

"In third place is…" The superintendent opened the envelope. "Alan Drexel from Marshall High School."

There were shouts and hoorahs from members of the audience, along with the applause.

"Second place is Carol Hasaki from Santa Monica High School."

Carol took her place next to Allan as the applause continued.

"And this year's winner of the Los Angeles Unified School District's Musical Competition and the recipient of a five-hundred-dollar scholarship...is Letica Camacho of Hollywood High School!" Griffin announced enthusiastically.

Letty smiled big, wiping the happy tears from her face.

Angela, Lucy, and Johnny stood up and applauded. Angela mouthed, "I love you *mija*."

\* \* \*

Brother Kenneth and Marvin were set up in the alley off of Wilton watching Victor walk up to Cosmo's house. He had trailed the teacher daily after he made his call and Cosmo turned him down.

Victor took out a set of picks and jimmied the lock on the front door. He was inside just as if he had a set of keys.

"What has that boy got going with some music teacher? We done trailed him and the teacher for the last three days." asked Marvin.

Brother Kenneth never took his eyes off the house. "Patience, Marvin, obviously Mr. Vega believes this Cosmo Turner must know something he is interested in. Della was a little shy on details. She asked us to watch Vega and report back to her. That is what we are doing."

Victor carefully went through the drawers and cupboards. He didn't want to give Cosmo any reason to believe his house had been broken into. If the teacher was in contact with Hagen, a break-in might cause Cosmo to alert him or shut down contact. Victor found Hagen's postcard on Cosmo's desk in the den. He picked up the card, turned it over, and studied the message. He looked at the photo of Twain on the front and then read the message again.

Victor set the card down. He grabbed a pencil and copied the message on the notepad on the desk. He tore off the sheet of paper and slipped it in his pocket. He quickly tossed the rest of the house, paying close attention to the phone bill sitting on the kitchen table. No long distance charges. Nothing out of the ordinary.

Victor checked his watch. Twenty minutes in and he hadn't come up with anything besides the postcard with an odd message. Victor quietly walked out the front door as if nothing was amiss and got into his car.

"What the fuck?" said Marvin. "The guy was in there for twenty minutes and doesn't come out with a fucking thing?"

"Our boy is searching for something. He believes Mr. Turner is the key." Brother Kenneth gestured for Marvin to follow Victor's car. "We shall continue to follow Mr. Vega and report to Miss Rio."

Marvin sighed, threw the car into gear, and kept two cars between them as they followed the Chevy.

* * *

Ezekiel stood across the street from the Palladium. Don had come in to Los Angeles to do some business. Victor tagged along. Don parked the car on Sunset and told Victor he'd be back in an hour. Ezekiel wandered over to Wallach's Music City. He was surprised by the widow display showing the Rolling Stones' latest album. Ezekiel thought they looked scary. He walked around to the front of the store and watched the people in the listening booths. A salesman came out and told Ezekiel he was disturbing the customers and would call the police if he didn't leave. Ezekiel moved on.

He crossed the street and walked over to the Palladium. He could hear music coming from the auditorium. Ezekiel didn't see anyone taking tickets, so he ventured inside. A young lady was at the piano playing. Ezekiel didn't know the piece of music, but he instantly recognized it was Letty up on stage. He watched as she played the concerto, amazed at her ability and how she had grown. Angela turned around and looked back at him. He saw Lucy and Johnny were with her.

Ezekiel took a step back. As soon as Angela turned and faced the stage again, he made a hasty exit from the auditorium.

Ezekiel paced back in forth. He wished Don would show up. Coming to Los Angeles had been a bad idea. Ezekiel had only come along because Don didn't care to make the drive alone and asked him to come. Seeing Letty and Angela brought back a rush of bad memories. Ezekiel inquired as to the time from nearly a dozen different pedestrians over the next twenty minutes.

He eyed the auditorium with suspicion. Ezekiel wasn't sure if Angela had seen him. He began to get a headache. Ezekiel took out a bottle of aspirin and swallowed three tablets dry.

The Palladium doors opened, and the people poured out onto Sunset and Argyle. Ezekiel ducked into the shadows so as not to be seen. He watched the people coming out. Angela and Letty were nowhere to be seen. He wondered if Carmen was with them.

"Hey," said Don, walking up from behind him.

Ezekiel jumped, startled by his friend.

"What's up?" asked Don.

Ezekiel shrugged his shoulders and didn't say anything.

Don chuckle. "I scared you. What, were you going to rip off somebody's car?"

"No," Ezekiel replied sheepishly.

Don glanced across the street at the Palladium. "What's that all about? Kinda early for a concert to get out; it's only one o'clock."

"It's some kinda school recital."

"Come on. I want to hit Tommy's for lunch. I'm buying."

The two men walked down the block and got into the car. Don pulled out into traffic. Ezekiel slid down in his seat as they passed the Palladium.

"What's up?"

Ezekiel sat up once they had passed the auditorium. "Nothing, man. Thought I saw some old vatos from the hood."

Don laughed. "And they want to kick your ass?"

Ezekiel frowned and looked out the window. "Yeah, something like that."

Don glanced over at Ezekiel, who had cleaned up himself for the drive into town. "Man, you look a lot better than you usually do."

Ezekiel remained silent, staring out the window.

Don shrugged his shoulders and turned on the radio. Aretha was singing about wanting respect.

Ezekiel wished he hadn't come to the city. He fought back tears. He fought back the bad memories. Letty played the piano beautifully. She had become a beautiful young woman. Ezekiel wiped his eyes with the back of his shirt sleeve. A smile crept across his lips as Don made a right onto Western and headed south toward Beverly Avenue. The headache eased. The thought of a Tommy's chili burger replaced the bad memories.

"I think I'm gonna have a double," said Ezekiel.

Don chuckled. "Whatever you want, brother. It's a good day."

Ezekiel nodded his head. "Yeah, it is. Thanks for asking me to come along."

\* \* \*

Cosmo and Nola entered the house. Nola hung up their coats and went into the kitchen. Cosmo went down the hall to the den. He suddenly got an uneasy feeling. He checked the bedrooms. Nothing appeared to be disturbed, yet Cosmo had a feeling that someone had been inside the house. He stepped inside the master bedroom, opened the top drawer on the dresser, and lifted the stack of white handkerchiefs. The five twenties he kept for emergencies were still there, and as were his gold cuff links. If someone had been in the house, they weren't interested in valuables. Cosmo shrugged off the feeling and crossed the hall into the den. That's when he noticed it.

The notepad was not at the top of the blotter pad where he normally kept it. The pad sat in the middle of the desk. The post card he had received was backside up. Cosmo sat down at the desk. He picked up the pad and looked at it. Nothing. He took a pencil and rubbed it lightly across the page. Someone had written down the message from the postcard.

Cosmo had been surprised when the card came. It had a Sacramento cancelation stamp. He didn't know anyone in Sacramento. The message didn't mean anything to him. It appeared to be just a strange series of words. He liked the photograph of Mark Twain and had decided to keep it. Someone had obviously broken into the house and copied down the message on the postcard. Cosmo didn't want to say anything to Nola and alarm her. Cosmo was about to go down to the kitchen when the phone rang.

Cosmo picked up the receiver. "Hello?"

"Hey, Big Daddy," said Michael McGuire.

# 46

# *The Hunt*

Dominic Torelli stopped at the Ace and dropped off Della's cut. He admired Della. He thought her a smart business woman and soft on the eyes. He enjoyed their brief visits. They were seated in Della's office. Dominic was enjoying a Johnny Walker neat.

"So, Della, when're you gonna give this place a facelift?"

Della spun the dial on the floor safe, opened the door, deposited the cash, and shut it. "Never. It'd scare my customers away."

Dominic chuckled. "You're a smart broad, Della. You know whose hand butters your bread. Smart enough to know that if you knew anything about a hit in San Diego, you wouldn't keep that information a secret."

Della didn't bat an eye. She maintained her composure. "Of course, I would call you if I knew about a hit."

"What about a drug heist?"

"That too. What is this about, Dom? You can shoot straight with me."

Dominic took a sip of his scotch and looked at Della, trying to read her. "One of our guys got whacked awhile back. The guy we think was behind it ran. Considering all the traffic that comes through here, my friends hoped that you might've heard something."

Della's expression warmed. "Sorry, Dom. I read that Patty Bono was killed. It was in the newspapers. You guys still haven't found the shooter?"

Dominic shook his head. "No. The guy vanished like a ghost." He took another sip of scotch. "He'll turn up. They always make a mistake. When this mook does, he's gonna wish his mother was never born."

"I guess they want this guy pretty bad."

"Like a heart-attack."

Della put her arms up in mock surrender. "I wish I could help you, Dom. Nobody talks to a woman, especially one who runs a gas-stop gambling joint."

Dom finished his scotch and set the glass down. "You would tell me if you heard something?"

Della looked at the man and didn't bat an eye. "Of course. We're partners." Della stood up and walked Dom to the door, her arm on his shoulder. "Partners look out for partners. That's how it works."

Dom's eye studied Della. He broke a smile. "Yeah, that's how it works. See you next week, Della."

* * *

Brother Kenneth and Marvin trailed Victor. He made sure to keep at least two car lengths between them at all times.

"Where's this muthafucker going?" hissed Marvin. "He been to the library, some book store, and Triple fuckin' A. You'd think this muthafucker was goin' to Tahiti."

"He's hunting, Marvin. Watch your speed."

Marvin frowned. He was a good driver and didn't like the way Brother Kenneth would correct him. "Hunting for what?"

"I'm not certain. That's why we keep an eye on the man."

Victor headed west on the 405. Marvin moved over a lane.

"Please remain in the same lane as our quarry. You increase the chance of him spotting us in his mirror."

Marvin did a slow burn and moved back into the second lane of traffic three cars behind the Chevy. Victor took the off ramp for LAX. Marvin followed. Victor pulled into the parking lot and parked. He got out, opened the trunk, and took out a black canvas bag. Marvin pulled into a slot in the next lane. The two men got out of the Ford and followed Victor into the terminal.

"The muthafucker is flyin' outta here," whispered Marvin.

Brother Kenneth and Marvin followed Victor through the terminal to the desk of Western Airlines. Brother Kenneth motioned Marvin to remain.

"Stay with him. I'm going to call our employer."

Marvin leaned against the wall, watching the Western Airlines counter. Brother Kenneth walked over to the line of phone booths and placed a call.

"Henderson, Nevada please." He gave the operator the number and deposited four quarters. The line rang, but no one answered. He hung up, waited two minutes, and tried again. Ten rings and no answer. Brother Kenneth frowned. He left the booth and walked back to the Western Airlines desk. Marvin walked up holding two tickets.

"The muthafucker is going to San Francisco."

"There really is no need to used such language. It shows ignorance," chided Brother Kenneth with a roll of his eyes.

Marvin stuck out a chubby hand holding two plane tickets. "Fuck ignorance. The plane leaves in thirty minutes."

Brother Kenneth glanced at the ticket but didn't take it. "You will have to follow the man alone."

Marvin gave Brother Kenneth a questioning look. "What the fuck? You aren't comin'?"

"I was unable to reach our employer. Victor Vega believed the teacher had something to do with this. He must've discovered something in the man's house. We need to find out what it is and how it may pertain to our client."

Marvin frowned. He grabbed Brother Kenneth's arm. "Fuck the teacher. We was hired to trail this muthafucker. That's exactly what we gonna do."

Brother Kenneth pulled away. He wore an expression of discomfort. "I don't fly."

Marvin grabbed Brother Kenneth by the arm, only tighter this time, and moved in the direction to the gate. "You do now."

Brother Kenneth broke free of the big man's grip but continued walking toward the gate. "You know I'm going to shoot you if this plane goes down."

Marvin nodded his head. "I'm suppose' to watch your back. You suppose' follow that man. That's what we doin'."

"Ain't this a bitch," Brother Kenneth muttered under his breath.

Marvin smiled as they walked up to the gate and handed the flight attendant their tickets.

\* \* \*

Hollywood was still a white man's town, so Michael met Cosmo at Babe's & Ricky's on Leimert Blvd. Michael suggested it when he called. The nightclub was familiar ground for Cosmo. Michael was already seated at a table near the rear when Cosmo walked in.

"You beat me here," said Cosmo, offering his hand.

Michael stood. "Experience has taught me that it is generally wise to arrive first."

The two men shook hands and sat down.

Cosmo looked at Michael. "I'm here."

Michael didn't blink. "I need your help. Jimmy is in trouble. Has he contacted you?"

Cosmo chuckled. "You get right to the point. Not hi, Cosmo. How are things? Are you still teaching?"

A waitress came over.

Michael indicated to himself and Cosmo. "Johnny Walker, rocks, two please."

Cosmo shook his head. "No thanks. I'll just have a Coke, thank you."

The waitress gave a nod and dashed off to another table.

Cosmo saw Michael's expression of surprise. "I told Nola—she's my wife—I told Nola I was out getting the papers. I don't frequent the clubs much anymore."

Michael grinned. "I'm sorry. It's been a long trip. I just got into town." He noticed Cosmo's quizzical look. "I've been living in Italy. Congratulations on the marriage. I take it you are still teaching?"

"Yeah." Cosmo reached inside his coat pocket and removed the postcard and laid it on the table.

Michael read the message and looked at Cosmo. "When did you receive this?"

"Two weeks ago. Do you know what it means?"

"Jimmy is in San Francisco." Michael turned the card so Cosmo could read it.

*Coldest summer, Joey. belle vie, rank, division, horseman, tower, church, tag, decimal, precarious, much. Out.*

"Joey is our code name for being in trouble. The coldest summer was the one Twain spent in San Francisco. Belle Vie is the name of the bistro in Paris we would go to. Jimmy wants to meet at a coffee shop. My rank in the war was first lieutenant, so that's one. Our division was the forty-fifth. Forty-five. Horsemen refers to the Four Horsemen of Apocalypse. So, four. The address is 1454. Take the next six words and take the first letter from the first word, second letter in the second and so on then reverse them, Haight. The address of the coffee shop is 1454 Haight. It's a code Jimmy and I came up with during the war. Nothing elaborate, but it's been useful when direct communication was difficult."

"I think somebody may have seen that message," said Cosmo.

Michael was about to say something, but the waitress returned with their drinks. Michael laid a twenty on the lady's tray, and she disappeared off to another table.

"What makes you think that?" Michael asked.

"I think somebody broke into our house two days ago. Nothing was taken. But they took time to write down that message."

Michael slipped the postcard into his pocket and stood. "Thank you. You've been very helpful, Cosmo. I wish it was different circumstances we could've met over. If you will excuse me, I need to catch a plane."

The two men shook hands. Cosmo watched Michael disappear out the door. He finished his Coke and left the club. Cosmo stopped off and picked up a copy of the *Sentinel* and drove home. Nola had dinner cooked when Cosmo walked in. It was fried porkchops, mashed potatoes, and apple sauce. One of Cosmo's favorite meals. He kissed Nola and silently thanked his Lord that she had entered his life.

# 47

# *San Francisco*

Jimmy saw the man sitting outside at the Magic Mushroom Cafe. He had a perfect view of the coffee house from his apartment. Jimmy had watched the cafe every morning since he sent the postcard to Cosmo. He knew if Michael tried to contact anyone in the states, it would be Cosmo. The three men had a history together, and Cosmo was safe.

The first day Victor Vega showed up at the Magic Mushroom, Jimmy spotted him immediately. He didn't know Victor's name, but Jimmy was certain this was somebody who didn't belong. It was the black leather jacket and the dark shirt and slacks he wore that caught Jimmy's eye. Most in the neighborhood didn't dress like Mafia hitmen.

Jimmy knew it was time to move. He got the suitcase of cash from the closet, left the few belongings he had, and made an exit out the backdoor. Jimmy hailed a cab and had him go around the block. He slid down in his seat as the cab approached the Magic Mushroom. He wanted to get a look at the man pursuing him. Something else caught Jimmy's eye and diverted his attention, however. He thought he saw someone who looked familiar sitting at a table. He was about to sit up and wave, but he quickly slid down again when the man in the black leather jacket turned and looked at the passing taxi.

A pretty mini-skirted girl in her twenties walked by. Victor glanced in her direction, and then a Yellow Cab passed. He caught just a glimpse of the passenger. He wasn't sure, but Victor quickly scribbled down the license number of the cab.

Brother Kenneth and Marvin sat on a bench at a bus-stop across the street. Brother Kenneth perused the *Chronicle*. Marvin appeared to be reading a paperback but fidgeted on the bench.

"Please sit still," Brother Kenneth whispered to his companion.

"How long are we going to watch this guy?"

"Patience. You got me on that plane. We're going to let this play out. Maybe there's some cash in it for us."

Marvin smiled. "I like that."

"Vega is obviously waiting for somebody. We're going to find out who it is and what Vincent Vega's interest in them is before we kill him. Our employer didn't say anything about a time schedule."

Victor sat at the table for another thirty minutes and then left. Brother Kenneth and Marvin gave him a few seconds' start and then crossed the street. They followed Victor like two jackals trailing unsuspecting prey.

* * *

Michael took a cab to the Magic Mushroom, ordered a double espresso, and waited. He saw a man in the black leather jacket sitting at a table, but he didn't give the man much thought. Michael's eyes scanned the street for any sign of Jimmy. People started to drift out onto the street after a while. It was obvious that many of the neighborhood's denizens were late risers.

There was no sign of Jimmy. If he was watching the café, that meant Jimmy lived close. Michael studied the buildings across the street. He decided that the one with the brown paintjob that sat just one up from the corner was the best choice. A second-floor window offered a clear view of the coffee house, but from the bistro's view, one couldn't see into the apartment.

A Yellow Cab passed. Michael's attention was on the buildings. He was certain that the brown building would be the one that Jimmy would use.

Michael left two singles on the table, got up, and crossed the street. He strolled down to where the brown row house stood and continued around the corner. There was a cab stop just up the street where two cabs waited for passengers. Michael continued around the back of the buildings down a narrow alley.

Sure enough, the brown building had a wooden staircase running down its back. Michael climbed the stairs to the second floor and tried the door. It opened. Then he proceeded inside the house, walking to the hall. Loud music came from one of the units on the floor above.

Michael continued down the hall until he came to the front unit on the right corner. He spotted the folded matchbook near the bottom of the jam, then knocked gently on the door. There was no answer. He knocked again. When there was still no answer, Michael tried the door. It opened. Michael stepped inside and closed the door behind him.

The room had all the appearances of a hasty departure. Clothes hung in the closet. Michael checked the jacket. It was a tailor Jimmy favored. Michael quickly cased the flat. The aftershave in the bathroom was one Jimmy used. Michael checked the nightstand. He found a postcard exactly like the one Cosmo had received. Michael was certain this was Jimmy's room. He walked over to the window and looked out at the coffee house. The man in the black leather jacket was walking down the street. Michael spotted the two Negroes trailing after the unsuspecting man.

Michael sat down on the bed and looked about the room. His gut told him that Jimmy had left the building. Michael reached into his pocket and took out a piece of jade with a Chinese character carved on it. It had been given to him by Walter Sing, his partner from long ago.

He had given the jade to Michael just before he died. Michael exited the apartment and hailed a cab from the stop.

"Where to?" asked the driver.

"Chinatown," Michael replied.

*  *  *

Jimmy checked into a single room, rent by the day tenement in the Tenderloin District. He was on the second floor in the back. Jimmy made it a practice never to get a room any higher than the second floor. If you had to jump, third floor and above would sure result in injury or death. A bare lightbulb hung from the ceiling. The room hadn't seen a coat of paint since Coolidge was president.

Jimmy laid his worldly possessions on the bed. A razor, a toothbrush, and two pairs of BVD's. He also had two-hundred grand in the suitcase. That bought a lot of underwear.

Jimmy pulled a pint from his jacket and took a long pull from the bottle. He had to focus. That was foolish to have exposed himself, thinking it was Michael he saw at the café. Michael was smart. He took his money and left the country.

Jimmy sat down on the bed and ran his hand through his hair. He didn't know who the man in the leather jacket was. Jimmy needed a plan. His first order of business was to get out of town. San Francisco had become too hot. Jimmy knew he couldn't go to Mexico. Emilio Hernandez would hand him over to Frank in a heartbeat. Jimmy decided he would make a run for Portland. The mob wasn't big up there, and it would buy him a few more months.

Jimmy would have to retrieve his car from the parking garage and get the second suitcase from the bus depot locker. He decided to stay in the room until the following evening when he would get the car and suitcase and make his run north. Jimmy took another pull from the bottle and smiled. He had a plan.

* * *

Michael sat in William Wong's office. It was on the third floor of the Cal-Fed building downtown. Wong was the bank manager. He was more importantly the son of Ah Wong, the leader of the Chinese Consolidated Benevolent Association in San Francisco. The CCBA was the outgrowth of the early Tongs who controlled Chinatown.

William was in his mid-thirties and dressed in a fine-tailored suit. He looked at the jade piece Michael had given him. "Your grandfather is still spoken of with reverence in our society. How may I be of service to you?"

Michael laid a small photo of Jimmy on Wong's desk. "My friend is in trouble. I believe he is in the city, and I need to find him."

William picked up the photo and looked at it. "James Hagen, formerly James Grazzi."

Michael arched an eyebrow. "You know him?"

William handed the photo back to Michael. "I do not know your friend, Mr. McGuire. I do, however, know who he is and what his business is. He was once your partner, then he became James Hagen and ran an aviation company until the government investigated him and he went bankrupt. We know he had been importing heroin and that some people believe your friend to be responsible for the death of Patrick Bono. We do not deal with the Italians or Mexicans. We have our own sources for such things. We do not meddle in their business. They do the same. Have I left anything out?"

Michael was surprised at the depth of Wong's knowledge. He kept it hidden behind a deadpan expression. "No. Are you able to help me? I want to get Jimmy out of the city."

It was William who arched an eyebrow this time. "That would not be looked upon kindly by certain people you and James have worked with."

"Only if someone were to inform them," Michael replied coolly.

William handed the jade piece back to Michael. "I like your loyalty." He picked up the telephone and punched in a number. William said something in Chinese and hung up the receiver.

"Your friend has left his apartment on Haight. Our men will locate him if he is still in San Francisco."

Michael didn't bother to hide his surprise. "You knew Jimmy was in the city."

William smiled. "There is little that happens in the city that my father is not aware of. We have kept an eye on James out of self-interests. We don't want a bloodbath in our city. Mr. Grazzi's problems are not ours, and we are happy to assist you in taking him out of San Francisco. Violence is never good for business."

"But you don't know where he has gone?" Michael asked.

"No. We did not have eyes on him this morning. We will soon enough."

"There is one other thing."

"What?"

"I think Jimmy is being followed by someone."

Michael gave William the brief rundown of the events earlier at the café and how he the man in the leather coat being tailed by two Black men. He gave precise and accurate descriptions of all three men.

"I am impressed with your attention to detail of these men. You have a good eye, Mr. McGuire."

"It comes from making movies for thirty-six years."

The two men stood and shook hands.

"I will be in touch. Where are you staying?"

"The St. Francis."

\* \* \*

Jimmy waited in his room on Eddy St. He debated shaving off the beard and cutting his hair and decided against it. If somebody could pick him out now, they were sure to spot him clean shaven.

Jimmy went downstairs and paid the guy working the front desk for another day. This wasn't a house that cared about names, as long as you had a fin for the room. He bought a newspaper and went back to his room. Jimmy had purchased a sack of oranges from a street vendor before he checked in. He ate two. He read the newspaper. He studied the map to Portland. He played solitaire. Jimmy also checked the window every so often. The room did not offer a very good view of Eddy St. and had none of Larkin, the nearest cross street. Jimmy hadn't spotted the man in the black leather jacket, or anyone else who looked suspicious. The district was populated primarily by alcoholics, drug addicts, and folks who had been beaten so low that a basement flat looked like a penthouse to them. The Tenderloin was home to the destitute, the disenfranchised, and the discarded. Anyone standing around casing the place would have to deal with a constant stream of street folk looking for a handout or a sucker to rob.

Jimmy tossed a card toward his hat sitting on the floor. The ace of hearts sailed directly into it. Jimmy snapped his fingers and smiled. He checked his watch. Five o'clock. He would be able to leave soon. Jimmy looked about the room.

The case was hidden under the bed. He didn't want to leave the case, but he also didn't want to take it with him to the parking garage. He thought it better to take a bus. A cab could be traced. The Ford was Jimmy's secret, and he didn't want it traced back to him. It was his only set of wheels. According to the bus schedule, he could reach the garage in three stops. Jimmy figured he wouldn't be gone from the room more than thirty minutes. That should be more than enough time to get to the garage, collect his car, and return to the rooming house on Eddy to pick up the suitcase. He would go to the bus station, collect the second suitcase, and head north.

* * *

Victor sat in a room on the opposite side of Eddy St. A sawbuck to the dispatcher got him the name of the driver who picked up Jimmy. A double fin to that cabbie got him the address where Jimmy was dropped. Victor knew money talked when it came to obtaining information. He rented a room across from the rooming house Jimmy had checked into. Then Victor waited. He saw Jimmy go to the window and check the street below.

Victor thought about going over and confronting Hagen, but he had no idea how many were in the building. It could expose him to too many witnesses. So, Victor waited and watched. He chuckled upon seeing a black minister all dressed up in a gray suit, white shirt, and black bowtie preaching on the corner.

Victor had no time for priests or preachers. He had one man on his mind and when and where to separate him from this life.

Brother Kenneth stood on the corner with his bible. Marvin sat on the sidewalk smoking a cigarette. Whenever a pedestrian passed, Brother Kenneth would exhort the passerby to accept the word of the Lord and praise Jesus. Nearly all ignored him and went about their business. When someone would engage Brother Kenneth, Marvin would keep an eye on the building. Brother Kenneth and Marvin had dogged Victor from the time he left the café. When he checked into the rooming house, they remained on the street. Brother Kenneth had called Della and given her a report. No, Brother Kenneth hadn't seen the man Victor was trailing. Della told him to watch and wait and only kill Victor once he had eliminated the man he was pursuing. Brother Kenneth didn't ask who Vincent's target was. He answered to the affirmative and hung up.

Jimmy left the rooming house at exactly 7 p.m. He didn't see anyone tailing him when he grabbed the bus on Van Ness and headed south toward the Mission District.

Kevin Lo stood on the corner of Larkin smoking a Kool and talking to a young woman who had walked down the street when the *gwelio* passed him. Kevin was one of dozens of men William Wong had put on the streets to find Jimmy Grazzi.

When Jimmy passed on his way to the bus stop, Kevin grabbed the woman, hugged her close, and kissed her. The young girl pushed away and frowned. Kevin grinned. Then the woman marched off, indignant.

Kevin watched as the *gwelio* got on the bus. A man wearing a black leather jacket, white t-shirt, and a San Francisco Giants baseball cap hurried by and caught the bus just before it took off. Kevin took a drag off the Kool and stubbed the butt out with the toe of his shoe. He looked up just as a dark sedan came around the corner and followed the bus. Kevin shook another smoke from the pack and walked over to the pay phone on the corner. He lit the cigarette and exhaled as he dropped a dime into the box and dialed.

"Please tell Mr. W. that the target has been spotted." Kevin gave the address he had seen Jimmy come out of. "It appears he is being followed by a guy wearing a black leather jacket and a Giant's cap. Two spades in a black Mercury rental rolled past right afterwards. I think they're tailing the bus."

"Stay there and keep a lookout," replied the caller before hanging up.

Kevin walked over to the closed market and leaned against the front. He smoked his cigarette and watched the rooming house on Eddy. The *gwelio* must have been someone important, but Kevin didn't care. He knew he had an extra hundred coming that night because he had spotted the *gwelio* first.

Walter Wong was watching *Rawhide* when the call came. He picked up the telephone and listened. "Good," he replied. Walter hung up the phone and dialed another phone number. "Mr. McGuire's room, please."

Jimmy wasn't sure if the man who got on the bus was the same one, he had seen earlier at the Magic Mushroom Café. The man had his hat pulled down, and he sat in the first seat. Jimmy had taken a seat across from the rear door. The man remained on the bus when Jimmy got off. "I must be getting paranoid," Jimmy said to himself as he walked up the street. The garage was on the next block.

The bus continued up the street. As soon as it had gone a block, Victor jumped up and pulled the cord. The driver frowned. "This ain't a stop."

Victor smiled. "Sorry, I didn't realize that last one was mine."

The driver stopped the bus and let Victor out.

"This ain't a limo service," said the driver as he closed the door.

Victor walked briskly down the street. He saw Jimmy enter a parking garage. Victor hailed a passing cab and got in.

"Where to?"

"Sit here for a bit," Victor replied as he kept his eye trained on the garage's exit.

The dark sedan driven by Marvin was now situated one block down from the cab.

"Sit tight and let's see what percolates," said Brother Kenneth.

Marvin sighed. "This is some boring shit."

"Patience, Marvin. Patience."

Jimmy rolled out of the parking garage behind the wheel of his Ford Galaxy. The cab made a U-turn and followed after the Ford. Marvin waited a beat after both cars had passed. He slipped the rental into gear and trailed the cab.

Jimmy pulled over and parked on Polk. He planned to stop at the bus station and grab the other suitcase on his way out of town. He was only a block away from the rooming house. If the place was being watched, he didn't want to give up the car's license. He got out of the Ford, walked to the corner, and turned down Eddy St.

"Stop here!" shouted Victor.

The cab driver hit the brakes.

Victor tossed a ten at the man, jumped out of the cab, and started up the street.

"The mark's going back to his place," said Brother Kenneth.

Marvin made a left, drove down a block, and made another left. He had to cut a car off to do so. The other driver laid on the horn and flipped Marvin the bird.

"There," said Brother Kenneth. "Pull over."

Marvin could see Jimmy approaching down the street. He pulled over and parked the rental.

Victor stopped at the corner. He crouched down behind a row of trash cans and watched as Jimmy proceeded down the street. A man stepped from the shadows. He appeared to confront Jimmy. The man lunged at Jimmy, and he hit the pavement. The assailant knelt down and rummaged through Jimmy's pockets. Victor dashed toward them.

"What the *fuck?*" exclaimed Marvin when he saw the attack.

Brother Kenneth put his hand on Marvin's shoulder. "Steady. Let's see how this plays out."

The two men sat in the rental as Victor raced up to the scene of the attack. Victor had his gun out. The assailant looked up. He was a white junkie who looked to be about twenty going on fifty. The junkie lunged at Victor with his knife. Victor fired. The junkie staggered for a moment and collapsed on the sidewalk a few feet from Jimmy. "Fuck, fucking, pendejo," Victor spat on the dead junkie. He rushed over to see if Jimmy was dead.

Grazzi groaned.

"Stay here, I'll call the police," said Victor.

"No, no police," whispered Jimmy. "Help me up. My place is just a few doors down."

Victor helped Jimmy to his feet. Grazzi was bleeding badly, a gut wound. Victor put his arm around Jimmy and helped him up the street and into the rooming house.

"Ain't that a muthafucker?" said Marvin.

"Why you always have to talk like that?" Brother Kenneth said.

Marvin frowned. "What?"

"Cuss and such."

Marvin looked at his companion for a moment and broke into a big laugh. "We 'bout to shoot this muthafucking Mexican and you worried 'bout my fuckin' language?"

Brother Kenneth arched an eyebrow. "Be ready."

"I was born fuckin' ready."

Victor helped Jimmy up the stairs to his room and sat the wounded man on his bed.

"You shot that prick. Thanks," Jimmy said in a low tone of voice. It hurt to even breathe. "You better clear out. I can handle myself." He reached into his pocket, took out a wad, and peeled off five bills and held them out to Victor.

The hitman looked at the money and then at Jimmy. "You don't know who I am?"

Jimmy's vision was hazy. He tried to focus on Victor's face. "Sorry."

"Cinnamon Carlyle sends her love," Victor whispered. He jammed his hand into Jimmy's wound and squeezed.

Jimmy groaned loudly. He shoved Victor away.

The door suddenly flew open.

Brother Kenneth marched in. He fired two shots from his Smith & Wesson .38, one to the heart, the other a head shot. Vincent fell like a sack of cement to the floor with a thud. Marvin stepped into the room his gun drawn. Brother Kenneth stuffed his pistol into his belt. Marvin kept an eye on Jimmy while Brother Kenneth tossed the room and discovered the suitcase under the bed.

Marvin pointed to Jimmy, who now laid on the floor. "This one ain't dead."

"Ain't our concern."

"We was supposed to wait until Vega killed this whiteboy."

Brother Kenneth set the suitcase on the bed. He glanced down at Jimmy. "Don't think he's going to make it. We weren't paid to kill him." He popped the locks and opened the suitcase. "Sweet Jesus." He starred down at the case full of cash.

Marvin's eyes widened in surprise, which quickly turned into a huge smile. "Goddamn, no wonder this dead muthafucker was after the whiteboy."

"Gentlemen," said a voice.

Bother Kenneth and Marvin turned.

Michael McGuire stood in the doorway. He had his coat to the side so his holstered gun was accessible.

"You going kill both of us?" asked Brother Kenneth.

"The fuck yo—"

Marvin never finished his sentence. The gun seemed to leap into Michael's hand and he fired. The big man hit the floor dead.

Brother Kenneth raised his hands slowly. He had never seen anyone pull a pistol with the speed and accuracy the white man had. "This room is getting crowded."

"You can join 'em."

"It was Nicole," groaned Jimmy.

Michael kept his gun trained on Brother Kenneth and knelt down close to Jimmy. "You, okay?"

"It was Sullivan all the time," Jimmy wheezed. He coughed blood. He placed a key into Michael's hand and then expired.

Michael rose to his feet. He looked at Brother Kenneth. "Talk."

Brother Kenneth told how Della Rio had hired him and Marvin to kill Victor. He pleaded ignorance about Jimmy. Michael pressed the gun hard against the black man's temple.

"I swear," said Brother Kenneth. "The bitch got a place outside of Vegas called the Ace of Hearts. Her office is behind the bar."

Kevin Lo raced into the room. He saw the dead bodies on the floor and looked at Michael.

"Come on, we have to go. The police are coming," Kevin urged Michael toward the door.

Michael closed the suitcase and picked it up. He handed Brother Kenneth two packets of hundred-dollar bills. "Tell your employer the job was completed. No more. Understand?"

Brother Kenneth gaped at him. "Understood."

Michael smiled. "If I could find Jimmy, I can find you. Remember that."

He and Kevin exited the room. Brother Kenneth looked down at Marvin. The wail of sirens could be heard in the distance. Brother Kenneth bent down and stroked Marvin's cheek. "Should've had patience, brother." He stood and made a hasty retreat down the rear stairway.

* * *

Michael eased back in his seat. He was flying to Los Angeles on a red-eye. He had retrieved the second suitcase from the bus depot. Michael kept that one and gave Kevin the suitcase taken from Jimmy's room with the instructions to give it to William Wong.

Michael made sure he paid tribute to the Tong. There was plenty of mess to clean up in the rooming house, and the money would cover that. Jimmy was dead. Michael wished he could've remained to see Jimmy got a proper burial, but that would've been risky. As the plane made its way down the coast to Los Angeles, Michael had only one thing on his mind: Nicole Sullivan.

# A New Arrangement

Los Angeles Tribune Headline – Morning Edition – September 14, 1965

## Aircraft Tycoon Dies in Tenderloin Tenement

### Howard Silver

James Hagen, the former head of Allied Aircraft, was found murdered in a San Francisco rooming house on Friday. He was the apparent victim of a robbery. "It appears that Mr. Hagen was lured to a tenement for the purposes of robbing him," said SFPD Capt. Mark Kinsella. "This is a tough neighborhood with many undesirables." The police did not indicate who was responsible for Hagen's murder. Capt. Kinsella went on to say, "There were a number of bodies at the scene. the case is under investigation, and SFPD is handling this case with the utmost attention." Hagen was a pioneer with the fledgling aircraft company that called San Diego home. During the war, the company rose to prominence, producing as many as two hundred planes in a week. "Our record was two hundred and fifteen," said Peter Bixby, the company's former Director of Morale. "This is a tragedy for all. James was a proud American who worked hard for his country in a time of need," stated his former wife, Claire, now married to New York Senator, Wyatt Bassham. A funeral will be held at the Alcala Cathedral on Thursday.

Dominic Torelli walked into the Ace. He brushed the bartender aside and entered Della's office. She was on the phone and looked up when Torelli marched in.

"I'll have to call you back. Someone just walked in," Della said to the person on the phone and hung up. She fixed Dominic with a cool look. "To what do I owe the pleasure of your company?"

Dominic placed a newspaper on Della's desk. It was folded to highlight a single article, Hagen's obituary. She glanced at it and didn't miss a beat. "So, what does this man have to do with me?" Della asked, bored.

"Maybe you'd like to tell us," Dominic replied in a monotone voice.

Della didn't waver. She looked at Dominic with the innocent eyes of a child. "I never met the man."

Dominic sat down on Della's desk and leaned close. "You never sang at a war bond fundraiser at Hagen's house as Cinnamon Carlyle? You and your brother, Marcellus, never tried to squeeze Hagen over some photos?"

Della was quiet. The air hung heavy in the room. "My brother is dead," she finally replied.

"Dead because you scammed the entire bunch, sweetheart." Dominic was impressed with the woman's moxie and cool exterior. "Do you really think we're that dumb? That we didn't know who you were all these years? You were allowed to work because your business didn't conflict with ours and you were smart enough to pay tribute. Now your business is our business, and we don't want any problems, understand?"

Della's eyes flashed hate. "Don't you talk to me like that."

Dominic chuckled. "Don't worry, we ain't going to make you turn tricks. You won't even have to pull cons like the one in Dallas. You're going to sit tight and let us make our drop. Of course, our financial arrangement is going to change."

Della shot out of her chair. "This is my club. You can't come in here like some—"

Dominic backhanded Della hard across the face, cutting her off. "Sit down and listen. The only reason you haven't joined your boy, Victor, is because you *do* own this place. We need your name on the deed. The only way we can keep it that way is for you to stay alive. You can keep the money from the slots. We're now taking the tables, and we're putting our own dealers in the house to make sure."

Della rubbed her cheek and glared at Dominic. "What if I don't accept your offer?"

Dominic shrugged his shoulders. "That wouldn't be good for either of us, but it would be worse for you. Believe me, you don't want to go down that road."

Della collapsed into the chair and was silent.

"Look at it this way," said Dominic, "you keep the Ace and your life."

"I didn't have anything to do with what happened in San Diego. That was Victor."

Dominic had a bemused look on his face. "You knew."

Della didn't say anything.

Dominic stood up and adjusted his tie. "I wouldn't suggest trying to leave town either." He ran his hand down Della's check. "You work exclusively for us now." With that, he tipped his hat and exited the room.

Della brooded. She hated men. Every man she had put her faith in failed her, first Marcellus and now Victor. She had escaped James Hagen. She had escaped the Rodriguez brothers. She would escape Dominic Torelli.

* * *

Michael McGuire read the newspaper. He sat at the big table in the dining room of the Oso Negro, sipped his coffee, and sat back in the chair. It was a beautiful fall morning. The sun was shining, and the air was crisp.

Jimmy was dead. Laurel and Nicholas were strangers. He had let it all slip away. *Strappare Grande* was picked up by Warner's and dumped. It tanked at the box-office. The studios weren't interested in Michael or any of his projects. As far as they were concerned, Michael could go back to Italy. The Italians loved him. Michael didn't want to make movies in a foreign country. He had done that. It wasn't the same as having a premiere at the Chinese or Egyptian. He didn't have the passion any longer for making movies.

Michael set the paper down and washed his dishes. He realized there was only one thing left for him to do. Before that, he had to go to Jimmy's funeral.

*49*

# *Coming to an Understanding*

It was sunny the day when James Hagen was buried. The light streamed through the trees at the cemetery as the people took their seats. A large group had come to pay their respects, and most were former employees of Allied Aircraft. Pete Bixby gave the eulogy. Michael sat in the last row. The press was there, and Michael preferred to remain anonymous. Surprisingly, other than one reporter who wanted to know when Michael's next film was coming out, the rest paid him little attention.

Michael lingered after the services. He allowed others to view the coffin one last time. One or two people came up to him and offered their condolences, but most in attendance were unaware of Michael's connection to James Hagen. Claire was a no-show. Michael wasn't surprised. It would have been a political landmine to navigate for her Senator husband. Brenda Williams, XELA's secretary, showed. She came over to Michael. They talked about the old days at the station. After a few minutes, the conversation ran dry. Brenda bid Michael farewell and left for the reception.

Someone had gone to the time and expense to hold a reception for Jimmy at the Butcher Shop, a steakhouse in Mission Valley. Two men approached Michael. The man in the lead was Michael's age. He had a moustache and was dressed in a tailored black suit. The man to his left walked a step behind. He was built like a lineman and was two decades younger.

The older man held out his hand. "Frank Bompensiero."

Michael shook his hand.

"This is a sad day for our friend, Jimmy," said Frank.

Michael knew Frank had gone apeshit when Jimmy took off. He had put out the word and offered ten-grand for anybody who could find Jimmy, but he stayed hidden. His sole mistake was sending the postcard. Jimmy had violated the cardinal rule for anyone on the run: Never contact someone from your past. He paid for it with his life. The irony of Jimmy's death was not missed by Michael.

Michael nodded and replied with a simple, "Yes."

Frank looked at his bodyguard. The big man raised his eyebrows and held his hand out palm up.

"Look, Michael. I know you and Jimmy were *fratelli*, the war and all the stuff afterwards."

"Jimmy was like my brother," said Michael.

Frank took out a cigar case and offered Michael one. He declined. Frank removed a cigar and returned the case to his breast pocket. He bit the tip, spit it on the ground, and lit the cigar.

"Cuban. I have a guy who flies for the airlines bring me a case." Frank puffed on the cigar and exhaled. "Look, Michael. I know you want to do that fuckin' moolie cunt in Henderson."

Michael's eyes met Frank's. The gangster chuckled. "You, see? I'm right. Well, that's the reason I wanted to talk to you. You can't kill her."

Michael remained silent.

Frank sighed. "It would be bad for business for our friends in Nevada."

"I thought Victor Vega was the one who killed Patty Bono," said Michael.

Frank chomped on his cigar. "Look, Michael, you don't think I'd love to slit that bitch right up her snatch and watch her bleed out? But this is business."

Michael glared at him. "Your business is not mine. I made that very clear when I left the country."

Frank forced a smile. "Good, then we understand each other."

"Yes. I understand, Mr. Bompensiero."

Frank gave Michael a pat on the cheek and puffed on his cigar. He said "goodbye" and he and the bodyguard made their way down the grass toward a long black Cadillac.

Michael watched as Frank got in the car. The bodyguard closed the door and raced around to the driver's side before getting in. Then the Caddy slowly drove away. Michael stood alone at the gravesite. Two workers stood off to the side, waiting. Michael looked at the casket sitting at the bottom of the grave and placed his hand on it.

"It was an honor, my friend."

Michael placed his hat on his head and walked away.

# 50

# *A Year Later*

Cosmo and Nola watched the television. Looks of concern crossed their faces. Chicago was aflame as protestors burned and pillaged stores. They had gone down to Ensenada for vacation and returned to witness another city caught up in rioting. Los Angeles still hadn't recovered from the Watts uprising the previous year.

The dynamics at school had changed over the past year. Some of the teachers were more reserved in their interactions with Cosmo and kept him at a distance. Others, who had rarely said more than a, "good morning" before, now wanted to engage Cosmo. They asked if he had seen the Supremes on Ed Sullivan, or talked about what a great boxer Muhammed Ali was and how unfair the government was in their treatment of him. Cosmo would smile and let them talk. He offered little in the way of an opinion to his white co-workers.

Gun sales had skyrocketed since Watts. Whitey hid behind his door and wondered when the Zulus would rise and slaughter them in their homes. Cosmo shrugged it off. He had a new class starting and plenty of work to keep him busy. Nola got up and turned off the TV.

"I'm tired of watching people get shot and arrested."

Cosmo stood and held out his hand. "I won't argue." He pulled Nola to him and hugged her, kissing her gently on the lips.

Nola smiled. "I bet you won't."

"Did you have a nice time in Baja?"

"Yes. I wish we could've stayed longer."

Cosmo kissed her again. "You are beautiful, baby. I don't know why you wanted me. You could've had so much better."

Nola gave Cosmo a sly smile. She broke away and seductively strolled toward the hallway. Then she turned and coyly beckoned Cosmo with her forefinger.

"I'll show you why I keep you around."

Cosmo spread a big grin as he followed his wife into the bedroom. He knew he was the luckiest man alive.

\* \* \*

Michael waited in his Mustang. He was parked in front of the Ace of Hearts, second row back with the windows rolled up. The December air was cold. Michael checked his watch.

Della Rio, aka Cinnamon Carlyle, aka Nicole Sullivan exited the Ace and walked to her car, which was parked in right in front. She saw a small white cat licking an empty can of food. Della bent down.

Michael got out of his car and silently approached. He had cased the Ace for days and knew that Della left at 2 a.m. every morning. Michael had placed a can of food and the cat near Della's car a few minutes before she exited the building and returned to his car and waited.

"Oh, sweetheart—" Those were Della's last words.

Michael put a .22 slug in the back of Della's head. The frightened cat scrambled away. Michael jammed the gun into Della's mouth and pulled the trigger a second time. He then looked in both directions. There were no witnesses.

Michael walked back to the Mustang, got in, and pulled away from the truck stop casino. Four hours later, he was back in Los Angeles. He drove across the Sixth Street bridge and tossed the pistol in the river, which was running high this year. Thirty minutes later, Michael sat in the living room of the Oso Negro sipping a twenty-year-old single malt scotch he had saved for a special occasion.

It was three days before they showed up. Michael knew they would come. He had violated Frank's orders. There was a price to be paid. Michael knew that when he killed Della. That's what a man did for his partner. Michael was down by the site of the former family graveyard when he heard the cars approach. He casually walked back to the house.

The guns were laid out neatly on the table. There was a rifle in every room and nearly as many shotguns. Michael had a Smith & Wesson in his holster and another stuffed in his belt. He preferred barrel guns. They didn't jam. Michael picked up a rifle and went to the window. Three cars were heading up the long drive and pulled into the big cul-de-sac. Each vehicle had four men inside. They had sent twelve to kill one.

Michael checked the rifle and smiled to himself. Nicole Sullivan must have been very important for them to send that many men.

He walked over to the cupboard and removed the bottle of twenty-year old single malt and a glass. He heard the vehicles cut the motors and the men getting out. Michael poured himself two fingers and took a long drink.

"Fuck 'em all."

Michael set the glass down on the counter. Then he took a position. A shotgun was propped against the wall nearby. Michael figured he could take at least six of the bastards before they came through the door.

# 51

# *The Last Goodbye*

Howard Silver was one of the few who showed for Michael's funeral. The newspapers and studios didn't want to touch what happened at the Oso Negro. The papers kept their coverage sweet and simple. Michael McGuire had financed his final film with members of a foreign underworld organization and was murdered due to its box office failure. There were no lurid shots of the bodies strewn across the courtyard of the Oso Negro or of Michael's bullet-riddled body in the living room. LAPD closed the case. End of story.

Michael's funeral had more flowers than Holland in Spring. No one came. Laurel was absent. She had no desire to attend what she knew years ago would be Michael's final outcome. Frank thought it wise to keep any former associates away from the press. He and the boys were no-shows. Few in the current Hollywood hierarchy had worked with Michael. They knew him from his films, which they had studied in film school.

The studio honchos were no-shows, except for Sarah Royal. She had been reduced to a figurehead at the studio her father had founded. She had a title, but no real power. Sarah didn't give a damn what the others thought. She and Michael had butted heads frequently, but he was her friend and a big reason why she had lasted as long as she did at Royal. Every no show had sent flowers or an arrangement in their stead.

A good looking, well-dressed young man in his twenties came in the room. He had a small scar on his right cheek. The man walked up and viewed the body and departed. The reporter approached Sarah.

"Do you know who that was?" asked Howard Silver.

Sarah Royal shook her head. "No. Frankly, I'm surprised you showed." She shook her head at the empty room.

Silver grinned. "I'm a reporter. Naturally inquisitive. It really is a shame. All the movies he made sure made a lot of people happy. I know I liked his stuff."

Sarah smiled. "No, I think this is how Michael would've liked it. He was never one for the usual hub-bub that goes along with a Hollywood funeral, and certainly not his own."

Silver nodded. "Yeah, you're probably right, Sarah."

The reporter held out his hand. "Come on, I'll buy you a drink and you can tell me all about the new studio head who is banging that blonde starlet from Paramount."

Sarah smiled and took Silver's hand. "Why, it's sounds like you already know half the story."

The pair exited.

Michael's body laid alone in a room filled with beautiful fragrant flowers.

# 52

# *The Departure*

Ezekiel threw his rucksack over his shoulder and went to get his pay from old man Spahn. Ezekiel had been staying at the ranch ever since Spahn returned from his last visit to the hospital six months ago. The man's health was failing, and Ezekiel helped out at the ranch. He had learned to control the headaches through meditation and had stopped eating mushrooms. He cleaned himself up and with his trimmed beard now looked more like a western cowboy with his hat and jeans.

Don kidded Ezekiel about his "new look".

Ezekiel called Don, "Shorty".

The two men got along fine. The truth was that the ranch was failing. The studios no longer used the place to shoot, and few people came to rent and ride the horses anymore. There just wasn't enough work to warrant a second man. The ranch became a hang-out for vagrants and hippies. Ezekiel didn't care for them.

He wished Don well and walked up to old man Spahn's house, which looked more like a shack now.

"You sure you won't consider staying?" asked the old man.

Ezekiel glanced out the window at the group of long-haired women dancing around outside. A long-haired man with wild eyes sat in the middle of the circle as the women danced around him. He looked back at Spahn.

"No thanks. Those people are trouble. That fella leading them gives me bad vibes."

Spahn chuckled, "Charlie, he's no trouble. He and his family are helping out."

Ezekiel shook his head. He knew Spahn was enjoying the favors of Charlie's girls. "It's your place, but I'd watch out. That guy and his people are bad news."

Spahn laughed. "You're just jealous cause not one of 'em has tickled your wick."

"Good thing, too. You'll get the drips from them."

Spahn laughed again. "At my age, that's the least of my worries."

Spahn paid Ezekiel, and the two men shook hands.

"Know where you're going?" asked Spahn.

"Think I'll head up to Canada."

"Well, good luck, son."

Ezekiel stuffed the money into his pocket. Then he picked up his rucksack and headed out the door. The girls continued dancing around Charlie. He motioned for them to stop. His piercing eyes watched as Ezekiel walked down the drive to the main road. Charlie clapped his hands.

"Helter skelter is coming, children."

The girls danced around Charlie singing, "Helter skelter is coming. Helter skelter is coming," over and over again.

Johnny Camacho graduated from high school that June. Two months later, he was drafted. Two months after that, Johnny was on a military transport to Vietnam. Letty was a music major at U.C.L.A. Lucy was working part-time at a book store and taking classes at the community college. She still hadn't figured out what direction she wanted to go. Angela was on location in Utah working as a first AD on a Blake Edwards movie. She flew in just in time to see Johnny off at the airport.

The following summer, the powers that be in Los Angeles decided to have a plaque placed in Chinatown honoring the many who had come to *Gum Saan*. The speaker was William Wong. Cosmo Turner was the musical director at the dedication. Nola and their young daughter, Kendra, sat in the audience. After the band played a number, William Wong stepped up to the podium.

"I would like to thank the mayor and the board of supervisors for giving this plaque to the people of Chinatown and for recognizing the contribution we Chinese have made to Los Angeles. I would also like to thank Sean McGuire and his family. If it wasn't for Mr. McGuire's friendship, many of us would never have succeeded. It was the Sing Tong that provided many opportunities to us, and it was Mr. McGuire who took that first step and made Lee Sing his partner. For that, we are forever grateful."

The mayor forced a smile, leaned close to one of the supervisors, and whispered, "Damn McGuires, we just can't get rid of them, even when they're dead."

The supervisor chuckled. The crowd applauded. The band played another number. As the ceremonies broke up, a good looking, well-dressed man in his twenties approached William Wong and held out his hand. He had a small scare on his right cheek.

"I'm Nicholas McGuire. Thank you for what you said about my family."

William shook Nicholas's hand. "A pleasure to meet you. If you should ever need a friend, please do not hesitate to call me."

"Thank you," Nicholas replied.

"You should have been up on the stage. It was your great-grandfather who saved many Chinese during the massacre."

Nicholas scratched his jaw. "Probably not the best idea in this city. I am learning much about my father and family. My parents divorced when I was young. My mother kept me from my father's world."

William smiled. "And what have you discovered?"

"My great-grandfather and my father were both interesting men."

"Both knew the value of loyalty and friends." William handed Nicholas his father's jade piece. "Remember, you have a friend, Nicholas."

Nicholas took the small jade piece and bowed his head. "Thank you." He glanced over at the group of people gathered around the mayor and looked at William. "Don't you find it ironic that so close to an election the mayor finally decides to get a plaque up in Chinatown?"

William flashed a sly grin. "Politics. After gold was discovered, California became a land of myths. Like a myth, California never really was what it appeared to be. No, I am not surprised. This is just business as usual."

"True," Nicholas agreed.

The two men shook hands. They bid each other a good day and departed the square in different directions.

*The Bear* series is first and foremost a work of fiction. While many of the events depicted actually happened, and some real characters were thrown in for good measure, it is a total fabrication and bears as much truth as a politician on election day. The author encourages all to know their history. If you're fortunate to live long enough, some charlatan will come along and try to sell you fiction, proclaiming that it's your history. The author would like to thank his editor, Ashley Oliver. He would also like to thank all the readers who came along for the entire ride. *Hasta la vista, buckeroos.*

Printed in the United States
by Baker & Taylor Publisher Services